PETER MICHAEL JOHNSON

WHITE CLOUD FREE

V Press LC
www.vpresslc.com

Consistently committed to publishing
writing that 'Rises Above' as our motto states.

ISBN: 979-8-9854670-4-8
PRINTED IN U.S.A.

White Cloud Free

1361 W. Wade Hampton Blvd.
Suite F, PMB 162
Greer, SC 29650
(864) 334-5909

Praise for *WHITE CLOUD FREE*

"Imagine Joseph Conrad writing the great Peace Corps novel. *White Cloud Free* is heartbreaking, vast, and tough. Johnson splashes the colors of Latin America onto these pages."

—Darin Strauss, author of *Cheng & Eng*

"*White Cloud Free* is a haunting novel, with the authenticity and redemption that makes fiction worth reading in the first place. It's a brutal, beautiful, penetrating story. Peter Michael Johnson is the real deal. Beyond just being a good writer, he's generous to the reader."

—Mark Cirino, author of *Name the Baby*

"An amicable coming-of-age novel, a spiritual exploration of youth and a terrific primer on beekeeping. Highly recommended."

—Tom Franklin, author of *Crooked Letter, Crooked Letter*

"Peter Johnson's novel, *White Cloud Free* is a wonder…It is a stirring and compelling book. A must-read, it is a winner of the 2021 Seven Hills Review Novel Excerpt Contest."

—Lyla F. Ellzey, author of *Into the Unknown* and Seven Hills Review Contest Judge

"*White Cloud Free* is a well-structured thriller so convincing of place and characters the reader stops bothering to sort memory from enhanced memory, fact from fiction. The story has veracity; the narrative pace doesn't allow you to wonder about how true what had happened because you want to read on to what will happen. It's all totally believable, but you know you are being told a tale."

—Stephen Foehr, author of *BIX: Because I Exist*

For Ash
che rembyreko
who snuck into Brazil with me.

TABLE OF CONTENTS

PROLOGUE

I am 22 years old and it doesn't occur to me that my degree in English from New York University might not qualify me to save a fully grown cow from an angry swarm of killer bees. My buddy, Jack, on the other hand, is more reasonable about the whole endeavor.

"We've been in the Peace Corps for only two weeks," he observes, as we traipse across a pasture, his words punctuated by the soft popping sound of bees smacking into my veil as they try to find a vulnerable patch of flesh on which to martyr themselves.

"So?" I say, crossing my arms. It is the hour of the day just after sunset when it is not yet dark. The pasture is enclosed on all sides by a lush jungle and the thigh-high chartreuse grass is dotted with reddish earthen termite mounds that, in the waning light, look vaguely like phallic specters.

"So, I don't think we've been trained for this," he says simply, his face obscured by the veil. Jack is a giant man who was the starting offensive tackle for the 2001-2002 University of California football team. Owing to his size, he played football pretty much his whole life—and was quick to tell anyone who would listen that he hated every minute of it.

"C'mon, Jack," I implore. "You know that a situation like this won't be covered in our training. Besides, we're the only people who can do this. None of the farmers have a bee suit." Even though I've only known Jack for a couple of weeks, I suspect that appeals to heroism or adventure won't work on him. He is the hometown hero of his small farming town in Northern California. Unlike me, he did not join the Peace Corps to be the protagonist of his own personal odyssey; but rather, he travelled halfway around the world to escape all the lofty hopes that had been foisted on him.

Before he has a chance to demur, we are interrupted by a gurgled, miserable bellow of a cow somewhere in the grass toward the far side of the pasture.

"We can't just leave her out here," I say, setting off toward the sound. Jack plods after me, every step evoking a new wave of frenzied bees glancing off of my canvas bee suit. A few land on the veil in front of my face, vainly thrusting their tiny stingers through the gossamer as if to convey a dire warning from their berserk sorority.

The cow emits a few more anguished groans before I find her laying on her side, resigned to her fate, white from the honeybee venom sacs covering her body.

"Oh God," Jack whispers as he lumbers to a spot beside me.

I take a step closer and the cow makes a half-hearted attempt to rise to its feet, wriggling against its own halter which is attached to a lead rope stretched taut from a place where it is tied to a large clump of flaxen grasses. The beast collapses again with a hollow thud.

"Easy girl," I coo, brushing dozens of bees from around the creature's protuberant, wet black eye. Her enormous rib cage rises and falls with breath that is uneven and labored.

"Jack, go untie her," I say, motioning toward the place where the rope seems to be tied. A moment later the rope goes slack and Jack joins me where I am squatting over the creature's head, futilely swatting at the bees that continue to attack.

"What now?" Jack says. "Cows weigh like 1,000 pounds."

I grab the rope out of Jack's hand and begin to pull at the creature. "C'mon girl," I say encouragingly, jerking at the rope. She rocks back and forth a couple of times, finally heaving the front half of her body up on a pair of improbably spindly legs. She pauses for a moment in this twisted position and then collapses again with a sickening thud.

I look over at Jack who shrugs his massive shoulders.

"Well we can't just leave her here to die," I say. "Take her back legs and help me drag her back toward the village."

Progress is slow and halting as we drag the corpulent bovine over broken stalks of grass. I try to ignore the awful way her massive head skids and bounces across the ground in front of me, its roving globular eye somehow unperturbed by the whole ordeal.

The bees continue their ceaseless attack, though soon I am breathing so heavily that I barely notice it.

"Hold on," I say breathlessly, dropping the legs. "I need a break." A long avenue of matted grass extends away from the massive supine creature back toward the place, still visible in the distance, where we found her.

"This is horrifying," Jack says after a few moments of silence. "Like this might be the worst thing I've ever seen."

"What I find horrifying," I say, still gasping for breath, "is how much easier this is for you than it is for me." I emit a halfhearted guffaw.

My words don't seem to register with Jack as he stands transfixed by the massive animal between us.

"Hey, Hercules," I say waving at him. "You're not cracking, are you?"

"Fuck you, bro," he says, turning toward me. "This is fucked on so many levels. Totally fucked. What do you think we can do here, now, ever?"

Jack and I had initially bonded over our shared brand of gleeful cynicism that was a distinct contrast to the starry-eyed idealism that seemed to permeate the attitudes of our peers in the Peace Corps. Something in his tone told me that this wasn't just another jaded tongue-in-cheek comment.

"Let's get this over with," I say, grabbing the legs.

It is dusk by the time we drag the cow to the tree line along the far side of the pasture. There, we are joined by a group of barefoot, adolescent village children who are carrying smoldering cow patties, which emit plumes of thick white smoke. They quickly arrange more smoldering dung in a circle around the suffering beast. Jack and I take off our veils. I pretend not to notice when he wipes his glassy eyes.

The children methodically scrape the stingers from the cow's hide with kitchen knives they've brought from their houses. Without the stingers, I see that the cow is dappled brown and white. Its breathing is jagged and irregular.

"Hey, I have an idea," I say, pulling an Epipen from my pocket. "What do you think? Do you have yours?"

Jack rifles through his pocket and hands me his auto-injecting adrenaline shot. All the beekeeping volunteers were given one on the first day of our Peace Corps training.

"Where do I put it?" I ask, popping the safety cap.

"How should I know?" Jack says. "Somewhere soft."

"Didn't you grow up on a farm?" I say.

"My dad sold farm insurance," he says. "We leased our land to almond farmers. I don't know anything about cows."

"How about here?" I ask, stroking the coarse hair on its neck. "It's soft here."

Jack nods and I stab the cow with the Epipen. Almost immediately she takes a deep breath and her breathing becomes more normal.

"Holy shit!" I say, smiling. "It worked!" The children whistle and cheer in Guaraní—a language that is still very foreign to me.

Before long, we are joined by some local farmers who cluster around Jack. They have nicknamed the giant American "Ivan." The way they say it, the name sounds like "Ee-bahn."

"Ivan, you saved the cow," one farmer says in Spanish.

"Ivan, you carried it yourself," suggests another, patting him on the bicep. "You can carry a cow!"

Ivan is short for Ivan Drago, famed Russian antagonist of the Rocky movies. It turns out that everyone in Paraguay has seen Spanish-dubbed versions of Rocky IV. It does not matter that, except for blonde hair, Jack looks nothing like Dolph Lundgren. All the American beekeeping trainees in the village think the nickname is hilarious, except for Jack, of course.

In broken Spanish, Jack insists that the cow is still in a precarious condition. The nuance of his comment is either lost or ignored because the villagers have decided that they have just witnessed the sort of valor that they have come to expect from the Americans that they see in their favorite Spanish-dubbed Hollywood action movies.

While Jack chats with the villagers, I squat over the cow's massive head. The stingers have been mostly scraped from her body, but her breathing is already beginning to become labored again.

"Peter!" Jack exclaims, grabbing me by the shoulder, his voice bright for the first time that evening. "Did you hear that, Peter?"

"What?"

"They have called for the veterinarian!" he cries. "Peter, we might actually save her!" It is too dark to see his face, but I can tell from his voice that he is excited about this news.

"Look, you stay here," he says, his voice brimming with determination. "I'll go to all of the beekeepers in our group and get their Epipens and bring them back. We just need to keep her alive until the veterinarian gets here. Give her my shot if her breathing becomes labored again, okay?"

I sit vigil over the suffering cow until the vet arrives on the back of a motorbike. He is a middle-aged balding man who is indistinguishable from the villagers in his tattered shorts and flip flops. He seems neither surprised nor particularly interested when I explain, in broken Spanish, that I had administered six human doses of adrenaline to the cow to keep it alive. He nods sagaciously and deftly pours a big bottle of antihistamine down the cow's throat.

"What do you think, doctor?" I say in Spanish, when he has finished force feeding the medicine. "Is she going to live?"

The vet says something in Spanish that sounds both complicated and technical, but I decide the tone is hopeful.

"Let's go grab a drink, Jack," I say, slapping my gigantic friend on the back. "I'm buying."

We go to the one home in the village where we have seen folks gather to drink ice-cold Pilsen beer. The proprietor, Carlito, is a paunchy, curly-haired young man with a gregarious wife and a throng of smiling children. He has arranged a variety of patio furniture in front of his house where customers can sit and drink frosty 40-oz beers poured into glass jars under a flood light that illuminates his front yard.

"I make this toast to the great Ivan Drago," I say, holding a jar of beer in the air, "the myth, the man, the legend of Cumbarity—who single-handedly snatched an enormous beast from the jaws of death."

"And I toast Pedro Jones," Jack says ebulliently, "the man whose quick-thinking *actually* saved the day!"

Jack drinks beer like water and I do my best to keep up. We drink long into the evening, and, with every bottle, our toasts become increasingly outlandish and ridiculous:

"To the Samson of Cumbarity!"

"To Hippocrates Jones!"

"To the Brawn of Berkeley!"

"To Doctor Livingstone, I presume!"

It takes 6 or 8 of the 40-oz Pilsen bottles before Jack begins showing any effect from the beer. His words slurring, Jack leans in close to me to share a confession:

"I was beginning to think everyone was right," he says wistfully, his big freckled brow furrowed.

"Right about what?" I ask hiccupping.

"That I was not coming *for* anything," he explains. "But that I was just running away from my *responsibilities*. Coach, my dad, everyone said it. They had a whole intervention."

I nod because I can feel the mood shifting, though the truth is that I'm not sure I completely understand what he is saying. It feels like our friendship is too new to ask too many clarifying questions.

"What did your parents say," Jack asks, "when you told them that you were coming to Paraguay?"

"Everyone thought I had gone mad," I lie. The truth is that only my friends from college thought it was crazy that I joined the Peace Corps. My parents, on the other hand, were old hippies whose lifelong counsel to me had been to be "true to myself." Their support for my decision to spend two years teaching beekeeping in Paraguay had always been enthusiastic and unqualified.

"My whole life, all I wanted to do is get a job working with animals, whether it meant becoming a veterinarian, a biologist, or just a farmer," Jack says, almost as if to himself. "And everyone pretended like they supported my goals. I majored in fucking *biology* for God's sake. Do you know how fucking hard organic chemistry is? And I passed it while playing football for a good D1 program! Did they think I was taking those classes for fun?"

I nod, wide-eyed, as if I know how hard it is to pass biology classes at Cal.

"But as soon as I make a decision to actually do what I said I wanted to do, everyone acts like I've lost my mind. They say I have a 'responsibility' to go into the NFL draft," he says making air quotes with his massive hands. "What about a responsibility to myself? What about a responsibility to *my* dreams?"

"Fuck 'em," I say, waving my hand as if to dismiss these naysayers.

"Yeah, fuck 'em!" Jack cries, raising his jar of beer. "Saving that cow today made me realize that I am right where I'm supposed to be."

"A toast for the cow!"

"Hear hear!"

I am very hungover the next day and have a hard time concentrating in my intensive language classes which are scheduled for four hours every morning. I endure a seemingly endless series of exasperated sighs from my Guaraní language teacher, who can't seem to understand why I am having so much trouble remembering the greetings that I had recited effortlessly the day before. I am saved from this torture mid-morning by Don Antonio, the Director of the Agriculture Sector Programs, who is also the only Paraguayan national in a leadership position in the main offices in Asuncion.

Don Antonio is a jocular, stout middle-aged man with a meticulously groomed coif of thick salt-and-pepper hair and an unabashed reputation as a consummate ladies' man. He does not seem to be in a joking mood and leads me to his gleaming white Land Rover with the Peace Corps logo emblazoned on the door. Jack is already standing there—having been summoned from his language class too.

"Okay, gentlemen," he begins in his Spanish-accented English, glowering, "who gave the Epipens to the cow?"

I raise my hand.

"*Idiota*," he spits. "They aren't for animals."

"But Don Antonio—"

He puts his hand up to shush me.

"Each of those Epipens costs more than it would cost us to buy a new cow for the family," Don Antonio explains.

"But we saved—" Jack interjects.

"The cow is dead!" Don Antonio cries. "You did nothing except to cost our program thousands of dollars. We were very clear in our training that you are to use—oh, Jesus Christ, man. Pull yourself together."

But it is too late. Jack is blubbering like an enormous child. I pat him on the back and flash a withering glare at Don Antonio. Before long, some villagers and a few other beekeeping trainees have gathered to watch, aghast, as Jack cries hard, convulsing and sputtering, into his enormous hands. The scene is mildly terrifying: a giant man losing all composure like that. I am stuck in the awkward position of patting him on the back, while at the same time trying not to look at him during the public humiliation.

When he exhausts himself weeping, everyone sheepishly pretends like nothing notable has transpired.

By that afternoon I get word that Jack has quit the Peace Corps. He leaves without saying goodbye to anyone, including me.

A few days later, I walk past a group of kids playing on the street on the outskirts of the village. They are gleefully throwing clumps of dirt from the road into a nearby ditch, where the fetid, bloated carcass of the cow is being consumed by vultures and thick, pulsating swarms of black flies. The scene is both mesmerizing and awful.

For the first time since his unceremonious departure, I feel a twinge of relief that Jack has gone back home.

PART 1
MYMBA KA'AGUÝRE (Jungle Animals)

Chapter 1

CONQUISTADOR

The village of Táva Rã, Amambay celebrates my arrival with a big fiesta involving the slaughter of an enormous pig that they slice into bite-sized morsels to grill over coals. The pork is greasy and delicious and everyone except me gets extremely drunk on cane rum. Countless intoxicated men inquire with hot, sour breath about whether I might be interested in dating their sisters and daughters. I try to politely decline these offers in a way that does not insult the family—but find that sort of nuance hard with my limited language skills.

Late that night, a small group of drunken farmers walk me through the village to the home that they have prepared for me. Táva Rã is little more than a series of dilapidated, thatched-roofed wooden huts along a red dirt road, clustered around two tidy brick government buildings: a one-room schoolhouse and a small police outpost.

My sparsely furnished hut is on the outskirts of town and is not unlike all others in the village: board-and-batten walls painted seafoam green with a brown straw roof and a swept dirt floor. I am grateful to find that it has electric lights, if not running water.

"It is very well-built," one farmer says slurring his Spanish, pointing at the tree trunk that serves as a cross beam at the peak of the dwelling. "I helped to build it."

"And the latrine is far away from the well," another farmer boasts.

"And the bed is big enough for two," still another says lecherously. They all find this hilarious and begin to guess how many local women I will be inviting into my bed.

I assure the farmers that I don't plan on inviting any women to my house.

"That is because he will go to their beds!" one of the farmers yells. This sparks more conversation about the strategic location of my hut in relation to the homes of local single women.

When they have exhausted their repertoire of double entendres and gleeful speculation on my future relationships, they take their leave and I am left alone for the first time since my arrival in the village.

The silence is profound; and I stare into the darkness cataloguing all the small, seemingly inconsequential decisions I have made that have resulted in me now living in some God-forsaken corner of rural Paraguay.

The chain of choices goes back into the mists of memory, to a time when I was still a child. Even then, playing imaginary games with friends, I thought of myself as the hero of my own life story, a person capable of extraordinary fortitude in the face of the world's thorniest challenges.

Staring into the blackness with a deafening silence ringing in my ears, this view of myself appears patently naive. How had I failed to see it as such until now?

My strategy to combat the excruciating loneliness is simple: Work to the very limits of my physical abilities so that I am too exhausted to contemplate the existential dread that comes from living in such extreme destitution.

Fortunately, there is no lack of projects into which I can invest my time. When I am not improving my hovel—despite a profound ignorance of any skills associated with construction or carpentry—I busy myself helping local villagers capture killer bee colonies from the jungles. The capturing process, which is called *trasiego*, requires many hours of hard work in the stifling tropical heat while wearing full bee suits.

The villagers' enthusiasm for this suffocating work is directly correlated with the amount of cheap cane rum they have consumed. Intoxication makes my pupils loud, clumsy, and impetuous—not the most ideal qualities for managing killer bee colonies. But I am so desperate for human connection and purpose that I don't dare turn anyone away.

Besides, **Táva Rã** is the sort of place where rampant alcoholism seems less like vice than a perfectly appropriate response to the ubiquitous, soul-crushing poverty.

Because misery loves company, I become fast friends with the only person in the village who might be more miserable than I—a semi-homeless 12-year-old boy named Edén. Edén is a skinny, dark-skinned scamp with a mop of thick black hair, emotive almond-shaped eyes and a quick, cheerful smile that contrasts with his solid reputation for smoking, drinking, and petty theft.

Villagers who notice him lurking around my hovel tell me not to feed him or he will keep coming back "like a stray dog." The warning comes too late, though. I have already begun preparing a double portion of my evening meal, heaping bowls of rice and black beans.

We eat after sunset, when the intolerable jungle heat has dissipated some, and he peppers me with questions about *lostados unidos*. He loves my American music and insists that I play it on a small CD player whenever we are together. To pass the time,

I have decided to teach him chess, something I had played competitively in high school and college.

"Peter, I have a bet for you," Edén announces one evening. He speaks in a mix of Spanish and Guaraní—for my sake—but insists on using my English name, "Peter," instead of "Pedro" like everyone else.

"A bet, huh?" I say, my eyes narrowing. Edén likes to make the sort of one-sided bets that require no payment or risk from him.

"If I beat you in chess," he proposes, moving his bishop with a dramatic flourish, "then you must teach me to fight like Chuck Norris. Check." His favorite action hero is Cordell Walker, the protagonist of *Walker, Texas Ranger*, the Spanish-dubbed version of which has made it into syndication throughout Latin America.

"What do I get if I beat you in chess?" I ask, knowing that he has already lost the game.

"If you win, then I will get the *pique* out of your toes," he says beaming.

"What is the *pique*?" I ask.

"Peter, you don't know the *pique*?" he says incredulously. "How is it you do not know? Your toes, they have *bichos*."

"Bugs?" I say, scooting away from the table to examine my feet, which are bare except for the straps of the flip flops I am wearing. "Where?"

"They are under your nails, Peter," he says. "Do they not itch?"

I had noticed my toes had a strange itch over the last few days.

"Okay, I'll take that bet," I say shaking his hand. "Checkmate in three."

When he is satisfied that I have, in fact, beaten him, he dutifully kneels at my feet, sewing needle in hand, poking at my toes and squeezing them to extract the little black parasites and their creamy white egg sacs adorned with ribbons of blood.

"Hold still, Peter," he chides. "You have a lot of *pique*."

I want to tell him that it tickles, but don't know how to say it in Spanish or Guaraní.

"Peter, do they have *pique* in *lostados unidos*?" he asks, crushing one of the parasites between his thumb nails.

"No," I say.

"What kind of *bichos* are there in *lostados unidos*?" he asks.

"I don't know. Lots of the same ones," I say. "Mosquitos and flies and ants and bees." These are perhaps the only insects that I know the words for in Spanish.

"Hold still," he says squeezing the parasites out of my small toe.

"That hurt!" I cry.

"Stop being delicate," he admonishes. This is his favorite insult because he knows it bothers me.

I grit my teeth while he digs in another toe with the needle. Eric Clapton is crooning an old blues song.

"What is he saying, Peter?" Edén inquires. Edén had recently declared that Eric Clapton is his all-time favorite musician after hearing it for the first time a few days ago. He likes to play my one Clapton CD on repeat whenever we are together.

I listen to the lyrics for a moment, Clapton is half-crying in a falsetto about a "kind-hearted woman who studies evil all the time." I am not really sure I understand these lyrics in any meaningful way, but know Edén will not let me plead ignorance.

"It is about how difficult it is to find someone to love," I say.

"But it is not hard to conquer the *Americana*, Peter" Edén declares, digging in another toe with the needle.

"Conquer?" I ask through gritted teeth. "What do you mean by conquer?"

Edén drops my foot and turns to me with a sheepish smile: "You know, Peter." He makes a motion, as if revving an imaginary motorcycle: the Paraguayan sign for all manner of sexual exploits.

"What do you know about conquering women, Edén?" I inquire with a sly smile.

He turns back to my foot and pokes me with gusto.

"OW!" I yelp, jerking my foot out of his grasp. My cry echoes eerily in the hushed nighttime calm. A dog bays in response somewhere in the distance.

"You are so delicate, Peter," Edén says, pulling my foot back onto his lap. "I know that the *Americana* is *hakuietrei*."

"Is that right?" I say. "And how, exactly, do you know that American women are horny?"

"I see it in the movies, Peter," he says. "The *paraguaya* is not so *haku*. You must fight the *paraguaya* if you want to conquer her."

This is not the first time that I've heard him say something that is somehow both perfectly innocent and profoundly disturbing at the same time.

"Edén, I don't think you should be fighting someone you want to—err—conquer," I say, realizing too late that I no longer feel comfortable using that word. "And let's not use the word conquer anymore."

"What do you want to call it?" Edén asks.

I think about this for a moment, searching my limited vocabulary for an appropriate word. The chessboard on the table next to me gives me an idea.

"*Intercambio*," I suggest. "Relations with a woman should be an exchange. It is not a conquest."

Edén considers this for a moment, poking my toe with his needle. Then he asks this: "How much does it cost?"

"How much does what cost?" I ask, grimacing.

"You know," he says, "the *intercambio*. How much does the exchange cost?"

I realize, too late, that the word I chose may have been similarly ill-conceived:

"Not that kind of exchange," I clarify. "It is not a transaction. It is an exchange of—of—of—how you say it?"

Edén has finished his field surgery on my toes and stands, his curious eyes searching me for some clue as to what I am trying to convey.

"Thank you," I say, looking at my toes, which are bleeding from his handiwork. "It is an exchange of—how you say—of emotions."

Edén looks at me as if I am speaking a foreign language.

"How do you give *emociones*, Peter?"

I look into the night sky above as if the answer might be written in the stars. Clapton's guitar is wailing a soulful blues riff.

"It is like when you laugh," I say. "Sometimes it makes others laugh too, you know?"

He nods slowly as if the answer is dawning on him.

"So I need to make la *cuñakuera* laugh?" he asks.

"That is a good start," I say slapping him on the back.

"That is easy," Edén says blithely. "I can make women laugh easy."

"I am sure you can," I say, packing up our chess game.

"How many exchanges have you had, Peter?"

"I think this conversation is over, Edén," I say. "Goodnight my friend."

"I think I will go make some women laugh tonight," he says, almost as if to himself. A moment later he disappears into the darkness.

I close my door and secure it with a pair of poorly rigged latches that I installed myself. I turn off the light and lie in my bed, sweating in the sultry tropical heat, wondering where Edén goes at night.

Edén doesn't forget our chess bet and thinks talking trash will help him beat me. He often says outrageous and contemptible things in a vain attempt to distract me from my play. His smack talk reminds me of the hustlers playing chess in Washington Square Park near my NYU classes.

"Peter, there are rumors about you," Edén says, advancing his knight so that it is threatening to fork two of my more valuable pieces. His play is fairly obvious, lacking any nuance or subterfuge.

"Edén there are rumors about you too," I retort. Local villagers regularly warn me that Edén is a bad apple, a sort of Paraguayan Huckleberry Finn, transient, wild, uncivilized, and likely to steal from me if I don't watch him closely. Rumor is he had gotten kicked out of school years ago for selling cigarettes and cane rum to his classmates.

"But, Peter, the rumors about me are true," he boasts. "Are the rumors about you true also?"

"What rumors?" I ask, blocking his attack. As is our custom, Eric Clapton is serenading us with his version of an old blues song. It is my favorite time of the day—that somnolent hour, just after dark, when the nighttime cool lulls the whole village to sleep.

"The people say that you are a spy," he says in almost a whisper, advancing a pawn. Edén is employing his favorite form of psychological attack: Try to distract me with rumors he has heard from the local degenerates—drunks, gamblers, thieves, *narcotraficantes*—that he calls friends.

"If I am a spy" I parry, "what would I be spying on?" I have this idea that exploring these rumors, no matter how false and ridiculous, might force him to think critically about what he has been told.

"They say you want to steal Paraguay's *agua dulce*," he reports, moving another pawn.

I chuckle at the irony of being accused of wanting to steal the parasite-infested water that has given me a severe case of dysentery. I move aggressively, threatening his queen.

"It is not a joke, Peter," Edén says grimly. He moves a piece that fails to ameliorate his precarious position in the game.

"Yes, a very serious thing," I say sarcastically. "Do you want to take that move back?" I know that Edén will be much too proud to accept the offer. I take his queen off the board.

"Peter, if you are a spy the *pyraguë* will find out," Edén warns, moving a piece recklessly toward my king. "Check."

"The *pyraguë*?" I say, defending my king.

"Yes, the *pyraguë*," Edén repeats. He explains that *pyraguë* literally means "hairy soles," so-called because of their extreme stealth. The most lethal of the Paraguayan secret police, the *pyraguë* was organized by the long-deposed dictator, Alfredo Stroessner, who is said to still meddle in Paraguayan politics from his estancia in Brazil.

"What makes you think I am scared of the *pyraguë*?" I snort. "Would Chuck Norris be afraid?"

Edén nods slowly, as if I have said something quite reasonable. He studies the board between us. Depending on his strategy, he is four moves from losing the game. Then, for his first time in our play together, he lays down his king, conceding the game between us.

"You see that we are a few moves from checkmate?" I observe.

Edén nods, deflated.

"That is great!" I exclaim. "You lost, yes. But you also see what is coming. It may not seem like it, but this means that you are improving a lot."

Edén shrugs.

"Really, this is a good thing," I argue. "A month ago you were just learning how all the pieces move and now you are seeing many moves ahead."

Edén is unconvinced.

"Here's the thing, Edén," I say, in almost a whisper, eyes darting as if to ensure no one is listening, "I wasn't going to tell you this, but—"

Edén nods, sitting forward. "What, Peter?"

"Well, this is actually the first lesson in how to fight like Chuck Norris," I whisper.

"This?" he says conspiratorially, pointing at the chess board.

"Yes, Edén, *ajedrez*," I say. "You have to think many moves ahead. How do you think Chuck Norris is able to anticipate the attacks of his enemies?"

Edén nods with arched eyebrows, his mood visibly brightening.

"You have passed the first test," I say winking, as if I am some sort of wise, old sensei in my own strange version of *Karate Kid*.

"Now I get to learn the moves?" he asks, rising to demonstrate his shadowboxing skills around my patio.

"Strength comes from up here," I say sagaciously, tapping my temple. "Not from here," I say smacking my fist.

"Pa'i Roberto says my strength comes from my weakness," Edén recounts.

"Pa'i Roberto?"

"Yes, the *sacerdote*," Edén explains. The priest is a corpulent gray-haired man who I have seen only once in my short stay in Táva Rã. I am told that he comes every month from Pedro Juan Caballero, a nearby big city, to say mass and deliver communion in a nondescript hut that serves as the village church.

"I think you should ask Pa'i Roberto something," I say grinning. "Ask him if when he says strength comes from weakness if he means the Chuck Norris sort of strength."

"I will!" Edén exclaims gleefully.

Chapter 2

SENSITIVE CREATURES

At first glance, Pa'i Roberto's ecclesiastical garb looks suffocating. The pudgy old priest is stuffed into a starched white dress shirt, black vest, slacks, and a clerical collar wrapped tightly around his fat neck. His florid speech and refined mannerisms, though, exude the contrasting sense that he is somehow quite comfortable in the tropical heat.

"Of course your visit is not a bother," I say, welcoming both Padre Roberto and Edén to sit in plastic chairs opposite me. I am outside my hut in the late afternoon, tending to a steaming pot of beans cooking over a small metal stand that holds a tidy bed of blazing charcoal. Eric Clapton is singing softly in the background, an unplayed chess game set up for my evening ritual with Edén.

Padre Roberto speaks Spanish in quick staccato bursts, as if it is his native tongue. The Spanish to which I have become accustomed, the *campesino* version spoken in Táva Rã, is much more deliberate, almost halting—and only spoken reluctantly for my benefit.

"Can you please speak more slowly?" I ask, only catching half of what he says.

"Yes, of course," the pudgy old priest says, wiping his glistening brow with a white handkerchief. "I was just saying that it is good to meet you finally, Pedro. Our mutual friend has told me much about the American he has befriended."

I smile, imagining all the ways Edén's fertile imagination might have embellished what he told the priest about me.

"It is good that you have taught our young friend the *ajedrez*. The pope enjoys chess too." Padre Roberto looks oddly out of place sitting next to Edén, whose tattered, threadbare clothes look even shabbier by contrast.

"Edén, why don't you prepare some *tereré*," I say to my young friend, who dutifully hops up to prepare the various containers. *Tereré* is the cold version of the national loose-leaf tea. It is the Paraguayan custom to share a gourd of the cool drink with visitors on a hot day.

"That is very kind," Padre says, carefully pacing his speech. "You need only play a traditional polka instead of this American music and you would be living just like any Paraguayan!"

"This is Eric Clapton," Edén shouts proudly from somewhere in my hovel where he is preparing the tea. "This song is a traditional American blues song"—only he can't pronounce blues so it came out more like "eh-bus."

"Ahh, yes, the blues," Padre says. "I have heard of this music before. It is the music of the blacks, no?"

"Yes, that's right," I confirm, deciding not to complicate the conversation by adding that Clapton is actually a white Englishman.

"It is like the samba," Father says. "In Brazil the music of the African slaves became the samba."

"You sound like a scholar of music," I observe, stirring the pot of simmering beans.

"Do not tell Edén," he murmurs conspiratorially, "but I love Bossa Nova."

"Brazilian music?" I say.

"Yes, it is the most famous Brazilian music," Padre says. "Here in Amambay we get Brazilian radio stations from Mato Grasso. I grew up listening to Bossa Nova when it was actually *nova*."

Edén emerges from inside my hut carrying a *tereré* gourd and pitcher of water

"It is written that there is nothing *nova* under the sun," Padre intones. "Thank God."

Edén places the *tereré* on the chess table.

"Here you go my son," Padre says, thrusting a bill into Edén's hand. "Go get us some ice from Karai Amado."

Edén nods and dashes down the dirt road to the hut in the middle of the village where the proprietor sells long tubes of ice in thin plastic sleeves from the only freezer in town.

"He is a good boy," Father says as we watch him trot down the road. "It is hard to be good in a place like this."

I whistle as if to endorse his assessment. For a moment we sit there wordlessly, as if contemplating the observation.

"This challenge is made even more difficult by his belief that you are teaching him how to fight," Padre laments. "But I am sure this is one of his fantasies, no?"

I look at Pa'i Roberto, as if seeing him for the first time. He looks vaguely like a watchful old bulldog with his jowly cheeks and steady dark eyes. Despite the courteous rebuke, I find myself not offended, but feeling a strange kinship with the old man. We are both missionaries—of a sort—in this strange, sad village who have developed a fondness for the same mischievous kid.

"You know how he is," I say. "He hears only what he wants to hear."

"Yes, I know how he is," Padre says smiling indulgently. "That is why I worry."

"Padre, you needn't worry," I assure. "I will not teach him anything dangerous."

"You already gave him some dangerous ideas," he says, a kind smile contradicting the criticism.

"What is that?" I say incredulously. "I haven't taught him anything about fighting—"

"No, no, no, not fighting." he interrupts. "But might you have encouraged him to question how strength can come from weakness?"

I smile, despite myself, imagining how the conversation must have gone. "I apologize for that, Padre," I say, casting my eyes downward. "I didn't mean to cause a problem."

"I suspected that you did not mean to cause problems," he says courteously. "I can see that you and I both want what is best for the boy."

In the distance, Edén is trotting down the road with two cylinders of ice in hand.

"I wish there was something I—err—would teach him," I say struggling with the conditional tense, "that he can actually use."

"I am sure there is much you are teaching him," Padre says confidently, waving his hand as if to dismiss my comment.

"Chess won't help him much," I snort. "Not in this village."

"You are much more than a teacher," Padre counsels. "You are a friend."

"Yes, but I wish it could actually help him in some way," I say. "Like in his real life."

"Oh ho!" Padre calls. "You do not think friendship is real life?"

"Yes, it is real life," I concede. "But I want to be able to help him more than that."

"Like the food you serve every night?" he says pointing at the simmering pot between my knees.

"Yes!" I say. "Exactly. Something tangible. But more permanent. Like a skill or a trade. He does not want to learn beekeeping."

"Beekeeping?" Padre asks, wiping his brow with the handkerchief.

"Yes, the production of honey. *La apicultura*," I clarify. "It is my specialty. It is my mission here."

"He did not mention that," Padre says, a faraway look in his eyes. "I think I can change his attitude."

"Good luck!" I say flatly. I have often encouraged Edén to join me on my beekeeping expeditions. He has a preternatural knack for avoiding anything that sounds even remotely like work.

Edén approaches the hut short of breath with ice in hand.

"Thank you, my son," Padre says.

Edén smiles proudly and inserts the cylinders of ice into the pitcher. He pours the water into the gourd and passes it to Padre.

"Pedro tells me that he has invited you to learn beekeeping," Padre says, taking a gulp of tea. Edén's smile disappears as it dawns on him where the conversation is headed.

"I have invited him many, many times, Padre," I confirm, drinking my sip and passing the gourd back to Edén. "But he does not want to come with me."

"Perhaps he is afraid?" Padre suggests, winking at me. Edén pours himself a drink and sucks on the metal straw, his eyes darting from the old priest to me and back again. Clapton fills the silence with a musical lament about an unfaithful woman.

"I am not afraid," Edén replies defensively, refilling the gourd.

"It is okay to be scared," Padre consoles.

"I am not afraid," Edén insists through gritted teeth.

"Is that so?" Padre says, squinting as if trying to see something that is far away. "Then why don't you assist Pedro?"

Edén shrugs, looking slightly ashamed—an emotion I didn't think he possessed.

"I would like to propose a business deal," Padre announces.

Edén's eyes get wide. He likes deals almost as much as he likes bets.

"If you produce honey, I will sell it for you in Pedro Juan Caballero." Pedro Juan Caballero is the biggest city in the remote state, a border town that serves mainly as a busy hub for all sorts of smuggling between Brazil and Paraguay.

Edén seals the deal with a handshake and begins manic speculation about how he intends to grow our newly formed enterprise.

Padre Roberto, a twinkle in his tired, old bulldog eyes, appears quite satisfied that he has awakened an entrepreneurial spirit in the boy. He takes his leave soon thereafter explaining that he has a long drive ahead of him to get back home for the night.

"Thank you for the visit, Pa'i Roberto," I say, standing.

"It was a pleasure," he says shaking my hand. "I look forward to our visit next month." He takes a few paces toward the road and stops short, his index finger thrust into the air, as if remembering something he had forgotten.

"One more thing," he says, turning to face us. "You are a *creenete*, no?"

"A believer?" I say.

"A Christian, yes?"

For a brief moment, I contemplate telling him the truth: My hippie parents raised me to possess a healthy skepticism of all organized religion—especially Christianity. But the priest's visit had been the most interesting and pleasant I had had in my short stay in the village and the kinship I felt with him, in that moment, seemed to demand prevarication.

"*Sí, soy creente*," I say after what is perhaps a longer pause than I would have liked. I was never a good liar, but it feels easier, somehow, in a foreign language, as if everything I say is already some slightly skewed facsimile of the truth.

"Would you like to come to church?" he asks simply.

I feel sure that attending church would highlight my spiritual ignorance, so I say something that I think is quite clever: "I do not need a church to believe."

"I thought you might say that," Padre says, without elaborating further. "Goodnight, gentlemen."

While we eat our beans over chess that evening, Edén dreams aloud about our newly formed enterprise. He is quite sure that the arrangement will yield extraordinary riches. I can't bring myself to temper his enthusiasm with a more reasonable profits forecast. By the time I pack up our chess game later that night, Edén is fantasizing about life as a wealthy Paraguayan honey baron.

The next morning, I am woken from a deep sleep by the sort of racket that makes me sit bolt upright in bed.

"Peter, *despiértate*!" Edén calls out, banging on the wall right next to where my bed sits. The cool air in my hovel tells me it is some ungodly early hour of the morning. It takes me a moment to remember our conversation from the past evening and conclude he must have come to launch our beekeeping business.

"Okay, okay," I groan. "I'm up. Let me get dressed."

When I walk outside, I find Edén already tending to a fire that contains a pot of boiling water.

"I have the water for our tea," he says proudly, inviting me to sit in the chair next to him. Local roosters have begun their volleys of cockcrows to celebrate that hour of the early morning when the eastern sky shows the first dim blues of light.

"You're up early," I grumble as I sit down heavily next to my young companion.

"Yes, Peter," he says, rising to prepare the rest of the equipment for our morning tea. I watch groggily, arms crossed, as he deftly pours the boiling water into a thermos and then shakes pulverized leaves from a box into my bulbous gourd.

"I know of four beehives in the jungle near here," Edén announces, passing me the tea gourd.

"And where are we going to put the bees?" I ask.

"We can just make a lot of smoke and then take the honey and run," he says. "That is the Paraguayan way."

I tell him that the Paraguayan way is not sustainable, explaining that if he is to achieve his lofty business ambitions, he will have to learn how to capture the bee colonies from the wild and actually manage them.

"Manage the hives?" he asks. "What does that mean?"

"It's like having an animal on the farm," I explain, using the metaphor that has resonated with local farmers. "You have to make sure the colony gets enough to eat, is safe from predators and parasites, stuff like that."

"Predators?"

"You know, mites, moths, frogs, toads."

"How do you feed them, Peter?"

"You can feed them sugar water to increase the size of the colony if you're trying to prepare them for a flowering season," I say. "But usually they only need nectar from flowers."

"Nectar? What's nectar?"

"Look, Edén," I say, standing to stretch, "we can sit here all day talking about it and I'm not sure it will do you much good. It is easier to learn all this by doing it."

"Okay, Peter, let's do it," Edén says, rubbing his hands together, a big smile spreading across his face. I disappear into my hut and return holding two bee suits.

"First thing we have to do," I say holding them up, "is get you stung."

The smile evaporates.

"Stung?"

"Yes, Edén," I say, relishing the moment perhaps a bit too much. "We have to make sure you are not allergic."

"But you have special clothes so we do not get stung," Edén replies. "It is protection."

"You still get stung a lot doing this work," I explain. "Even with the veil and suit I get stung almost every time I go out."

Edén looks stricken.

"You've been stung before, no?" I ask.

Edén nods unenthusiastically.

"So you're probably not allergic," I say. "We just need to make sure. We can go to the hive I have out back. Come on, let's get dressed." I nod my head toward the back of my hut where I keep a demonstration hive.

Edén rises reluctantly to get dressed with me. The suits are one-size-fits all veil and long sleeve shirt combination with elastic bands at the waist and wrists. To protect our hands, we wear yellow rubber dish gloves. Edén is wearing shorts, so he must borrow a pair of pants from me, which are much too big for him. I use duct tape to belt the pants around his waist and fasten a pair of plastic grocery bags around his ankles like shoes. When he is all dressed he looks like some sort of hobo astronaut.

"All set," I say, squeezing his shoulder. His face is obscured by the veil, but his body language says that he is hesitant.

"This is a smoker," I say, placing a glowing coal into the tin fire chamber. "You squeeze it like this to produce smoke. The bees smell smoke and they think there is a fire. They gorge on the honey thinking they may have to swarm and find a new home. They won't attack as much if they're doing that."

"It is a trick!" Edén exclaims. Edén loves tricks.

"Umm, yeah," I concur. "It is sort of like a trick. But they'll still sting you. It will just make them less aggressive."

We walk toward the demonstration hive set behind a small hedge of bushes on a small platform behind my hut. The hive looks out onto a wide expanse of marsh, an ethereal mist rising above the flaxen stalks in the dim early morning light.

"Edén, listen," I begin. "Here is the real trick." I pause for effect as we find our places next to the bee box. "We need you to get stung not just because we need to see if you are allergic. We also have to make sure that, when you get stung, you are able to stay calm. The bees, they can sense if you are anxious. They know if you're breathing fast. They can even hear your heart beating. They are very sensitive creatures. If you are too loud or move too fast or nervously, they'll swarm onto you and then you'll be in real trouble."

My wooden demonstration hive is not like the bee boxes one might see in American farms. It is a Kenyan Top Bar hive that looks more like a trough than the rectangular box—called a Langstroth hive—that has become the most popular variety in the industrialized world.

The lid is just a plain wooden board that is stuck to the trough by bee propolis resin. I peel the board off the top, revealing 18 uniform wooden bars underneath arranged in a row that serve as a sort of second lid.

"You smell that?" I ask. The spicy propolis bouquet mingles with the smoke to produce an aroma like some sort of exotic middle eastern incense. Edén is unusually quiet. "That is how it is supposed to smell. Remember it. Smell is important in this work."

I look over to my companion who is standing as still as a statue, a few curious bees wandering over the veil in front of his face. I send plumes of smoke into the air between us.

"Edén, the bees are not aggressive right now," I say, rolling up a sleeve to reveal the naked flesh of my forearm. I place the arm next to his veil and a bee wanders from his veil onto my arm, stumbling over the blonde hairs.

"See? The bee is just curious. You will know when they are aggressive. You can even smell it."

Edén remains quiet.

"Edén, you can talk. You can move. They're not going to do anything to you."

The ensuing silence says that Edén is unconvinced.

"Let's get this over with," I declare. "Pull up your sleeve like mine."

"Wait, Peter," Edén whispers breathlessly, yanking his arm out of my grasp. "They can hear my heart beating fast?"

"Yes, they can sense when you are anxious."

"How do I stop it?" he asks, his words half choked.

"Stop what?"

"How do I keep my heart from beating fast?"

"Edén, are you afraid?" I say, perhaps a bit too cheerfully.

Edén does not answer and I sense, perhaps too late, that he is ashamed of his fear—which makes me feel like a jerk. He is always so full of bluster and bravado, I sometimes forget that deep down he is just a scared kid.

"When I first came out to work bees I was also nervous," I confess. "That is why we are doing this. The only way to become less nervous is to do this."

"But, Peter, you said that they will swarm me if I breathe a lot," he recalls. "You said they can hear my heart."

"Look, it is not that bad," I say, deftly snatching a bee wandering on the wooden bars. It does not like being pinched between my fingers and is desperately thrusting its abdomen about in a vain attempt to sting its captor.

"See how it is trying to sting," I say, holding the bee in front of his veil. "Now, watch."

I slowly place the angry bee on the naked underside of my forearm where she promptly martyrs herself, burying her stinger in my flesh and leaving a string of entrails as she buzzes away to her death.

"You see? It is nothing."

Edén is silent, his face obscured by the veil.

"See the small white ball?" I ask. "That is the poison sac. It is where the poison comes from. See how it is pumping? It will continue pumping poison for two or three minutes. This is why you need to remove the stingers." I demonstrate how to scrape the stinger from my skin with my thumb.

"It does not hurt you?" Edén whispers.

"Sure, it still hurts," I say. "But you get used to it. Come on, move your sleeve."

Edén remains still.

"Peter, how do you become less nervous if you are already nervous?" Edén asks. "How can I stop my heart from beating fast?"

I fall silent for a moment really listening to him for the first time. I wish there was some way I could comfort him—but I know this is one of those times, when doing is better than saying anything.

"You can't," I acknowledge. "All you can do is decide if you are going to do this even if you are nervous. A lot of people would never try this because they are too afraid. But I think you are brave. You are brave like Cordell Walker."

Edén very slowly moves his sleeve until a tiny patch of his brown skin is exposed. I snatch another bee from the top of the hive and quickly press it onto his flesh.

"Ow!" he yelps, quickly covering the skin with his sleeve.

"Wait, Edén," I say, holding him by the shoulders. "You need to remove the stinger, remember?"

He ignores my instructions, his gloved hand rubbing his arm where he was stung. I tell him that it will get itchy and much more swollen if he doesn't remove the stinger, but he doesn't seem to care.

"Edén, now let me show you what they look like when they're angry." With the toe of my boot, I kick the hive a couple times, jostling the box violently.

"No, Peter!" Edén exclaims. But it is too late, the hollow thuds are followed by a low buzzing sound emanating from inside the hive. Only a moment later we are both being attacked, the familiar popping sound of bees diving into our bee suits.

"This is what it feels like when they're angry," I explain. "And see, you're totally safe in the suit. Smell that? It smells like bananas. That is the attack pheromone. You can smell their anger."

I pump the bellow of my smoker, sending plumes of white thick smoke into the air around us.

"The smoke is not working, Peter," Edén says, a barely perceptible quaver in his voice.

"It is working," I murmur. "But it will take a little while. Stand still. Listen. Watch. Smell. Feel it. They will calm down. Just watch and wait. And I think you will find that you will calm down too." My beekeeping students, up until that moment, had all been half-drunk, desperately poor, subsistence farmers. They were the sort of pupils that tended to privilege practicality over poetry. But with Edén, it seems like the reverse is true: He needs me to discuss how it feels to manage a hive of dangerous bees—not just what to do.

At the far horizon, across the expansive swamp, the sky is blazing with a sunrise full of vibrant bloody oranges—tangerine, papaya, pomelo. Perhaps it is the adrenaline response triggered by the bee venom, or perhaps it is the rhythmic thumping of angry bees—or a combination of both—but I am suddenly aware that the dramatic, sublime moment requires reverence.

We stand together, plumes of smoke rising around us, the rhythmic thumping of bees on our bee suits dissipating slowly—almost imperceptibly—like the raindrops of a violent summer storm.

When the bees have calmed so too has my mind and I am left feeling exhausted, as if I had glimpsed some great mystery of life, which was so grand and elegant and expansive that my mind could not fully comprehend what it had seen. Part of me wants to ask my young friend if he felt it too, but I know, somehow, that words will only diminish the experience.

Chapter 3

HONEY FROM THE ROCK

With only a few hours of training, Edén decides to market himself as an expert beekeeper. He targets all the farmers who have captured bee colonies from the jungles with me and is satisfied to be paid in honey. He promises that his weekly visits to manage the hives will result in higher honey yields, making the arrangement a win-win for both parties.

The result of Edén's enterprise is that there is a marked increase in the number of local farmers that request my help capturing bee colonies from the wild. Even the laziest chronic alcoholics in town see this as an easy way to produce their own honey—for sale or trade or consumption—with little or no work.

Edén is a savvy entrepreneur and consummate salesman, ready to work with anyone in the village for the right price—with one conspicuous exception. He refuses to work for his own father and wants me to join him in his very specific beekeeping embargo.

"You should not work with him," Edén declares one evening, while we play chess. "He is a drunk." As is our custom, Eric Clapton provides a soundtrack to our evenings.

"Being drunk would disqualify pretty much everyone in Táva Rã," I remind him.

"But my father is worse, Peter," Edén replies. "He is a bad, bad man."

"He didn't seem that bad," I say. Earlier that day Edén's father paid me a visit, inquiring whether I could help him capture a bee colony like I had done with many others in town. He is a short, dark man with strong indigenous features and sad rheumy eyes. His breath smelled like cane liquor and his words were slurred, but he looked no better or worse than other drunks in the village.

"You don't know what he does, Peter," Edén says. "He will use it for bad things."

"What bad things?" I ask.

"He will use it to make my mother sicker."

"Sicker?"

"Yes, Peter, she gets *casos de los nervios*," he says, as if this is self-explanatory. "It is your move." This was more than I'd ever heard about his family situation, something I hadn't felt as if I had the opportunity to ask about until now.

"Don't worry about the game," I say waving my hand dismissively. "Edén, what do you mean by 'a case of the nerves?'"

"My mother is *un tavyron*," he clarifies. "She is not okay in the mind. She sees things that are not there. *Una loca.*"

Eric Clapton is singing "Floating Bridge," a song about the trauma of living through a terrible flood. It seems oddly appropriate for our conversation.

"But, Edén, what does this have to do with helping your father have a beehive?" I say.

Edén sighs heavily as if exasperated by a dense child to whom he must explain something exceedingly complex.

"I am saying that my father will use the honey he produces to try and go back to my mother."

I squint trying to imagine why Edén wouldn't want his parents to be together.

"Peter, if my father uses the honey as a gift to go back to my mother," he says in a tone that tells me that his patience is wearing thin, "then soon she will be pregnant again. But he will not stay. He will not help. He will go away. My mother should not have any more children. She already has too many and it is not good."

So many questions come to mind: Does he live with his mother? And siblings? Where does his mother live? Where does his father live? Is there any chance for reconciliation? But I can tell that Edén does not want to discuss it anymore. And besides, I suspect that the answers to these questions will only uncover deeper tragedy, misery, and dysfunction.

"Okay, Edén," I say, returning my attention to the chess board between us. "What do I tell your dad is the reason I won't help?"

"Tell him that you're too busy to do it yourself," he says. "And that I am your assistant. He is too proud to ask me for help."

When Pa'i Roberto returns to Táva Rã for monthly mass, Edén is eager to deliver the month's harvest: eight golden panels of capped honeycomb that he has collected, which we have sealed in small plastic containers. Though I am less effusive than my adolescent friend, I am also quite proud of what we have to show for our month's work.

We are sitting outside my hovel in the evening while Padre inspects our product.

"This is quite impressive," he says, prodding one of the soft honeycombs with his index finger.

"And the good thing about capped honey is that it will keep without refrigeration," I say. "They found honey sealed in pots in the tomb of King Tut. It was still sweet after thousands of years."

"The only thing you are missing is a brand," Padre says. "Do you have a name for your product?"

I defer to Edén who is sitting next to the old priest, beaming.

"Let's call it *miel Tres Leones*!" Edén suggests, as if suddenly inspired. *Tres Leones* is the most popular brand of cheap cane rum in Paraguay.

Padre Roberto flashes a knowing look at me and for a moment both of us fall silent, neither particularly eager to stifle the kid's enthusiasm.

"Why don't we just call it *miel de Edén*," I counter.

"No, Peter," Edén says, a look of disgust on his face. "Maybe we call it *miel* Eric Clapton?"

I shoot a look at Padre as if asking for his help. How does one explain trademark laws to an elementary school dropout from rural Paraguay? Padre just smiles as if he is immensely enjoying the absurd conversation.

"Okay," I say, nodding, as if I am actually considering the proposal. "But do you think anyone knows Eric Clapton?"

Edén shakes his head.

"What's wrong with *miel de Edén*?" I ask.

"I don't like my name," Edén says simply. I decide it best not to debate this point.

"Okay," I say. "I have an idea: What name would you want if you could name yourself? Maybe we can call it that name?"

"Yes, I like that idea," Edén says, nodding enthusiastically. "I like the name *Roque*." He explains that this is the name of his favorite soccer star, Roque Santa Cruz.

"So *miel de Roque*?" I say, looking at Padre for help. "A problem might be that it doesn't sound particularly appetizing to say honey from the rock."

"I disagree," Padre chimes in. "There is a beautiful psalm about a land so rich that when rocks are cracked open honey flows from them. Also, Pedro, your name means rock. So, it works on many levels. It is an inspired name."

"*Miel de Roque*!" Edén exclaims.

With the brand name settled, Father says he must get going, citing the long drive back to the city ahead of him. Edén is already wondering aloud about what our *Miel de Roque* logo should be.

"I almost forgot," Father says, pulling a paperback book out of a small leather satchel he brought with him. "This is for you, Pedro. I found an English translation."

He passes me a book with a weeping saint on the cover entitled *Confessions of Saint Augustine*.

"You know Augustine?" he asks.

"I have heard of him," I say. "I've never read this. Or anything."

"I thought you would like it," he says, gathering the plastic containers in his arms. "You may find him to be *un alma gemela*."

A 1,600-year-old Algerian theologian, my kindred spirit? I do not tell the old priest that it seems unlikely I will have much in common with the saint—any saint really—but promise, nonetheless, to read the book before he returns the next month.

I begin reading *Confessions* later that evening, after Edén has left me alone in my hovel. It is a slow start, full of florid language praising God with lots of Bible citations. But it is easy enough to skip the tedious parts and focus on the real story: the autobiography of a man tortured by the memories of his former self.

Having spent the better part of my first months in Táva Rã reflecting on the unique combination of hubris, folly, and naiveté that led me to join the Peace Corps, I couldn't help but feel some strange kinship with the author.

Like me, Augustine was a clever student, who, in hindsight, wonders about the ultimate value of what he had learned in his elite schools. It is not hard to question the utility of my degree in English, given my struggles with simple everyday tasks like handwashing clothes, splitting wood, and cooking food over an open fire.

Augustine describes excelling in his elite schools without much effort and how he adopts the values of his culture insofar as they advance the pursuit of pleasure. His education, his intelligence, is all vanity. He calls it "rich beggary and shameful glory."

It is strange how modern the saint sounds, how his words could be a description of my time at NYU. What was the point of it all? In hindsight, my life in New York City seems such rich foppery. My education had equipped me to write an incisive 20-page paper about dust bowl farmers in *Grapes of Wrath*, while remaining abjectly ignorant of the real-life struggles of those living in extreme rural poverty.

Augustine is so clearly done with it all. It is all just the trappings of a society that has forsaken noble ideas for the basest passions. It is all just a way for clever people to "tell of their own licentiousness and be applauded for it, so long as they did it in a full and ornate oration of well-chosen words."

Augustine gives voice to the vague suspicion that had been forming in my mind, like dark clouds gathering before a thunderstorm. The notion is almost too troubling to consider for very long: Is the Peace Corps simply an elaborate, misguided effort to cloak my selfish pursuits in altruistic garb?

"A curtain for error."

I want to see behind the curtain, to pierce the veil.

What had Augustine done? Had something been done to him? Did it require some God-forsaken place like Paraguay to change his thinking?

I turn off the light in my hovel and ponder these questions, turning them over again and again in my mind, staring into the darkness. Maybe Padre was right. Maybe this long dead saint is my *alma gemela* after all.

Having cornered the existing beehive market in Táva Rã, Edén expands his services to local farmers by offering to assist me, instead of them, in capturing bee colonies from the jungles.

Initially, I am reluctant to let him insert himself into the only remaining activity that connects me to the wider community. I have this idea that as long as I require the *campesinos* to participate in the *trasiego* process, I won't have completely abandoned my mission in the community.

Also, capturing colonies from the wild almost always involves long hours schlepping heavy tools and a bee box into the jungles to cut down enormous trees where the bees have made homes. It is hard work for two grown men, and I tell Edén that I don't think it is the sort of job he will be able to do.

But Edén is eager to prove his worth and is unrelenting in his quest to become the village honey czar. He knows enough about beekeeping to have learned that *trasiegos* usually result not just in the capture of a colony, but also a large honey harvest. He promises to split the harvest 50-50 with the farmers on whose land the colonies reside. The deal seems like a no-brainer to the farmers, who don't have to lift a finger for the honey.

"The most dangerous thing about this work is not the bees," I tell Edén, as we traipse through the jungle one early morning en route to our first *trasiego* together. "It's the tree. If it falls on you, you're done. Dead. Understand?"

"Si Peter," Edén says too quickly to have seriously heeded my warning. He resumes humming his favorite Clapton song. I decide that his Pollyannaish enthusiasm is going to get him hurt or worse.

"Stop, Edén," I command. I toss the heavy bee box that I am carrying on the ground between us. "Look at me." He stops and turns, impatience written plainly on his face. Under his arm he is carrying a machete, an axe, and an unwieldy two-man crosscut saw.

"Look, Edén," I begin, hands on my hips, "if you're going to do this with me, you need to listen. Cutting down a tree is hard work and it is very dangerous."

Edén rolls his eyes.

"Have you ever done this before?" I ask. "Have you ever cut down a tree?"

"Of course, Peter," he snorts. "Many, many times. All Paraguayans know how to do this."

"But you have never done it to capture a colony of bees," I say.

"Peter, this will be easy," he promises. "The hive is in a *kuri'y* tree. It is very soft, easy to cut down."

Something in my countenance must have betrayed my poker face. Somehow, he could tell that his specific knowledge of the relative density of the tree had impressed me. For the rest of our journey to the colony, he points at the various trees we pass, reciting the names that are derived from the ancient Guaraní inhabitants: *urunday, guatambu, peterevy, curupa'y, lapacho, caranday, ambay, timbo*.

He is right about the tree: The flesh of the *kuri'y* tree is relatively soft and, together, we quickly chop it down. It falls with a tremendous crash and the bees immediately swarm us aggressively.

In just a few short weeks, Edén has become quite comfortable working during the hive's berserk attacks. We carefully chop our way into the tree with a machete so that we may extract the honeycomb, some golden with honey, others heavy with larvae. The honeycomb is soft and fragile in the oppressive midday heat requiring that we delicately tie the panels to the topbars of the bee box.

When we have extracted all the honeycomb, the swarm, as if of one mind, abandons their attack on us. I take off my veil.

"Go ahead," I say. "You may take it off now."

Edén is unconvinced.

"You will be fine, Edén," I say. "You see? They are not aggressive anymore."

Edén slowly removes his veil, his mouth agape. It doesn't matter how many *trasiegos* I do, it always feels somewhat miraculous when the bees suddenly calm. The colony, only minutes before, had been attacking us with a terrifying frenzy. Now they seem a different species altogether. I don't dare ruin the moment with words.

We relish the peace for a time, watching the enormous heaps of pulsing bees on the tree in and around where we had extracted their honeycomb. Though there is still work to do, it does not feel like work anymore; the rest of the job feels like some sort of ancient sorcery.

I show Edén how to look for the queen, how to watch the amorphous masses dripping from the felled tree. How to watch with unfocused eyes, as if peering into a crystal ball, to see for those places in the heaps where the swarm seems to vibrate at a different frequency.

Before long, I catch a glimpse of the queen, whose coloring is not striped yellow, but a deep amber. I show Edén how to catch it—gingerly, not too tight, not too loose—between his thumb and index finger and trap it in a tiny matchbox.

Edén watches in awe as the vast army of insects marches in unison, as if compelled by some unseen force, into the wooden bee box, where we have placed their imprisoned monarch. The moment is exhilarating—magical—but instead of watching the swarm, I find myself watching Edén's astonished face.

Once Edén begins assisting with all the *trasiegos*, hardly a day goes by when we don't spend the better part of our waking hours together.

"Can I just stay here with you tonight?" Edén asks one evening as we are finishing our game of chess. Given the amount of time we are spending together, I had guessed he might ask this question and prepared myself to be firm in response.

"No," I answer, perhaps too swiftly. "I am sorry Edén, but you cannot."

He shrugs as if he is neither particularly disappointed nor surprised by the answer. Then he says goodnight and disappears into the darkness.

I find it hard to fall asleep that evening, and most evenings thereafter, my conscience plagued with guilt, heartbreaking images of Edén flashing in my mind. I can't help but imagine the boy bedding down among farm animals or, worse still, trying to get to sleep with his throng of wild, half-naked siblings, while his mother argues with the voices in her head.

I try to quiet my mind by thinking of the many good reasons why I shouldn't let the kid stay with me. It is probably against the law. The Peace Corps probably has some rule against it. The rumors would be brutal.

I had been in Táva Rã long enough to know that the locals were quietly suspicious of the motives of anyone who might choose to abandon a life in a wealthy country full of delicate, beautiful Nordic people to spend two years in a desperately poor village in rural South America. And because I reject overtures from the local women, it wouldn't take long for pedophile rumors to spread.

Still, my conscience is not satisfied by these perfectly reasonable objections. In my heart of hearts, I know I should simply let the kid stay with me. If I were the hero that Edén imagined me to be, I wouldn't let the laws, rules, and rumors get in the way of what is right. If I were a hero like Cordell Walker, I wouldn't think twice about contravening norms in service of some greater good.

To cope with the stubborn insomnia, I read *Confessions* long into the night, which only exacerbates the troubling thoughts keeping me awake.

Not only do I see myself in the life of the tortured Augustine, but I see Edén as the saint's young acolyte Alypius. Like me and Edén, the pair become fast friends mainly because perdition is only slightly less miserable in the company of another.

The pair wander through a rough and unforgiving world—not unlike the one I inhabit—only dimly aware that the greatest advances of their civilization, in which they had invested their hopes and dreams, are profoundly corrupt.

The only hope is radical conversion, a mystical garden experience, replete with the voices of angels.

Tolle lege, tolle lege

"Take and read, take and read," the angels sing.

And so I read on, sure that if I do so carefully enough, I will find rest at last.

Chapter 4

HARVEST

By my fourth month in the Peace Corps, the worst effects of culture shock—sleeplessness, anxiety, homesickness—are beginning to wane. I have lived in Táva Rã just long enough to become accustomed to the sleepy rhythms of the remote farming village, but not quite long enough to purge myself of the notion that I am the heroic, noble champion of my own personal odyssey.

Padre Roberto is to blame for these persistent delusions. The book he loaned me, Augustine's *Confessions*, has filled my head with vague hope that someday a dramatic epiphany will serve to give all my suffering some greater purpose.

I want to tell Padre about all my favorite passages from the Saint's autobiography. But on this particular visit, the old priest is not interested in a book discussion. He has another agenda.

"It is harvest season," Father murmurs. His jowly face looks especially serious. He is sitting outside my hut at twilight and seems to be talking mostly to me, though my young friend, Edén, is by my side, as always.

I purse my lips, annoyed that he wants to talk about the dull and obvious changing of the seasons instead of the profound literature that I had meticulously read straight through no fewer than three times that month.

Padre ignores my look and leans in closer, talking in a tone that is barely more than a whisper: "There are two harvests, one seen and one unseen."

I try hard not to roll my eyes.

"Do you know of both harvests?"

I shrug and look over at Edén who nods in agreement.

"There is the cotton harvest, and you will see that," Padre explains. "But there is also the marijuana harvest at the same time, which you will be wise to ensure that you do not see."

In all my time beekeeping in surrounding jungles and farms, I hadn't come across any marijuana plantations. In fact, I had mostly forgotten my Peace Corps boss' cryptic warning about narcotrafficking until that moment.

Padre explains that it is the month that I need to be very careful about what I do. I need to listen to Edén. I need to check with him before I go out into the community on my beekeeping excursions. I might see something that I cannot unsee. And I do not want to make myself a target.

Padre's dire warning solidifies Edén's role as my fixer, and my young partner seems to enjoy arranging my daily beekeeping jobs in the village. We continue our daily visits to local farmers, helping them to capture bee colonies, sometimes managing their hives, and things feel pretty much like they did before—until the harvest.

The cotton harvest is as remarkable as Padre said it would be. A severe, well-dressed man with shined leather shoes, slacks, and a blood-red collared shirt stations himself in an empty lot next to the village school. As if beckoned by his very presence, farmers from miles around bring bulbous, burlap sacks full of cotton to be inspected and weighed. He hands them each a wad of cash on the spot.

By sunset, his caravan of roaring diesel trucks leaves Táva Rã only to be replaced, soon thereafter, by another caravan. I ask Edén if this is the caravan for the marijuana harvest. My question makes him laugh.

"Noooo, Peter," he says. "Those people bring the *calecitahape*." The strangers in the center of town have brought the annual harvest carnival, Edén explains.

I ask Edén if it means the marijuana harvest has already occurred. His nod is slow and barely perceptible, eyes darting about, as if even this silent acknowledgment is tantamount to treason.

The carnival is tiny by American standards, but it is the biggest party I have seen in all my time in our remote village. It arrives in one tractor trailer out of which they construct stalls for a number of makeshift games of chance and a shabby little train for kids that goes slowly in circles around a winding track. Strings of flashing lights are festooned about, and two speakers blare bad cachaca music that echoes off distant hills. The whole spectacle is organized by the sort of unkempt, shifty characters one might expect to see at carnivals anywhere and is powered by electricity that is stolen from the overhead cables.

Edén tells me that the carnival is great fun—music, dancing, rum, games of chance—and that we should go together. I tell him that I don't plan on wasting our meager honey profits on cheap cane rum and parlor tricks. Besides, I recall, I've been to a party where everyone gets drunk, and it's tedious. I have no desire to spend my evening interacting with taciturn Paraguayans who become overly familiar under the influence of their favorite drink. They'll no doubt inquire about which local girls I have conquered. They scrutinize my responses, and I have learned there is no acceptable answer to this line of questioning. To lie that I have actually been intimate with local girls invites frenzied speculation and demands for specificity. To deny such relations provokes skepticism and, occasionally, pejorative comments about my sexual orientation.

Edén says that I'm being delicate and announces he is going to enjoy the festivities without me. For the first time in many months, I don't see him for a number of days. Worse still, due to Padre's warning to arrange all my work through Edén, I find myself without anything to do.

Over the course of the week, *los carnavaleros* blare the cachaca, beckoning farmers from distant villages to come enjoy the festivities. The farmers come at night, fortified by their favorite cheap cane rum, their pockets swollen with cash crop profits.

I have the sneaking suspicion that Edén is having the time of his life at the carnival. Apparently the festival is more interesting than chess, Eric Clapton, and my specialized knowledge of *Walker, Texas Ranger*.

From my stuffy hut, I imagine that Edén is reveling in the way the carnival subverts many of the same strict mores of rural Paraguayan life that have served to relegate him to his pariah status in the community.

There are few things in life more agonizing than enduring sounds of people laughing and having fun while one is trying very hard to feel sorry for oneself.

The deafening cachaca music shakes the board-and-batten walls of my hut late into the night. In the dark morning hours, after the insufferable music stops, I find that I have trouble sleeping. When I do sleep, my dreams are strange and carnivalesque and I wake up in fits while it is still dark outside, feeling anxious.

Worse yet, the carnival remains in Táva Rã much longer than I expect. It operates every night for at least a week and, as sleep deprivation compounds my loneliness and general malaise, I console myself by scrupulously listing in my mind all the ways that I have been underappreciated since my arrival in the village.

This may account for part of the reason why—on the final night of the carnival, after the music shuts off and gunfire subsequently erupts—I am not in the clearest frame of mind. I have spent the better part of the week demonizing my neighbors with such intensity that instead of taking refuge with one of them—which I might have done under any other circumstances—I choose to hide in a thicket of bushes behind my house, a machete gripped in my sweaty fist, enduring what seems like an endless phantasmagoria of bloodcurdling screams and intermittent gunfire.

My thinking isn't completely unreasonable, though. I can tell that the shooting is coming from the carnival and I imagine that my hovel on the outskirts of town might seem like a decent place for a desperate gunman—or perhaps a group of desperate gunmen—to take cover. The last thing I want to do is get in the middle of whatever is going on.

In some ways, the long silences between screams and gunshots are the worst parts. I am convinced the outlaws roving about the village might hear my breathing, which is rapid and shallow, impossible to calm. The harder I try to control my breathing, the worse it gets. I feel alternately faint and nauseous.

What an ignominious end it would be: My lifeless body, discovered rotting in the bushes, naked except for a pair of boxers, rigor mortis pulling the muscles in my hand tight around a useless machete. Paraguayan news media often featured grisly car accidents or bloodied assault victims, and I imagine the murder of an American Peace Corps volunteer would be an especially sensational story.

I hug my knees to my chest and think about all my friends and family back in the States.

My best friend from NYU, Joshua, is a first-generation Chinese-American who can't fathom why anyone would willingly choose to live for two years in a country like Paraguay, which is even poorer and less developed than the one his parents had so assiduously escaped.

If they could see me now, even my hippie parents back in Florida—who always supported my Peace Corps adventure—would have to concede that Joshua is right about the whole misguided endeavor.

Moreover, what in the world makes me think my degree in English qualified me to teach subsistence farmers how to capture colonies of killer bees from the wild? And besides, even if I'm not a complete failure with the whole beekeeping project, what makes me think I will have any lasting impact on the lives of people with whom I now live? It's worse than foolishness. It's arrogance, really.

The gunfire and screams persist throughout the night in sporadic bursts. Sometimes I can hear groups of men moving about in the darkness, speaking in hushed voices, and I wonder if they are the same seemingly simple farmers with whom I have been beekeeping.

I look toward the heavens to try and calm my mind. The nighttime sky in Táva Rã is incredible as there are hardly any lights for many miles around. It's infinitely bejeweled, and the dark spaces take on a special character that is perhaps more sublime than the stars themselves. There is a vertiginous sense of depth, layers even, as if peering out from inside some gigantic unbloomed flower with thin purplish petals.

I remain in the thicket of bushes, wary and still, tortured by mosquitoes and other creepy crawlies, even after the morning light gives the world around me a dim form once again.

As if in chorus with the early morning songbirds, I hear Edén.

"Peter, Peter," he calls out in a loud whisper. From my spot in the bushes, it takes me a few moments to realize that I am not imagining the voice.

I tiptoe to my hut where Edén gives me a once-over that makes it clear that I needn't explain how I had fared during the night. His wild mop of black hair and bloodshot eyes suggest that he'd had a similar experience. We say nothing for a moment.

I am reluctant to invite him inside, still worried about being cornered in my hut without an escape option, so I motion for him to follow me into the bushes.

We squat together, hiding, and Edén whispers so quietly that I have to put my ear next to his mouth to hear what he is saying. His breath smells like cigarettes and candy.

"I saw it, Peter," he begins. "I saw it all."

"What happened?" I murmur.

Edén shushes me with such intensity that I look around thinking that there is someone nearby. The conversation proceeds like this: Edén shushing me repeatedly, while I try to reconstruct the events of the past night based on the vignettes he describes.

I am initially skeptical of what I hear because Edén's penchant for Hollywood action movies is exceeded only by his facility for telling outlandish whoppers. And while Edén's status as an outsider makes him a great source of unbiased information about village life, his stories frequently incorporate a variety of magical creatures drawn from Paraguay's pantheon of mythological forest goblins, making it difficult to untangle facts from his fertile imagination.

But this story has no magic, no goblins, no obvious prevarication. Only a chilling series of events that seem entirely plausible:

A group of farmers from the outskirts of Táva Rã decided they did not like having lost their harvest proceeds at the carnival's roulette wheel and had brought pistols with them to emphasize the point. The *carnavaleros*, who were not unaccustomed to dissatisfied customers, were similarly armed.

Edén, who had a knack for anticipating violence from the often-inebriated adults in his life, foresaw the clash just before it began and melted into nearby shadows.

At least a few farmers were shot. There was a lot of bloodshed. The *carnavaleros* escaped relatively unscathed, at first, and took refuge in their tractor trailer. At some point, later in the night, they made their way to the tiny little police station in town in hopes of finding protection—shooting the whole way there.

The *Policía Nacional* are notoriously inept and often corrupt. It is said that the government does not provide them with ammo for their guns, and the officers only fire their weapons when their own lives are in danger. To make matters worse, remote villages like Táva Rã are the least coveted posts, where only the most ineffective officers are assigned.

Perhaps this is why, when the lynch mob arrived at the police station sometime in the early morning hours—Edén says there were maybe fifty or sixty men—the police promptly turned the *carnavaleros* over to the angry crowd.

The hair on my neck stands up as Edén describes how he watched nearby while a group of men threw the bodies of murdered *carnavaleros* into a well and then fastidiously deposited many wheelbarrows of heavy stones in after them.

"We must go to the police," I whisper.

Edén shakes his head vehemently.

"Not in Táva Rã," I clarify. "In Pedro Juan Caballero. Or the Capital."

"No, Peter," he hisses. "Let's go see Pa'i Roberto. He will help."

"This seems like something to tell the American embassy or the police," I suggest.

"Peter, they won't help us," he says exasperatedly. "The problem is that they will kill me if they find out that I talked. I need to get to Pa'i Roberto. He will help me find another place to live. I cannot stay in Táva Rã if I tell what happened. I need to go far from here."

My stomach turns over as I realize that this means I know just enough to be in grave danger as well and that my life depends, in no small part, on the prudence of a kid who seems to have demonstrated precious little good judgment in his short life.

Still, I have the nagging sense that we are in this together, so I nod gravely.

Edén flashes a broad, rakish grin, which serves only to reinforce my misgivings.

With the rising sun, I can't help but feel a little hopeful—like somehow the daylight signifies an end to the nighttime madness.

This hope is quickly extinguished, though, when it becomes clear that no one in the village is leaving their homes. There is perhaps no ritual more fixed in our small subsistence farming community than that hour, just after sunrise, when groups of barefoot men walk leisurely to their farms, hoes perched on their shoulders, machetes dangling from their hands.

Were it not for the distant sounds of farm animals, the village might look abandoned.

I glance at my young partner who is lounging on one elbow and appears wholly unmolested by the morning heat. Beads of sweat are gathering on my forehead, and I know it will soon be intolerably hot.

I need to formulate a plan to leave Táva Rã. Even under normal conditions, leaving the village can be difficult. The nearest city, Yby Yaú, is 80+ kilometers away—following a hilly, winding dirt road—making it all but impossible to reach by foot in one day. The only practical way out of Táva Rã is to catch an old bus that is painted in festive colors and decorated on the inside with magazine cutouts of half-naked women. The bus passes through Táva Rã in the early mornings, irregularly, and only when the roads are dry. There is no way to accurately predict when it will come. I've heard that if I want to catch the bus, I need to listen for the horn and have my bags packed and ready to go.

Even if I were to catch the bus, it would be hard to explain why I am leaving with Edén.

I ask my adolescent co-conspirator what he thinks we should say.

Edén makes a variety of suggestions, all of which rely on his favorite strategy for deceit: admit to the indulgence of some shameful vice—preferably something for which one is already suspected—in order to distract from an ulterior motive. He assures me that the villagers will believe me if I confess to any permutation of the story that I am surreptitiously visiting various local women at night:

"Just say that the Paraguaya have made you crazy with lust," Edén proposes in Guaraní. "And that you must visit Pa'i Roberto for penance."

After some thought, I say, "I am not Catholic."

Edén insists his story will work anyway. It seems absurd to debate with a 12-year-old kid about the merits and drawbacks of falsely confessing to adultery.

"I don't think I—err—I can tell this to people in Táva Rã," I say, struggling to express the conditional tense in Guaraní.

"Do not worry, Peter," Edén says. "You can say it."

"No, you don't understand," I say, frustrated. "I know I can say it. I just don't want to say it to the people who will think I am sleeping with their wives and daughters."

"You are being delicate," Edén counters.

"I am not being del—" I stop suddenly as an idea pops into my mind.

"What is it Peter?"

"I *am* delicate, Edén," I say smiling for what feels like the first time in a while. "Very delicate."

The idea is simple: the gunfire of the previous night has so traumatized me that I must avail myself of the Peace Corps' mental health services. The deception depends on the same underlying principle that makes Edén's lies so persuasive: confess to something so humiliating that no one suspects it is a lie. Edén agrees that this alibi will work.

"Peter, you are so delicate," Edén says, winking.

"What will you tell people?" I ask.

"Tell who?" Edén asks sullenly. The mood becomes serious again. While Edén often brags that he has the freedom to do whatever he wants, I know that he would readily give up that freedom were he to have a family who cared for him.

"Well, we should have the same story," I offer. "People will wonder why you are traveling with a delicate Yankee."

"I can be your translator," Edén suggests, his mood brightening.

"You don't speak English," I counter.

"Eh ah," he says in mock offense. "Have you ebah lo-o-o-ve a woman so much ees a shame and a seen. Annnnd all the time you know she belonnnngs to your best freen."

He continues singing his favorite Clapton song. Edén originally liked the Clapton CD for the blazing guitar licks, but when I explained that just about every song is about some form of infidelity, he begged me for the album's liner notes so that he could dedicate himself to memorizing the songs. He carries the little booklet of lyrics everywhere he goes.

We pass the time like this— Edén singing his favorite Clapton tunes—me discussing the meaning behind the lyrics and soon it feels like any other morning.

At some point around midday, Edén's Clapton impersonation is interrupted by a child calling my name from somewhere on the other side of the hut.

I decide that if children are out and about, it must be safe to leave my hiding place. I shush Edén and rise to meet the child near the front of my hut who tells me that someone is calling me from Asunción and that I need to come to the village phone. Edén joins me in my hut, and I dress quickly, wondering aloud who might be calling. I had never received a call in all my time living there.

Edén looks concerned: "Maybe it is the *pyraguë*, Peter," he warns.

As I walk out the door, I tell Edén that it seems unlikely that the secret police call people on the phone.

The only phone in the village is kept in a house that is distinguished from all the others by its enormous cell phone antenna, which looks like a strange flag atop a series of lashed-together bamboo poles.

There is a small crowd gathered outside the house. I know a few of the farmers in the crowd from my beekeeping work in the village.

One of the farmers, Karai Vidal, nods at me as I approach. Vidal is a stocky man with light curly hair and icy blue eyes, who likes to make jokes about how his eye color suggests that his mother probably had an affair with a *rubio* who looks like me. He does not seem to be in a joking mood, and I pretend not to notice that he has big brown streaks of dried blood on his blue jeans.

"I got a call," I say in Guaraní to no one in particular, looking mainly at the ground.

"Finish as quickly as you can," says the proprietor, a portly older man named Karai Amado. "There are people who need to use the phone." Amado runs a little general store out of his home in addition to selling minutes on the cell phone. I sometimes buy beans and stale Brazilian cookies from him. There is a strange quiet, and I have the palpable sense that I am interrupting some sort of conversation that they don't want to have in front of me. I kick the dirt trying hard not to look at any of the farmers.

After what seems like an eternity, the phone finally rings. It is Don Antonio, my boss in the Peace Corps.

"Are you okay?" he asks in English, eschewing the singsong *mba'echapa che irũ* he normally uses to greet volunteers.

"Yeah, I'm good," I say perhaps too quickly, glancing at the group of glowering farmers who are listening intently.

"It's all over the news. I'm relieved to hear your voice," he continues. "Peter, are you sure you're okay?"

I pause for a moment thinking about how I can say something that the farmers won't understand. I know they don't speak English, but I worry they might be able to decipher something I say.

"Yeah, I'm fine," I say. "A little shaken up is all."

"I will be there as soon as I can," he says. "I'm leaving right now. Should be in town tomorrow morning depending on the roads."

When I return to my hovel, Edén is listening to Clapton's "Mean Old World."

"He is singing that the world is angry," I interpret.

"Who called you, Peter?" Edén asks, uninterested in the music lesson.

"It was Don Antonio from the Peace Corps," I say. Everyone in Táva Rã knows Don Antonio from the time that he visited to evaluate the community's ability to host a volunteer. "He is coming."

Edén nods.

"I think we should tell him what you saw," I say. "He will help us."

Edén considers this. Eric Clapton croons achingly about lost love.

"He can drive you to Pedro Juan," I offer. "And take us to Pa'i Roberto. Then you will know what to do about reporting—"

"Peter, shhh," he says, eyes wild. "People listen." He motions with his head toward the back wall while leafing through his cherished Clapton liner notes. He thinks memorizing the lyrics to the Clapton songs will make him fluent in English.

After some time, he looks up from the booklet and motions for me to come close. I kneel next to him and he whispers this: "Don Antonio has to take me to Pedro Juan Caballero to see Pa'i Roberto, Peter. I need to be far away from here if I am to say where the bodies are."

I nod gravely.

In the hottest part of mid-afternoon, the village finally comes to life and we see the first of the gleaming white Land Rovers arriving in Táva Rã. The SUVs are all emblazoned with official-looking insignias on the driver's side doors and are filled with serious Paraguayan men in citified white button-down shirts. I hear my neighbors using words I haven't heard before and quickly learn how to say "prosecutor," "district attorney," and "detective" in Spanish.

A hope forms in my mind: perhaps the investigators can piece together what happened the previous night without the help of Edén and me. I share my hope with Edén who shoots me a thumbs up while he sings the refrain of "Kind Hearted Woman."

The day turns to evening and we fall back into our regular nightly routine. I cook beans over a fire while Edén plays the part of our official DJ. We play chess and Edén beats me for the first time. I do not tell him that I was distracted by the silhouettes of old carnival equipment looming nearby, the lights flashing brighter as the evening sun sets like an uncanny memorial to the men who ran it the night before.

Edén asks to spend the night. I tell Edén that I will let him stay over—but only this one time—because of what seems like extraordinary circumstances. The truth is that having him with me makes the night seem slightly less terrifying.

After I turn out the light, we lie like sardines in my double bed. His breathing becomes very slow, and I know he is sleeping. I wonder where he would have slept had I not let him stay with me. The thought makes me sad and I try to think of more pleasant things—things I remember from the States. Before long, I fall asleep too.

I do not remember my dreams. In the darkest part of the early morning hours, a loud crash wakes me and Edén. We sit bolt upright and hardly have time to clear the cobwebs before we are snatched out of bed. There are many hands on us—like vice grips—the sort of hands that have been strengthened from years of farming with hand tools and clutching thick ropes attached to large farm animals.

When we get outside, I notice there are at least a dozen men, maybe more, including the two Táva Rã police officers who are not wearing their uniforms. I recognize some of the men from my beekeeping work. They toss Edén on the ground and say something in a tone that makes me think it is derogatory. Edén runs away immediately.

The air is sultry and the grass is cool. It's moist against my cheek. The men push my face to the ground, and someone sits on my legs while two men pin my arms. I think of all the times I had seen local men slaughter fat pigs—tying them to trees, straddling the gelatinous beasts and efficiently puncturing the jugular with surgical accuracy. The scream of a pig bleeding out sounds strangely like that of a human child.

I struggle, but to no avail. The men don't say much. What little they do say to each other is difficult to understand. I hear them using the Guaraní word for kill, *ejuka chupe*, and begin to beg them, half in Spanish, half in Guaraní, to spare me. I tell them I have money and they say something pejorative about Americans.

"What did you tell Don Antonio?" a gravelly voice booms in Spanish. Out of the corner of my eye I can see that it is the Police Chief, Don Esteban. The police assigned to Táva Rã are both young, in their twenties or early thirties and come from the Capital. The chief is a short, swarthy, barrel-chested man with squinty, darting eyes. When I first arrived in Táva Rã, full of hope and ambition, I visited the local police station—a one room brick building in the center of town—to explain my mission in the community. Esteban said that he would be happy to buy honey from me to mix with his rum and then inquired, his deputy smiling encouragingly, whether I would be interested in visiting local whorehouses with them. I politely declined, feigning nonchalance, and had avoided the policemen ever since.

"He is coming to Táva Rã," I grunt, thinking this information might help save my life.

"What did you say to him?" the Chief asks again, through gritted teeth. He kneels onto my back making it hard to breathe. I hear people saying things using the word *ejuka*. I think about my parents and struggle with all my strength against the hands holding me.

This is what the end is like, I think with sudden clarity. *Just like the rest of life. No different.* And I am filled with the overwhelming sense that my life was a long string of opportunities, none of which I had fully embraced.

Then, suddenly, as if I have acquired superhuman strength, the men pinning me to the ground release me in rapid succession. And then I know why: the bees. They are attacking. They are swarming in the aggressive way that only killer bees do when their hives are threatened.

I have never dealt with an aggressive swarm without my veil and the bees immediately descend on my bare skin in sheets. The men are running in every direction shouting *ipochy la cava*.

In the melee, I am joined by Edén, who guides me to the river running through the marsh behind my hovel. The bees follow us all the way there and soon we are in the cool water being carried what feels like a long way from Táva Rã. When we finally pull ourselves ashore I feel drunk on adrenaline and bee venom.

We scratch the stingers off each other's bodies, hundreds of them. It is warm everywhere that I am stung and it feels like I am wrapped in blankets even though I'm soaking wet and it is the middle of the night.

Edén carefully removes the Clapton liner notes from his pocket, which are soaked, but otherwise seem to have survived the swim without disintegrating. With the care of a surgeon, he carefully peels each page from the next. While tending to his precious booklet, he explains to me that he had taken the hive behind my house and turned it over in the shadows near where the men were interrogating me.

"They would have killed you, Peter," he says matter-of-factly.

I nod somberly.

"How do you say sting in English?" he asks after a pregnant silence. He is finished tending to the Clapton booklet and we have resumed extracting the stingers from each other.

I grumble the translation, annoyed by the way he does not seem to be taking our predicament seriously.

"I esting de sheriff," he croons. "And I esting the deputy!" He is beaming at his new version of one of his favorite Clapton covers.

Despite my general annoyance, this is funny, and I can't help but laugh. It is a deep belly laugh—the sort of laugh that feels more like catharsis than mirth. Edén joins me laughing and then promptly begins singing his new version of *I Shot the Sheriff* with deep emotion. I realize I don't know much about the song and wonder, briefly, if it is supposed to be literal or symbolic.

Bee venom is coursing through my veins, making my whole body warm. The intoxication produces a euphoria unlike any drug I've ever taken. I remember the cow that the bees killed early in my Peace Corps training and wonder if this is what she felt as she was dying. It's not nearly as painful as I would have thought.

My Peace Corps-issued Epipen is back in my hut and with our blood full of bee venom, I know we are in real medical danger without treatment. I don't know how to avoid anaphylactic shock—but it seems like walking will help.

While we walk, Edén sings his new version of *I Shot the Sheriff*. He seems a bit too buoyant for someone who had just been attacked by a lynch mob and a swarm of killer bees.

We walk through jungles and farmland and more jungles and creep past cows and skittish horses and oxen. Nervous dogs howl at us. I don't know where we are, but we keep walking until my bare feet are raw and sore, and the sun begins its ascent into the morning sky.

The warmth and euphoria have given way to swelling and a dull ache. With the rising sun, I feel like I'm seeing the world for the first time. It is like the pain somehow put filters on my mind, reducing what I see to its essential elements.

Or maybe I was sleep-deprived and high on bee venom.

Chapter 5

PANÉ

Thank God for Chuck Norris—and for all the lesser Hollywood tough guys whose movies and television shows have made it into syndication in Latin America. Sometimes all you need is someone who believes you are tough to start believing it yourself.

At least, for me, that becomes my main motivator, my reason to push through the pain. My skin is swollen taut from all the bee stings. The heat that initially comes from the stings becomes excruciating agony. Every inch of exposed skin feels like it has been bludgeoned—even the skin under my ears, the soft spot under my jaw, my eyelids. But Edén, having watched too many bad American action movies, expects me to have the grit and perseverance of his favorite heroes.

The pain is so severe that I vomit. But I press on, mostly because my young friend expects me to and I don't want to let him down. American arrogance isn't always a bad thing.

Edén and I walk and walk until my feet are raw and bleeding.

Occasionally farmers out in their fields watch us with a sort of befuddled look that expresses their surprise at finding some half-naked *gringorubio* traipsing through their fields accompanied by a young Paraguayan singing American songs off-key. Edén eventually pilfers me some clothes off of a clothesline but the curious gazes persist.

Edén seems to be having the time of his life, unfazed by both the bee stings and the previous night's trauma. He smiles and sings. I, on the other hand, am plagued by thoughts about the men who want to finish the job they had begun the previous night. Would they come with dogs? Would they come in pickup trucks? Would they come on horseback?

I try to convey the seriousness of our situation to Edén, but he only nods and continues singing. The sun rises to its apex and it is uncomfortably hot and humid. I am very thirsty, but I feel that I ought to be able to last as long as my young companion who has endured it all without whining about water—so I walk, gritting my teeth.

We follow a red earthen road that cuts a narrow path like a scar—just big enough for an ox-cart—between verdant farms on both sides. Small, tidy, thatched-roofed homes occasionally appear where women are sweeping dirt or doing laundry or drinking tea or caring for a throng of half-naked children (they all seemed to contain a throng of small children). The children pause their play to watch us, mouths agape.

"We need to find a phone," I say. I am sure that if I could just pass a message on to the Peace Corps office, they would find a way to rescue us.

"There is no phone this way, Peter," Edén said. "But do not worry. We only need to walk a few more kilometers, and we will be safe."

A surge of adrenaline makes me dizzy, and we fall silent for a time while I try to regain my footing.

"Why do you think we will be safe in a few kilometers?" I ask after a long silence.

"We are going to the Aché place, Peter," Edén says quietly.

"The Aché?" I whisper. "What is that?"

"The Aché are a kind of native people, Peter," he says. "No one will try and find us there."

"Why not?"

"Because they have strong magic, Peter," he explains. "You can fall in love with their women, and then they'll eat you."

I ask him a few more questions because I am sure I am misunderstanding him. But, no, I understand what he is saying perfectly well. We are headed down a bucolic ox-cart path toward an indigenous group notorious for black magic and cannibalism. While my ultra-rational first world sensibilities tell me I needn't fear these people, the Aché, something continues to nag at the fringes of my mind, a sort of intuition, which says there must be some kernel of truth to these rumors.

Subsistence farms with varied crops and little homes give way to mechanized plantations with nothing but soy as far as the eye can see. We have arrived in Brazilian soy country. Brazilians are slowly taking over most of the eastern part of Paraguay, near the border.

The uniform landscape makes me anxious: in a soy farm, there is nowhere to hide.

"Further on up da road," Edén sings, "some'un is gunna 'urt you like ya 'urt me. Baby you jus wai' an' essseeee." He winks. I grimace.

We walk for hours, Edén singing the whole time, until, in the distance, we spot a thick patch of jungle where the soy abruptly ends.

"The Aché place, Peter," Edén announces, pointing at the jungle.

Up close, the jungle is dense, almost a wall, a good place to hide. Even if there is truth in the whole cannibalism thing, I calculate, surely the native people who are living there have given up their old ways by now.

Before I enter the jungle, I think briefly of my old Boy Scout training. They had always counseled me not to wander around in wild places where I could get lost. But none of the wilderness survival rules seem to apply when there is the prospect of a lynch mob in pursuit.

The jungle is so thick that I quickly abandon trying to walk in a straight line, instead heading in whatever direction seems like it will involve the least amount of effort. Still the hike is slow. We carefully avoid the thickest underbrush, much of which is alive with biting ants and spiny plants. The shade of the thick canopy overhead provides relief from the oppressive heat but also invigorates mosquitoes and biting flies, which descend on us in thick clouds.

I notice that the journey through the jungle should feel just like old times, a reminder of those halcyon days when Edén and I were capturing colonies of killer bees from the wild. But the lynch mob has changed even my memories—casting a long ominous shadow over them, turning them into just precursors of the violence and terror that would be visited upon me. The realization makes me feel a heavy sadness.

We walk for only a short while before I begin to suspect that we are lost. I have no idea what direction might lead back to the soy field. Edén has stopped singing, and he looks unsure too, though I suspect his trepidation is less about being lost than it is related to his worry that we are making our way toward purported practitioners of the occult.

Before long, we find a lightly-trod game trail which slowly becomes more defined. Then it turns into a clear footpath. Then, the first sign of humanity: we surprise a pair of small half-naked children with sticks in hand who are walking toward us. They turn on their heels and scamper out of sight.

A warm relief surges through me. Edén, on the other hand, looks stricken.

"We have arrived, Edén," I say smiling.

"Peter, do not look at the women," he warns.

"What if I want to fall in love?" I tease.

Edén is not amused.

We pass a series of small lean-tos with thatched roofs. Some are occupied by lounging families who watch silently as we pass. Other lean-tos are vacant. One contains the two boys we had surprised on the trail earlier. I approach the lean-to and clap loudly, as is the Paraguayan custom. Edén is making it obvious he intends to avoid all eye-contact and fixes his gaze at the ground. A short barefoot man with a tuft of wild black hair and vaguely Asian features stands up to approach us. He wears tattered polyester pants and a Paraguay national team jersey.

"Greetings sir," I say, employing my most formal Guaraní greeting.

"Hello," he replies in Guaraní. I glance at Edén whose eyes remain fixed on the ground.

"Is this the Aché place, sir?" I ask.

The man nods. The two boys from the trail peek out from behind a nearby tree to watch the exchange.

"Do you have water?" I ask. "I am very thirsty, sir."

"Juan Mbejyvagi," the man says pointing down the trail. I have to ask him to repeat himself a few times before I understand that he is giving me a name.

I say the name a few times under my breath as we set off down the trail again. As we walk, I turn to my companion.

"You are being rude," I scold. "They do not have magic, Edén. They are not going to eat you."

"Peter, I know a man who was eaten by them," he protests. This is like so many conversations I have had with Edén over our chess board in Táva Rã: Edén claiming to have firsthand experience of some magic that turns out to be no more than a rumor he has heard among the drunks and degenerates he calls friends.

"Edén, how could you know someone who was eaten?" I ask. "If he was truly eaten then he wouldn't be around to tell anyone about it."

The logic of this statement gives Edén pause. We walk for a little while, passing more of the open-walled homes variously occupied or not. Edén still dares not look at the occupied homes.

"No, Peter, it is true," Edén protests. "They have magic."

"You cannot believe everything you hear," I counsel. "Is everything they say about you true?"

"Yes," he says flatly. "And more."

I would chuckle if I weren't so thirsty.

We walk into a small clearing where a rutted dirt road, barely wide enough for a car, runs in both directions, disappearing into the jungle on either side. Along the road there are a few board and batten shacks, including one that has a sign in front of it that reads ESCUELA PRIMARIA. In every direction, a great living wall of green looms.

Behind the school, there is a rustic well marked by a wooden post where an old plastic oil bottle hangs attached to a rope. I rush to the well and pull water out of the ground. It is cool and delicious. I drink greedily, until my stomach feels heavy, —and pass the bottle to Edén, who drinks more timidly.

Behind us I can hear snickering from the schoolhouse. I turn to find a group of children at an open window pointing and laughing at us. I smile and the faces quickly disappear.

An Aché man with a deeply creased, broad face and heavy eyelids appears from one side of the schoolhouse. Like the man we met on the trail, he looks vaguely Asian with high cheekbones and dark black hair. His dress distinguishes him from the other men we had seen: he wears a collared blue button-down shirt, pleated pants, and shined leather shoes that matches his belt.

"Greetings," I say, using my formal Guaraní greeting. "How are you this afternoon?"

"I am good," he responds. "How are you?"

"We are good," I say looking over at Edén, who has stopped drinking water and is looking at his feet again.

"We are looking for Juan Mbejy—" I say, forgetting the strange name I heard only moments ago.

"Juan Mbejyvagi," he said. "Yes, I am Juan. What is your name?"

My jaw drops. I look at Edén who glances up from the ground with wide eyes. He has studied the lyrics of his favorite American music enough to know when someone is speaking English.

"You speak English?" I say incredulously.

"Yeah," the man says smiling. "What's up?"

"Are you an American?" I ask. His English has no trace of an accent.

"No, no," he laughs. "I am Aché. What did you say your name is?"

"But your English—"

"Yeah, raised by Canadian Mennonites," he interjects casually. "How can I help you?"

I glance at the school where the two open windows are packed with the faces of curious students.

"Do you have a telephone?" I ask.

"Not here," he says. Edén must understand what we are saying because he gives me a look that said I told you so. "But there is one in Táva Rã. Just ask for Karai Amado. You need to walk, this way—"

"That's not going to work—" I interrupt, choking back tears. If it weren't for the faces of all the students watching me, I might have wept. There is something deeply comforting about being able to commiserate with someone in your mother tongue, which cannot be replicated when speaking a language that is not your own. Somehow, talking about my ordeal in English makes the whole thing seem more real—more perilous.

Juan listens patiently while I relate how I had come to arrive in his reservation. If Juan is surprised by what I tell him, he hides it well. When I finish the short narrative, he turns toward the school and says something in another language that sounds vaguely like Guaraní but is not.

After he speaks, the students—whose handsome school uniforms contrast conspicuously with their bare feet—file out of the school, walking in all directions, murmuring intensely with one another, glancing furtively back at Edén and me.

"Come over to my house," Juan says motioning to a tidy house with a thatched roof across the dirt road from the school. "You must be famished. My wife will fix us something. Will you tell me your names?"

I apologize and introduce myself as we walk a few steps toward his home. I turn to introduce Edén but find that he has not joined us. He stands still, next to the well, still holding the bottle of water.

"Edén, come," I say in Guaraní. "He has invited us to his house."

Edén shakes his head, vehemently.

"Edén, do not worry," I cajole. "Come now."

I turned to Juan who has stopped to watch the exchange. He shrugs.

"He is scared of you," I say to Juan in English, choosing my words carefully so as to not offend him. "He has heard terrible rumors about the Aché."

"Come now friend," Juan says to Edén in Guaraní. "You are much too skinny for us to eat you. Let us fatten you up first."

Edén's eyes get wide but can't help himself when he hears me chuckle. He smiles sheepishly and follows warily behind us, keeping his distance.

"You will need to eat," Juan says warmly, patting me on the back as we enter the dark cool of his sparsely furnished home. A rough-hewn kitchen table occupies the center of the main room, where cool radiates deliciously from the fresh-swept dirt floor. Two matching sets of open windows on opposite walls allow a slight breeze. Various tools, ropes, leather straps, and farming implements hang neatly from a wall across from where I take my seat. Juan calls to his wife who answers from the next room.

"What do you speak?" I ask. "It sounds like Guaraní."

"It's our language," he says. "Aché."

"How do you know Aché if you were raised by Canadians?" I ask, realizing after I say it that it sounds like a much too personal question for our short acquaintance.

"That is a long story," Juan says. "Much too long for right now. We have more immediate problems to discuss. First, you need to eat. Please."

Juan's wife enters the room carrying two heaping bowls of oil-fried *manioc*. She is a petite Aché woman with short black hair, shy demeanor, and laugh lines that make her appear kind. She is older, probably in her 40s or 50s, but still very attractive. I know, suddenly, why these women are rumored to bewitch people.

"Thank you," I say. "I mean, *aguyje ndeve*."

She nods.

Edén, who has cautiously joined me at the table, is meticulously avoiding eye contact with Juan's wife, but nevertheless quickly begins shoveling heaps of the oily starch into his mouth. I try to exercise more restraint, but my own hunger overwhelms me, and we all eat in silence for many minutes. When Edén and I have eaten our fill, we become thirsty again, and Juan summons his wife who brings us cups of tepid water, which we drink until we feel sick.

"Rest, now," he says, standing. "I am going out to let the tribe know that we need to gather so we can decide how to help you."

Juan shakes Edén and me awake after what seems like a very short cat nap. We had both nodded off sitting upright in our chairs. Judging from the shafts of sunlight pouring through open windows on one side of the house making dust in the air twinkle, it is late afternoon.

"Okay, now we can talk about what will happen next," Juan says.

Edén and I rub our faces.

"You will hear the women soon," Juan continues. "It may frighten your friend. But you need to calm his fears."

I nod apprehensively, and we both look at Edén, who clearly does not understand what we are saying but can tell that we are talking about him. He gives us both a dirty look that says he doesn't appreciate us speaking in English.

"Do you think you can calm him?" Juan pleads.

"I don't know," I say. "I am not sure why he would be alarmed in the first place."

"There is very little time," Juan insists. "You know this boy, and it appears he trusts you, so you need to think of a way to ensure he remains calm. Lie if you must. We have some customs that will appear strange to you and your friend here. If he thinks we are going to eat him, he may run away. He cannot run away if you want our help. I am a Christian, thank God, and, truth be told, I do not believe in all of the things that my people do. Well, that's not exactly true. I do. I just believe it in a different way."

I squint at Juan, confused by what he is trying to tell me.

"It is too much to explain the whole thing right now," Juan continues. "What is important is that your friend does not show his fear. We are not Indians like you see in the movies. We do not have a chief. Well, we do have a chief. I am the Chief. But that is only because the government requires it of us. But I do not decide things like you think a chief might. We decide important things like this as a tribe. We must all agree."

I tilt my head to one side. The more he speaks, the less I understand.

"Look," he says, placing his small knobby hands on the table and looking up at the thatched ceiling as if searching in vain for the right words. "We can help you, but it will take some convincing from me. I can convince them, but you need to be there. Both of you. You will see lots of yelling and crying and chanting and singing. Some people will be very sure that we should not help you. They will yell and scream. The women might give you drinks and you must drink what they give you. I will have to convince them that we should help you both. It is a dangerous thing to help, and some of them will not want to do it."

I nod, wondering what kind of extreme pageant requires this elaborate warning.

"My people believe in something called pané, and it is sort of like karma, but for hunting. It is the life force of my people. It is the force that attracts animals. It is also what attracts women. Think of it as the force that brings out the animal in us.

"There is not good pané or bad pané. There is only pané. My people are traditionally a hunter-gathering people, and we live and die by the hunt. Even now, though jaguars no longer roam our jungles, the hunter of hunters still haunts our dreams.

"You have arrived here, being hunted by both men and the bees, so they will say your pané is very, very strong. I cannot argue that point. You have the sort of pané that only a great hunter should have. If you were an Aché man you would go immediately into the jungles and would not return unless it was with a large dead animal. But you are a white and whites do not know how to hunt like the Aché. A man who is being hunted becomes a great hunter because the animals come to him. But a man with strong pané who does not know how to hunt is as good as dead."

I don't like the way he is framing my predicament—but I nod nonetheless.

"I will argue that our greatest hunter, Karai Jakugi, take you to the Mennonite colony where I grew up. It is a full day's walk and you will leave before sunup tomorrow—if I am persuasive."

"Perhaps you could take us—" I stammer.

"No, that is impossible," Juan interjects, waving it away as if it were nonsense. "As I did not grow up hunting, my people would never let me take you, even if I wanted to."

"I could pay you to just take us," I plead, remembering when I had said the same thing to the men pinning me to the ground back in Táva Rã.

"It is not my choice alone," he reminds me, accentuating the point by thrusting his index finger into the air. "We must agree. It is our way and it cannot change. They would never let me take you with your pané. I did not grow up hunting like they did, and they would think it a death sentence. My role here is to be a teacher and to represent the tribe to the Amambay and Paraguayan government."

"I would pay anyone to take us," I implore. "I don't have any money now, but as soon as I—"

"No, no, no," Juan says, shaking his head vehemently. "I need you to trust that I know what I am doing. Just make sure that the boy does not ruin it."

I nod, wondering what I could say that would convince my skittish young friend that the Aché are going to help us. Edén's anti-authoritarian streak is firmly rooted in his own preternatural knack for self-preservation. I know that his refusal to trust anyone but himself is the only way he knows how to survive in a chaotic world that is populated with mean, often-drunk adults. It seems unlikely I can compel him to trust me over his own survival instincts.

On the other hand, I know that Edén does not think of his stubborn defiance as some pathological opposition to authority. Rather he likes to think of himself as a simple rebel, cut from the same cloth as his favorite Hollywood heroes, whose subversion of the laws and customs of their communities are just means to a higher, more just end. I have spent enough time talking about the finer points of *Walker, Texas Ranger* to know that Edén considers Chuck Norris the final authority on all moral matters.

"Remember how we discussed that Walker knows *m'buya* power?" I ask. On more than a few occasions Edén had asked about a mystical American Indian who raised Chuck Norris' character, Cordell Walker. Edén has told me that he believes Chuck Norris has superpowers consisting of a mixture of East Asian martial arts and American Indian mysticism.

"Yes, Peter," he says, his mood brightening.

"This is like in Walker, Texas Ranger," I say cryptically. "Juan will help us learn *m'buya* power."

Edén thinks about this for a moment and then nods sagaciously. I decide not to say anything more because it seems like the innuendo is sufficient to convince Edén that the Aché are not going to try and eat us.

What happens later that afternoon and extends into the evening as the sun sets, is like a dream. We are sitting in Juan's house, feeling satiated and drowsy when we are summoned by otherworldly voices to a small bonfire in the center of the village. The call is more like wailing than song that repeats in unison.

We walk with Juan to the bonfire—though, in my exhaustion the whole thing is surreal and even my own movements seem to occur outside of my own volition. I sit on the ground, mesmerized by the fire and, occasionally, by dramatic exchanges between the Aché, all in a language I do not understand.

Often the women wail things in unison, and then men nearby, upon hearing these cries, rush upon the women and scream at them in response. Both men and women are so ardent that they seem to be on the verge of violence.

Juan does not participate in the drama, watching it impassively with Edén and me.

Children—many of whom I had seen at the school earlier in the day—watch, occasionally laughing and playing, from the bushes and shadows nearby. As night falls, a pot of dark liquid is passed to me, and Juan tells me to drink. It tastes like dirty water and tree bark and makes my mouth numb.

I pass the pot to Edén, but Juan does not let him drink.

More strange cries and heated debates ensue, I think, but the rest becomes unclear because I get violently ill from what I have consumed and rush into the bushes nearby at least a few times to vomit, leaving big heaps of *manioc* on the moist jungle floor. When the sickness subsides, I return to the fire, my head spinning.

More cries and agitation, but in my debilitated state it somehow becomes clear that this is all ceremonial. I notice that the words are all the same, and the confrontations dancelike, the quarrelling parties unperturbed as soon as their frenzied solos are finished.

Soon I am naked and a pair of old women are scrubbing my body with some sort of dark liquid—perhaps the same thing I had imbibed—and it numbs my skin. I pass out. Or maybe I simply fall asleep, but I do not remember anything else.

The next morning—it must be very early because it is still dark out—Juan wakes me. Edén is sleeping on the floor next to me. We are sharing a blanket, having slept under the kitchen table in the middle of Juan's home. I do not feel terrible and try to remember what had happened the previous night. Even at that moment it does not seem real.

"Jakugi will take you to the Mennonites," Juan says. I am still naked, and upon seeing my stained skin, I remember, vaguely, being scrubbed by the old women. I get dressed and am brought to an Aché man who had a small rifle slung over his shoulder.

"This is Karai Jakugi," Juan says. I extend my hand and he offers a limp, calloused hand of his own. "Jakugi does not speak English, but he understands Guaraní."

"Good morning, sir," I say in Guaraní.

He nods and sets off at a brisk pace, leading us into the wild.

Chapter 6

CONSCRIPTION

Our Aché guide, Karai Jakugi, expects Edén and me to follow him in silence. And he doesn't just expect a run-of-the-mill quiet either; he expects a hunter's silence. Whenever either of us whispers or makes any sound, really, he frowns at us with the intensity of a schoolteacher giving an important examination. So we do our best to follow him without incurring his contemptuous gaze.

Edén and I are led through the jungles of the Aché reservation to a creek, which meanders out of the jungles and into the Brazilian soy fields that extend like a sea of green to the horizon in all directions. Juan remains in the forested edge of the creek, walking silently and efficiently along the bank. Edén and I do our best to mimic his silent steps, as we follow behind. Except for the occasional sound of a branch snapping or the swishing of leaves brushing against our shoulders, we walk in silence.

At intervals, Karai Jakugi stops suddenly, swiftly swinging the .22-caliber rifle around in order to shoulder it, aiming down the sights into the trees or some particularly dense patch of underbrush. It is as if we are hunting the whole time, though he never fires.

I formulate a long litany of questions that I want to ask him, but I know he will probably just glower at me for speaking. I want to ask him what he is seeing and hearing, I want to ask him about the Mennonite Colony, about his own people, about the *pané* from which I am purportedly suffering. But I stay quiet instead. It is perhaps the only thing my skilled guardian expects of me.

I will do whatever he asks because I am immensely grateful that he is taking us to the Mennonite Colony where there will be a telephone from which I will be able to call the Peace Corps offices or the US Embassy. I feel certain that if I can just call my fellow Americans that they'll come rescue me.

The journey takes all day and we do not stop the whole time, except occasionally to drink sips of water directly from the creek. The water smells vaguely like the chemical runoff from the stuff the Brazilians spray on the soy, though it tastes more like metal than chemicals. Having eaten heaps of oil-fried *manioc* before setting out, both Edén and I are able to walk the whole day without feeling the acute hunger that had marked the previous day's journey.

It is nighttime when we arrive at the Mennonite Colony. Juan stops and turns toward Edén and me. The creek has turned into more of a river and the only sounds around us are that of cicadas and the water sluicing swiftly past us between the banks.

"*La colonia menonita*," Karai Jakugi says pointing at the electric lights twinkling in the distance. I can just barely make out our guide's silhouette in the moonlight. It is the first thing he has said to either of us in what must have been at least 16 hours together.

"You will take us there?" I say in Guaraní after what feels like a long silence.

"*Nahániri*," he says, shaking his head.

"You will not take us?"

He shakes his head and sets off upriver without speaking another word. Soon he is swallowed by the darkness, and gone, leaving Edén and me standing alone in the darkness. My legs ache from the two day's walking and I want nothing more than to sit down and rest, but I fear I might suffer from debilitating cramps if I do so.

"Let's go then," I whisper to Edén in Guaraní.

Edén begins humming his favorite Eric Clapton song, but I quickly shush him. It feels much less safe without our armed escort. Visions of violent Paraguayan lynch mobs return to mind and my pace quickens. It seems certain that once I get to the Mennonites this whole nightmare will be resolved.

The twinkling lights are farther away than they appear from the river. We are again traipsing through farmland but the crops are no longer only soy, a variety of plants, some of which I recognize as beans, corn, and sweet potatoes.

As we get closer to the lights, a sparse row of tidy houses appears on the crest of a distant rise. The nearest house has one twinkling light over the front door and another, ampler light, a sort of streetlamp, illuminating the front of a big pole barn, a tractor, and a small water tower. I hurry toward the home, but as I get close, a throng of angry dogs rushes upon Edén and me, barking with such frenzy that we both instinctively stop in our tracks.

Edén pretends to have a stick; I yell "no" authoritatively, but it only gives the dogs pause for an instant before they resume their aggression.

They lunge at us, nipping at our bare feet as we occasionally kick at them futilely. Fortunately, both Edén and I manage to avoid a serious bite from any of the dogs before they are called off by a tall slender man who runs toward us in a state of half-dress, holding a pair of unclipped overalls in one hand and a shotgun in the other.

When his eyes adjust to the darkness, he puts both hands on his gun, letting his pants fall around his ankles.

"Please do not hurt us," I plead in Guaraní. "There are just two of us here and we have no weapons."

"Why are you here at night?" the man asks in perfect English. I probably should have anticipated that he would speak English. After all, his community had taught the language to Juan. But until that moment I hadn't thought about it and the casual use of English surprises me. For the second time in as many days, hearing someone speaking my mother tongue makes me want to weep. I croak something about needing to find a telephone and being pursued by killers.

"Why are you here?" he asks again, unmoved. With his shotgun at his hip, his silhouette is imposing, the lights of his house behind him.

I realize that I must sound like a crazy person, arriving at that time of night talking of killers. What could I tell him that would make him realize I wasn't crazy— or at least that my madness was justified?

"Juan Mbejyvagi said I should come," I plead. "I need help."

"You came from the Aché reservation?" he asks incredulously.

"Yes," I say, sensing his mood shifting. "We left before sunup. An Aché man— Karai Jakugi—brought us along the river the whole way here."

"Oh my." The man bends over to pull up his overalls and clips them over his shoulder.

Edén and I stand there, unsure what to do. The dogs are still whimpering in the shadows.

"Come, come," he says. "You will stay with us tonight."

I approach the figure cautiously and Edén follows behind me at what he feels like a safe distance from both of us. Closeup, I can see that the Mennonite is even taller than he appears at a distance—at least a foot taller than me. He has a short chinstrap beard and thin hair that hangs over his ears. He yells something at the dogs in a foreign language I can't immediately identify. The dogs obediently skulk off to the hidden places from where they had come.

As we enter the circle of light beaming from the front of his tidy farmhouse, the man's craggy face came into focus. He is much older than his imposing silhouette and voice had seemed. He is in his 50s or 60s, white-bearded, with deep creases on his gaunt cheeks and forehead.

"I am Daniel," he says, extending his enormous, calloused paw to shake. He invites us into his house, where, sitting at a huge kitchen table, there is a crowd of young people of all ages—presumably his children—in various states of daytime dress and pajamas. Standing at the kitchen sink, a lady in an old-timey floral dress, clearly his wife, side-eyes us. The kitchen is appointed with the sort of modern appliances that are rare among the Paraguayan campesinos with whom I have been living. There is a refrigerator, a stove and oven, and even a microwave. Despite these conveniences, there is a pioneer charm to the kitchen. The countertops are made of butcher block and various cast iron pots hang from pegs over the sink. Cheese cloths cover an assortment of dishes that are arranged tidily on the counters. The whole place smells like some sort of delicious dish they cooked earlier that evening, causing me to feel sharp hunger pangs.

Edén joins me just inside the doorway, his eyes filled with apprehension, and we stand there, pretending not to be bothered by the way the young people ogle us, the younger ones slack-jawed. The boys all dress like their father—overalls and work shirts or pajamas that look like long underwear. The girls wear floral dresses like their mother or frilly nightgowns. Metal cups and an assortment of small plates are arranged on the kitchen table, untouched.

Daniel goes into the kitchen and speaks to his wife in a Germanic language. I note only the words "Aché" and "Juan Mbejyvagi" in all that he says. She says nothing while he speaks.

"Come, sit down," Daniel says, clearing space for us at the kitchen table. "You must be hungry."

I nod and motion for Edén to join me. The floors of the house are concrete, though there are throw rugs all over. I avoid walking on the rugs, given that my bare feet are caked with dirt from the day's journey. I am aware that I must stink. The tidy living room is full of wooden rocking chairs and wooden benches that look vaguely like pews. They seem to be arranged in such a way that they are facing a large wooden console against the far wall where a huge family bible sits opened on a wooden platform.

The wooden plank walls are painted pastel green and are sparsely decorated except for a finely crafted cuckoo clock hanging on one wall, and a wooden calendar with movable numbered blocks on another. There are large windows in the center of every wall, replete with glass panes, something I have only seen in houses in the Paraguayan capital. All the windows are framed with matching lace curtains.

"Is German your language?" I ask, approaching the table where his family is gathered.

"In a way, yes," he explains. "Our ancestors were originally from Germany and we still speak an older form of German. And Russian. More recently, we lived in Canada, so we also speak English."

"Wow," I say.

"And I speak Spanish, of course," Daniel says, then beaming at his throng of children, "and my kids speak both Spanish and Guaraní."

"But you keep the German?"

"Yeah, our bibles and church services are all in German, so it remains with us. We lived in Russia too—between Germany and Canada—and some of us still speak Russian."

The kids clear spaces for Edén and me to sit at the kitchen table. As soon as we sit down, Daniel's wife places a piping hot bowl of brown beef stew in front of us.

Edén and I are famished, and the stew is so good that we burn our mouths scarfing it down. The whole family watches us eat in silence.

"Would you like another helping?" Daniel asks as I finish my bowl.

I nod. Daniel's wife takes my bowl to spoon soup into it from a pot on the stove.

"I am being rude. I should explain—" I say.

"—We will talk about your predicament tomorrow morning," Daniel interrupts, looking meaningfully at a couple of the little kids clustered around the table.

"Oh, yes," I say, inferring that he didn't want to talk about it in front of the kids. "Of course."

"We'll figure out our next steps tomorrow," he says. "Let's just get you a hot and a cot as the folks at the Salvation Army used to say."

I am so grateful for his graciousness that I become teary-eyed and excuse myself to go to the bathroom. Their bathroom has running water and an actual toilet, the floor is tiled, as is the shower, which is appointed with an electric water heater like I have seen in my few visits to the capital.

I look at myself in the mirror while I gather the resolve to return to the table and avoid crying in front of Daniel's kids. My short sandy blonde hair is wild, standing up in places and matted down in others. I am badly sunburned on my nose, cheeks, and forehead. My eyes are an even more shocking green in contrast to my ruddy skin. I am still wearing the threadbare ill-fitting clothes Edén had pilfered from the clothesline the previous day. I wonder if I still look so obviously American to anyone.

Tomorrow I will call the Peace Corps offices and this whole terrible ordeal will be over, I think, and try to smile at myself in the mirror. My mouth grins, but my eyes tell the true story of how I am feeling: exhausted and scared.

Tomorrow I will talk to Don Antonio, I think. He will be relieved to hear from me and will enlist the clever embassy folks to come get me and Edén. I wonder briefly what Don Antonio might have done when he showed up in Táva Rã and I wasn't there like I said I would be. Maybe he has already called the embassy—the thought is comforting. My heart sinks when I realize that if he has contacted the embassy, he has probably also alerted the *Polícia Nacional* about my disappearance. And if the crooked cops in Táva Rã are an example of the character of the wider police force, I don't want the Paraguayan police to be looking for me.

The thought gives me vertigo, shortness of breath, and the odd sensation of a totally blank short-term memory—like a sort of amnesia—and the terror of not knowing where I am located geographically or in time. But I splash water on my face and eventually my senses return to me, and I go back to the dinner table.

I finish my second helping of the stew and my eyes get very heavy. My legs and feet ache, and I want nothing more than to lay down. Daniel leads us to a room at the back of the house that is full of bunk beds and not much else. He explains that we are welcome to use the shower and Edén agrees to take the first one.

I lay in my bed, waiting for my turn in the shower, and, very quickly, I fall into a heavy dreamless sleep.

I wake with a start in the darkness, an incredible pain in my gut.

I hop out of bed and, for a moment, I don't know where I am. After the cobwebs clear, I stumble toward the bathroom where I spend at least twenty minutes coping with the most explosive dysentery I have ever experienced. Sipping from the river was not as harmless as I thought. When the cramps subside, I return to bed, still breathing heavily from the whole traumatic episode.

I lay down in the bed and stare into the darkness around me.

"Are you from the USA?" a boy's voice quietly asks.

"Yes," I whisper, not wanting to wake up all the slumbering kids in the room.

"Where in the USA?" another boy's voice asks.

"Leave him be, Obadiah," says still another with a deeper voice. I have obviously woken up everyone in my clumsy dash to the bathroom.

"It's okay," I say. "I'm from Florida. But I went to college in New York City." Everyone, even the Paraguayans from Táva Rã, seem to know New York City and Florida.

"Do they have farms where you live?" asks a voice from the bunk above me.

"Yeah," I say. "They grow a lot of oranges there."

"Do you have a farm?" the boy asks.

"No," I say.

It is quiet for a time. Then one of the older boys with a deeper voice speaks: "What's war like?"

"Excuse me?"

"Sorry, never mind," the voice says hastily.

"No, it's okay," I say. "I just wanted to make sure I heard you correctly. Did you ask what war is like?"

The room is quiet for a moment, then the voice murmurs, "Yes."

"I guess I have to say I don't really know," I say. "I've never been to a war."

"But isn't the USA in a war with the Holy Land?" the voice asks.

"I guess we are," I say. "But it's not like I really notice much to be honest." I realize after I say it that I sound flippant, so I add, half-apologetically, "I should notice more, I suppose."

"Do you eat a lot of pancakes?" the boy in the bunk above me asks.

"That is a dumb question, Obadiah," says the low voice across the room. "Of course he eats a lot of pancakes."

I do not feel compelled to point out that not all Americans eat a lot of pancakes.

"I love pancakes," the boy laying in the bunk above me observes.

"Everyone loves pancakes," the older boy says disdainfully.

"I've had pancakes with weal maple sywup," a young voice announces.

"Stop talking about pancakes," the older boy growls. Then to me: "Sorry."

"It's okay," I say, happy the darkness is hiding the broad smile on my face. "I miss pancakes."

"My dad's parents were from Canada; and they used to make real maple syrup," the older boy explains. "Relatives from Canada still send us maple syrup every year. The weather just isn't cold enough to make maple syrup here."

"Ahh," I say. "That makes sense. Why did they leave Canada?"

"The draft," the older voice says. "We are pacifists. Couldn't stay."

"Oh," I say, not sure what to think about that. It seemed an error to flee a prosperous and orderly country like Canada for a corrupt and poor country like Paraguay solely because of a military draft.

"Some of us stayed," he explains after a long silence. "Some of us left."

I suspect that the boys in the room wish their family had stayed, if not for the order and prosperity, at least for the pancakes.

"I am a beekeeper," I say. "I know honey isn't the same as maple syrup, but maybe you could make honey. It's pretty good on biscuits."

"You're a beekeeper?" the deep voice asks eagerly.

"Yup," I respond nonchalantly.

"I am going to the agriculture school next year and I want to study *apicultura,*" the deep voice says proudly.

"Depending on what you grow, it can be really good for your crops," I say sagaciously.

"Yeah, we grow everything," the voice says. "Everything we eat, we grow here."

It is quiet for a long time. A few boys sound like they have drifted back to sleep, their slow breathing whistling in the dark.

"Are you awake?" the older boy across the room whispers in the darkness.

"Yes," I hiss.

"Ask for whatever you need," he whispers.

"What?"

"Ask my dad for what you need," he repeats.

"What do you mean?"

"If you ask for something," he whispers. "By our faith, we are obligated to provide it."

I think about this for a moment, not really understanding what he is trying to say.

"What I mean is that you have to ask," he explains, still whispering. "If you don't ask for it, then he has no obligation."

I don't know what to say about this, so I say the only thing that comes to mind:

"Okay, thank you. I will."

It becomes quiet again. Eventually I fall asleep. I probably have strange dreams, given my thoughts right before bed—maple syrup and military conscription—but, if I do have dreams, my sleep is so deep that I don't remember them.

Daniel rouses me before dawn and motions that I should let my companion sleep. He ushers me to the kitchen table where he has prepared steaming cups of French-press coffee. It is still dark outside.

"This is great coffee," I gush. "I have been drinking *maté* for many months now. I forgot how wonderful a good cup of coffee is."

Daniel says nothing, appearing to be lost in thought, studying my face with his baby blue eyes. He looks especially tired, as if perhaps he hadn't slept that night.

I finish the cup of coffee and decide it is time to have the discussion that he had avoided the night before.

"We came from Táva Rã," I say. "We saw some really—"

Daniel is shaking his head. Then he says, "I know."

"You know?"

"Yes," he says mournfully. "I visited our leaders yesterday after you went to bed. You are wanted by the *Policía Nacional* as part of an investigation that they are conducting. There are many rumors. It sounds very serious."

"I need you to just take me to the *cabina telefonica* in town," I say. "I need to call the American Embassy. They will sort it all out."

He nods his head, rising, then sits again, opening his mouth, then closing it again, looking conflicted about what he wants to say.

"They are waiting for you," he says finally. "The *policia*, they have been patrolling our town since yesterday. They are officers that are unfamiliar to us. We do not know them."

"You cannot take me to the phone?" I ask, my heart suddenly beating wildly in my ribcage.

"I can take you to the phone," Daniel clarifies. "But you may not get your call. An officer is parked in front of the *cabina*. It is up to you."

I am at a loss for words. Then I remember what the oldest boy had said the night before: *Ask for what you want and we are obligated in our faith to give it to you.*

"Daniel, we need to get to Pedro Juan Caballero," I croak, on the verge of tears. "Can you help me get there? I need to get there without the police finding me. The police are corrupt. Edén has seen some very bad things and the police don't want us to tell anyone about it. You have to believe me. We did nothing wrong."

I fall silent, not sure what else to say, my eyes silently beseeching the old man across from me. Close up his skin looks like the leather of an old catcher's mitt with two lively blue eyes set into it. Daniel sits for a time, as if deep in thought.

"There might be a way," he says, sighing heavily, almost as if in resignation. "You might be able to get to Pedro Juan via the *campesinos sin tierra*. It is a dangerous option, but it is the one place you can be sure no police will find you. The squatters have been forcefully evicted from the land on several occasions already. This means that both they—and the Brazilians on whose land they are squatting—are likely to be armed and suspicious of anyone they do not know. So it is not without risk."

During my training, I had been warned, on threat of termination, to steer clear of *campesinos sin tierra*. Americans photographed nearby or even rumors of their presence at squatters' encampments could spark a diplomatic crisis, threatening the very existence of the Peace Corps in the country. But I figure the rules don't apply in my particular extenuating circumstances. Still, I am not sure how going to a squatters' camp will help me achieve my ultimate goal.

"How will I get to Pedro Juan Caballero?" I wonder dejectedly. "We need to get there. We have a friend there who will get us both to safety."

"They are supplied at night by smugglers who stay off the main roads," Daniel explains. "If you need to get to Pedro Juan Caballero, then they'll get you there and avoid the police the whole way."

"Okay, Daniel," I say, feeling suddenly exhausted by the prospect of more secretive travel through rural Paraguay. "I am requesting that you take me to *campesinos sin tierra*."

He nods and tells me to get my sleeping friend. He'll drive us most of the way there.

"We need to get going," he says. "The darkness is our friend."

Chapter 7

SNARES

Edén and I are packed into the bed of Daniel's truck under many sacks of grain. The ride to the squatters' camp is long and suffocating and terribly uncomfortable, but I know that this is a far better fate than the many nightmarish things that would happen to me were I discovered by the men in pursuit.

The truck stops at last and Daniel pulls the heavy sack off of us. It is light out, the sun beginning its ascent in the eastern sky.

"You just follow this road and you will find them," Daniel says, pointing toward the horizon. Nothing but rows of soy can be seen for miles in every direction. "I cannot take you any further."

Edén and I climb over the sacks to hop out of the truck.

"Here, take these," Daniel says, passing two sacks with bottled water and provisions through the open window of his cab. "We will pray for you."

Without another word, he makes a U-turn and leaves us standing on the road in a cloud of red dust.

We begin our journey up the red dirt road in silence. I think mostly about my parents, wondering if they had already gotten a call from the Peace Corps offices in Asunción. Given the violent circumstances surrounding my disappearance, my parents would no doubt fear the worst. My dad would probably drop everything to fly down and help with the search. I feel sick imagining the sort of fear and grief I might be causing them.

Edén senses the shifting mood and begins loudly singing a Clapton blues song from his favorite CD:

> Ayyyy yam e-dreefting like a e-ship en da sea
> Ayyyy yam e-dreefting e-dreefting like a e-ship en da sea
> Ain't got no one to care fo meeeee

"Enough already," I growl in Guaraní as he repeats the same verse. Edén ignores me, beaming, singing louder still.

"Enough already!" I roar, grabbing him roughly by the collar.

He quiets and squints at me as if I am some exotic animal he has never seen before.

"Listen you child," I spit, shaking him roughly one more time before releasing him, "it is not the time for songs. We need to think about how we will approach these people." I nod at the road ahead.

"Yes, yes, of course," Edén says genially, adjusting his shirt, which has been pulled askew.

"I don't think we should tell them about Táva Rã," I say, collecting myself. "The campesinos have enough problems without having to worry that you might bring more trouble to their community."

I glance over at Edén who appears completely unmolested by our precarious situation. His black hair is wild, sticking up in places, and he has a faraway look in his dark eyes.

"Did you hear me? Are you listening?"

"Yes, Peter," he says. "We say nothing about Táva Rã."

"Good," I say, returning my gaze to the horizon ahead of us. "Okay, let me see. What should we say is the reason for our visit?"

Edén does not answer right away, and when I look at him, he simply shrugs.

I dream up a few backstories. Maybe I'm a reporter or an activist or a speculator. But my threadbare, tattered clothes don't match those lies. What would I tell the *campesinos*? More importantly, what would I tell Brazilians on whose land the squatters are living? No good story comes readily to mind, but I am too proud to ask my young friend for help—even if he is the best liar I know.

Before long I spot, in the distance ahead, a red pickup truck parked in the middle of the road. Even from afar, I can tell it is a Toyota Hilux—a small pickup that is popular in rural Paraguay. I have never met a subsistence farmer who owns anything more than a small dirt bike, and I suspect that the truck's owner is Brazilian. The vehicle is so far in the distance that I can't tell if there are people in the cab.

"Okay, Edén," I say. "That is probably a Brazilian."

Edén stops and nods in agreement.

I think for a moment. What am I going to say? I don't even speak Portuguese. And what if the Mennonites are right—what if the Brazilian (or Brazilians?) parked up ahead suspect me of being a radical gringo organizer? I have the terrible urge to turn around.

"Do not worry Peter," Edén says. "I speak Portuguese."

Edén often brags about his English fluency—so I know better than to believe anything he says about his foreign language skills. In his mind, memorizing Eric Clapton lyrics is proof that he speaks English.

"No, you don't," I say curtly, still trying to think of how we will approach the Brazilian up ahead.

"Yes, I do," he says. "Peter, I speak it very well." Then he says something that sounds like Portuguese, but, since I don't speak it at all, I have no way of knowing.

"Edén, you do not speak Portuguese," I say, more forcefully now. "Just because you have learned a few Brazilian songs doesn't mean you speak their language."

"Peter, I do speak their language," he says. "Do not worry."

I badly want to shake him again but restrain myself.

"Edén, you do not speak Portuguese any more than you speak English," I say as witheringly as I can. "Stop speaking. I need to think."

Edén opens his mouth as if to say something but then thinks better of it and simply crosses his skinny brown arms. I rub my temples as my heart races. I have to come up with a plan—and fast.

"Okay," I say to Edén finally. "When we approach them, I will do the speaking, okay?"

Edén rolls his eyes but knows better than to argue. We continue.

I don't know what I will say, exactly, but have formulated this vague idea that I will feign ignorance. I will simply pretend I am a local American missionary out for a stroll with my young friend.

As we get closer to the pickup truck, I can see at least one man in the cabin, his elbow sticking out of the window. The radio plays upbeat cachaca dance music. My legs feel like jelly.

We get closer still, and I can see that the man has a cigarette in his fingers, but his face is obscured by the dark cabin. When I can smell the cigarette smoke, I speak, in what I hope sounds like a casual tone.

"Good afternoon," I shout in Spanish. The truck is an older model Hilux, the body rusted and dented. It is parked perpendicular to the course of the road, as if to block any passing traffic. A handsome, mustached man comes into view, his face tan with a square chin and a flat wide nose. He is alone, watching us impassively as we approach.

"How are you?" I say, perhaps too loudly, as we get within a few feet of the truck. I hook my thumbs in my waistband in a way I hope looks casual. I scan the horizon, nodding—as if assessing the landscape—in the hopes that it disguises my heavy breathing. The cachaca music is a ludicrous soundtrack to this exchange. Still the Brazilian does not say a word. After what feels like a long time, I realize he does not intend to respond at all.

"See you later," I say with a quick nod, sauntering to the front of his truck, motioning for Edén to follow. As soon as I step in front of his truck, he slams his hand on the horn, holding it there. I jump and stumble, gripping the bumper of the truck to steady myself. The sun is reflecting off the windshield in such a way that I can't see the man's face. I make my way back to the driver side door.

"What's up," I say, in Spanish, feigning nonchalance.

"*Prohibido*," he says thumbing toward the road on the other side of the truck. He takes a long drag from his cigarette.

"What's that?" I say. I can hear him perfectly fine but hope to give myself a few moments to think of something else to say.

He turns off the radio and flicks the nub of his cigarette into the dirt next to where I stand. Lugubriously, as if it is a great imposition, he climbs out of the cab, slamming the door behind him. He is about the same height as me, but broader, and wearing a thin collared short sleeve shirt, blue jeans, and worn cowboy boots. He stations himself about six inches from my face and repeats himself in a tone that implies his patience is wearing thin. I can smell the cigarette on his hot breath.

"*Esa camino es prohibido?*" I ask, feigning surprise.

"*Sim, prohibido.*"

"*Por qué?*"

He says something in Portuguese that I do not understand.

"*No fala portuguese,*" I say, trying my best to act like I don't understand from his tone that he is quite adamant that I should not pass.

He spits in the dirt. After a moment of silent reflection, he grabs me by the shoulders and forces me to turn around. When I try to turn back to face him again, he pushes me so hard that I fall to my knees. I turn awkwardly on my knees to look at him and see him flicking his large fingers at me as if to express that I better head back from whence I came.

I take my time getting to my feet, my mind racing. What am I going to do now? It would be hard to pretend I don't know exactly what he wants me to do. I make a big production of brushing the dirt off my pants, trying to think of my next move.

Then Edén speaks. In Portuguese—or, at least, it sure sounds like it. Before I can shoot him a dirty look, he is in conversation with the Brazilian. I try my best to arrange my face in such a way as to pretend that I am not alarmed by what sort of things he might be saying to a man who is clearly not averse to expressing himself by means of violence. The exchange seems to last a long time, though it could be only one terrifying minute. While they talk, I can't help but notice the Brazilian has what appears to be a large knife in a leather sheath attached to his belt. I slowly backpedal toward where Edén is standing, readying myself for the prospect that we might need to make a break for it.

I don't know what they are saying, but I can tell that they are talking about me by the way the Brazilian keeps glancing at me with a knowing smirk. Then he gets back into his truck, a mean grin on his face

"Let's go," Edén says to me in Spanish, pulling me by the elbow.

I let him pull me around the truck, watching the Brazilian the whole time. Is he really going to let us pass? I dare not say a word to Edén and simply walk, in what I hopes looks not too rushed, nor too slow, down the road.

When I feel like we have put enough distance between us and the truck, I murmur the question that is burning in my mind:

"What did you say?" I ask.

Edén glowers at me, shaking his head.

We walk for a while at what I hope looks like a casual pace. When the truck has disappeared from view, I try again.

"What did you say?" I say again, arranging my face into what I hope looks something like a grateful smile. I am in no mood to smile—feeling utterly exhausted from the adrenaline.

"Nothing, Peter," says Edén, who does not return my smile.

"Clearly you didn't say nothing," I say, patting him on the shoulder.

He scowls and swats my hand away.

"I'm sorry, Edén," I say. "I should have believed you about the Portuguese. I apologize, okay?"

Edén nods, quickening his pace. I run up to him and grab him by both shoulders, trying to force him to stop and look at me. He does so, but only after a short struggle.

"Edén, what did you say?" I plead.

Edén growls something in Guaraní, which I do not understand.

"I don't understand what you're saying."

"Please, Peter, I will not say it." he mumbles, eyes cast downward. "There are some things that you do not want to know." Something in his voice and eyes tells me to let it drop.

The squatters' camp is little more than a mishmash of orange and blue tarps lining the road. From a distance, it looks as if the rustic settlement might be abandoned. Based on our Mennonite friend's dire warnings, I imagined we would see a bunch of armed tough guys patrolling the perimeter of the camp—or at least one or two people standing guard.

Instead, we are almost in the camp before we see the first signs of life: Dozens of gaunt and miserable *campesinos* huddled under the tarps. Around the tarps, the soy is trampled and yellowing in large concentric circles.

When we are close enough to be heard, I clap—as is the custom. A young man rises slowly and steps out of the tarp nearest us. He is barefoot and dressed in dirty rags.

"Hello, sir," I called out in Guaraní. He nods. We approach slowly. Everyone else watches quietly from their places in the tarps.

As I step closer, his face comes into focus. He has short coarse hair and shockingly bright green eyes. A dozen or so paces beyond him, in the shade of the tarp, a small group of people lounge, quietly watching the exchange.

"Sir," I begin in Guaraní, "My name is Peter. My friend here is Edén."

"Hello, friend," says the campesino, walking toward us, "My name is Fulano."

"Hello, Fulano," I say automatically. "How are you?"

"I am well," he says, flashing a mostly toothless smile. It is obvious by the state of things at the camp that this is just an empty pleasantry. We shake hands. His hand is large and calloused, but surprisingly gentle. I can smell that he hasn't bathed for a long time.

"Friend," Fulano continues, "what do you have with you?" He is looking at my burlap sack in my hand.

"Food. Water," I say.

"Friend," he says. "Can we have it? My woman and child have been here for a long time, and we do not have enough to eat and drink. My woman makes very little milk."

Something in the way he speaks—quiet and earnest with unblinking, sad eyes—makes it hard to hold his gaze. Edén and I hand over our sacks without a second thought. Fulano nods and takes the sacks to his tarp.

Before we know it, a group of eight or ten emaciated, barefoot men approach us from other tarps, begging for anything we can give them.

"You have no food, but you have money," says one rail-thin older man with hollow cheeks and black eyes. "*Rubio*, we know you have money."

I explain that I don't have money and that I don't even have my documents.

The man and a few others become angry, calling us liars, pressing in on all sides.

Edén and I turn out our pockets, which mollifies them. They return to their tarps looking forlorn.

Fulano returns to us, having delivered our sacks to the women in his tarp.

"Come to my *carpa*," he says motioning toward his group of *campesinos* huddled in the shade of a bright blue tarp. "It is very hot now, and I invite you to rest with us."

Edén and I follow Fulano to the tarp—scarcely high enough to sit under—which is stretched from a square frame of lashed-together branches, back to where a series of stakes keep it fixed to the ground. In front of the tarp, in a ring of red earth cleared of the yellowing soy, is a pile of smoldering gray embers and a black, lidded cast iron pot.

Crowded under the tarp's shade, a group of five men and two women sit in silence. One of the women has a fat, stoic baby in her lap. The women are taking furtive bites from the Mennonite milanesa sandwiches, as if to hide the food from the emaciated men around them.

At first glance, the tarp seems to provide hardly enough shade for all the bodies gathered in it, but the campesinos lethargically rearrange themselves so that we each have a small space to sit. Off to one side of the tarp are a row of plastic bags, backpacks, plastic jugs and bottles, presumably full of food and supplies. I pretend not to notice that the severe man, sitting cross-legged next to me, has his hand on a black-blue revolver with a worn wooden grip laying idly in his lap.

"Greetings," I say in Guaraní, taking the seat cleared for me. The men nod. The women avert their eyes. The chubby, squinty-eyed baby with a mess of black curly hair studies me. The smell of all the unwashed bodies is overwhelming.

I have the urge to make some sort of small talk, but worry it will seem forced and trite, given the circumstances. Instead, I sit in what feels to me like an awkward silence.

"You speak Guaraní," the man with the revolver observes, breaking the long silence.

"Yes," I say. "I speak it some."

"You are not a Brazilian?" another asks.

"No, I am American."

"The *torre gemelos* fell," says another man from the far side of the group.

"What fell?" I ask.

"You know, the *terroristas*," the voice clarifies. "They made the big buildings fall."

"Ohh," I say, suddenly understanding the owner of the voice has decided to greet me with his knowledge of September 11—an event that I had experienced firsthand my senior year at NYU. "Yes, the terrorists made our buildings fall."

"There are lots of terrorists in the United States?" the man next to me asks. He had a long, hooked nose and sad brown eyes. His hand is still placed casually on top of the revolver in his lap.

"There are some," I agree. "Maybe not a lot."

There is a long silence where the group seems to consider this.

"You like Bush?" the man next to me asks.

"He is okay," I equivocate.

"And Pamela Anderson?" asks a shirtless gray-haired man in front of me, grinning lecherously. The woman carrying the baby stifles a giggle and says something I don't immediately understand. Edén laughs. Suddenly everyone is guffawing, a few of the men miming toward me that they, too, appreciate the actresses' big knockers.

I nod, forcing a stupid grin onto my face.

A lively debate ensues. I don't understand everything that is said. But the general gist of the debate is about what type of woman is preferable for a wife. A few of the men explain that they prefer women with hips like a cow so that they can bear many children. Others argue that women with Pamela Anderson boobs can feed a veritable throng of progeny. The women do not seem embarrassed, in the least, by any of this, though they still do not look me in the eye when speaking.

At some point during this conversation, I look over at Edén, who sits cross-legged next to me, thoroughly enjoying himself. His boyish brown eyes are darting from person to person as they debate the human reproductive arts, a big, guileless smile on his face. He catches my eye and the smile fades.

Near dusk Fulano invites me to accompany him as he goes to check traps, which he has set in distant soy fields. We venture into the rolling sea of green—far into the places beyond the horizon where the animals won't hear or smell the people gathered at the squatters' camp.

"There are lots of animals," Fulano explains in Guaraní as we hike through the soy at a brisk pace. "They hide between the rows. They live in the ground. They fly in. The animals still live here, hiding."

I survey the field around us. It seems unlikely that there are any animals left. There are only rows and rows of knee-high green soy as far as the eye can see.

"You appear as if you do not believe," Fulano says, studying me with his intense green eyes. "You will see."

Sure enough, in the first trap we check, we find a fat dove flapping around upside down, its leg caught by a string. Fulano efficiently wrings the bird's neck and then re-sets the trap, which requires he bend a long supple branch down toward a notched branch encircled by an open loop of string, into the center of which he deposits a handful of corn kernels.

"You see," Fulano says after he sets the trap. He holds the dead bird like a prize.

"Yes," I say. "You get something every day?"

"Most days," he says. "My woman is giving milk to the baby. She needs the meat."

I nod.

He takes a string from his pocket and loops it around the bird's neck, handing it to me like a strange ornament.

"You carry," he commands.

I take the bird, pretty with its blue, gray, and white feathers. It feels very light in my hand, and I wonder how much meat one could get from the tiny creature.

We wander through the soy fields checking traps for a long time. Most of the traps are empty, but a few had snagged birds. We check traps until it is almost too dark to see.

"Okay, we return to camp," Fulano announces at last. He has snagged two doves and two birds that Fulano simply calls *pajaro*. Even with the four birds tied onto the string, the catch feels very light in my hand. We set off through the soy field toward camp. Fulano takes one bird from my string and begins plucking its feathers as we walk.

"It seems that there is not enough to eat at camp," I observe. Even the poorest people in Táva Rã always seemed well-fed. It is the first time I have seen rural people who are hungry.

"The Brazilians block anyone from coming on the roads," Fulano explains. "So we cannot get supplies to us, except by those who come at night. They sneak in on their dirt bikes, which they must drive through the fields. It is very dangerous."

I nod and tell him we saw one of the Brazilians on our way into the camp.

"How did you get past them?" he asks, incredulous. "They let no one past."

"I'm not sure," I confess. "Edén speaks Portuguese and said something."

"He is a clever boy," Fulano observes. "You said you need help from us. But how can we help you? We have nothing here."

We walk for a little while in silence, the sound of dirt crunching beneath our feet, while I try to decide how I can ask for the help we need without alarming him with the true precariousness of our situation. Fulano finishes plucking the bird and hands the warm fleshy creature to me, grabbing another from the string to pluck.

"We need a ride to Pedro Juan Caballero," I say simply. "I was told that we may be able to catch a ride from here."

Fulano finishes plucking the bird in his hand and exchanges it for another on the string.

"Because you gifted me the food you had," Fulano begins, "I will ask if they will take you to the city. But I cannot speak for whether or not they will take you. You are a stranger and we are very careful. I cannot say whether the transporters will permit you to ride with them."

I nod, appreciatively.

"When I get to the city, I can pay them," I offer. "We have a friend there."

"Who is your friend?" he inquires. I have resolved to share as few details as possible about our journey so that we won't alarm our new friends—and so that they, in turn, cannot share any useful information about our ultimate destination with the pursuing lynch mob. Still, I suspect I need to do as much as I can to convince his friends to give us a ride, and I decide I should take a small risk.

"*Pa'i Roberto*," I say. "A priest there."

In the distance orange campfires flicker. Fulano stops and turns to face me, his silhouette black against a navy sky.

"I do not know the priests in Pedro Juan," Fulano says. "But our transporters who are coming tonight will. I will share this information with them. If *Pa'i Roberto* is with us, they will take you. If he is not in unity with *movimiento campesino*, then…"

He does not complete the sentence. I wonder, briefly, if I have made a terrible error by sharing this information. I have no idea what Padre thinks of the squatters' movement and, even if he is sympathetic, whether he is bold enough to publicly support them. But there is no taking back what I have said to Fulano and we trudge back to camp.

The women make quick work of the birds, which are gutted and fried in oil in their cast iron pot along with heaps of *manioc*. I haven't eaten since the morning and the smell of the fried food is intoxicating. The women serve me and Edén first. I shove my serving toward Fulano's wife, but the campesinos are insistent and unrelenting.

So I eat, somewhat guiltily while the hungry campesinos watch encouragingly. I finish quickly, wanting seconds, but refrain from asking for it. Much to my relief, neither does Edén.

It is dark and, though I am still hungry, I am also exhausted. Edén and I lay down near the campfire, mesmerized by the dancing flames. Soon we both have fallen asleep under a sparkling canopy of brilliant stars.

Sometime in the dark early morning hours we are awakened by the sound of growling motorbikes. I hardly have time to remember where I am before the four motorbikes are idling loudly in the center of the squatters' camp dropping supplies.

Fulano is already talking to the men on the bikes, and, after a short conversation, he darts back to Edén and me.

"You leave now and they will take you to Pedro Juan," he yells, short of breath. He grabs both of us by the wrists, his strong calloused hands pulling us through the darkness.

"*Jajotopata*," Fulano says, waving, as we climb onto the back of two of the dirt bikes.

I grab onto the waist of the broad-shouldered man driving the motorbike who smells vaguely like whiskey, exhaust fumes, and gasoline. I glimpse Edén's face on the back of another bike. He is beaming, which—for some reason—makes me feel calm.

We hurtle into the dark soy field, going much too fast to be safe, all four motorbikes growling in unison like a pack of wild dogs, either predator or prey.

Chapter 8

EPIPHANY

It is still nighttime when I catch my first glimpse of Pedro Juan Caballero, which appears in the distance like a terrestrial constellation. My arms are slick with sweat and shaking violently from exhaustion, having spent many hours tightly squeezing the torso of the driver, who callously ignores the obvious perils of careening top speed through a network of washed-out dirt roads at night.

To the driver's credit, his caravan of dirt bikes speeds from the squatters' camp to the city without so much as crossing a paved road, avoiding the most obvious places where we might be spotted by *Policía Nacional*. Even once we are clearly within the city limits, the caravan sticks to dark side streets and the web of footpaths crisscrossing the empty lots throughout the city.

It is my first visit to Pedro Juan Caballero and, from what I can see on the back of the dirt bike, the city is much prettier from afar. Up close it is a dusty city made up of a patchwork of slums, utilitarian commercial buildings, faded billboards, empty lots, and an occasional walled or gated residential compound featuring coils of razor wire that glint under the streetlights.

Father Roberto's church is a modest building in the center of town that looks out onto a tiny patch of greenspace that is the yard for his humble rectory.

There is no sign of Padre's car and a frightening thought crosses my mind: what if he is not home? What if he's out saying mass in a village somewhere? But I am not forced to contemplate the terrifying thought for very long because soon a light comes on in one of the windows and I can hear someone moving around inside.

Padre opens the door half-dressed wearing only slacks and an undershirt, his stoutness emphasized by the way he takes up most of the doorway. For a moment he does not recognize Edén and me, but as soon as I start speaking, he grabs me by the arm and pulls me close, as if inspecting my face for wounds—either physical or psychological.

"I can't believe it," he mutters, eyes darting from me to Edén and back again. Then, recognizing the cohort of motorbikes just behind us, he shakes his head, as if rousing himself from a dream.

I begin explaining that the men on the dirt bikes have given us a ride and that I hope that Padre could reimburse them for their troubles, but before I can get out more than a few words, Padre is already speaking with one of the men in rapid-fire Guaraní. After a short conversation, the men, as if of one mind, leave us standing in front of Padre's rectory, the echoes of their roaring motorbikes reverberating down the streets.

"I cannot believe my eyes," Father muses, ushering us inside the rectory. "You appear like ghosts!"

"I feel like a ghost," I agree. "I feel like it has all been a dream."

Padre's home is functional if not pretty. The kitchen, into which he ushers us, features a variety of modern appliances including a refrigerator, propane powered stove, and small sink with running water. Instead of cabinets, he has a series of mismatched free-standing shelves. He busies himself preparing *maté* for us, while I try to explain the story of how me and Edén had arrived at his doorstep at an ungodly hour of the morning.

I have scarcely begun the story when Padre interrupts.

"We know all about it," he says. "The violence in Táva Rã has been in the news. It is also said that you are *desaparacido*. In Amambay, disappeared always means dead. You have risen from the dead, Pedro."

"Yes, I owe my life to Edén," I say flashing a smile at my young friend. "He saved me." Edén, sitting across from me at the kitchen table, puffs his chest out, an enormous toothy smile spreading across his face.

I try my best to tell Padre about what happened after the lynching, Edén eagerly heightening the drama with exaggerated details. As I relate the story, I realize that it has been many days and nights since I was attacked. The memory is so lucid, so clear in my mind, that it feels like I have been snatched out of my hovel by the farmers only minutes ago. But in telling the story, I realize no fewer than three days have passed since then. I can still smell the grass, feel the hands on me, hear the gravelly voice of the ringleader, Don Esteban. At the same time, the whole ordeal seems a whole universe away from Padre's cozy kitchen where I am sitting.

Padre doesn't allow me more than a brief moment to silently reflect on the strange way memory constricts time while stretching distance before he shares his plan.

"We do not have much time," he says. "The men who brought you will soon talk to others in town. They may be talking already. We need to leave now."

We have scarcely begun sipping the tea when he rises from the table to get dressed. We cannot waste any more time, he warns.

He leads us to his small bedroom where he finishes dressing in priestly garments. He says that we need to get Edén on a bus to Ciudad del Este. The city is part of what is known as the *zona tres fronteras*, the tri-border area, where a sprawling metropolis has grown at the intersection of three countries: Paraguay, Brazil, and Argentina. Edén, who doesn't have any identification—much less a passport—will have to walk through the open border from Ciudad del Este, Paraguay to Foz do Iguaçu, Brazil, and then on to Puerto Iguazú, Argentina.

Once he gets to the Argentine side of the border, Father explains, Edén can buy a ticket to Buenos Aires without being asked for identification. Father says this all matter-of-factly, as if asking a 12-year-old to sneak across no fewer than two international borders in order to travel thousands of miles, alone, to one of the largest cities in the world, is some sort of reasonable plan.

"Padre, this is crazy," I say incredulously. "Surely you do not suggest that he simply run from those bad men in Táva Rã. We need to seek justice. They are murderers and almost killed me!"

"Edén, please go and sit in the kitchen," Padre says. "I need to speak alone to Peter."

Edén shoots us both a dirty look as he obeys the priest.

I find a seat at a small desk in his room and Padre sits on his bed, now fully dressed.

"Father, it seems like this is a very extreme solution," I begin. "I think if I contact the American embassy, they will make sure we are protected."

Padre nods thoughtfully for a moment, his intelligent dark eyes steady.

"Do you really think they will help both of you?" he asks. "Or do you think it is possible they will simply turn him over to the local authorities who are investigating the crime?"

It is my turn to silently contemplate what has been said. I had been so sure that calling the Peace Corps or the American embassy would solve all my problems. They would make sure justice was served. I hadn't thought through what they might do with Edén.

"But how are we supposed to ensure justice for those who were murdered?" I ask. "If we just run away, the bad men will not be punished for their crimes."

Padre takes a deep breath, as if he does not relish what he will tell me next: "Peter, there is no guarantee that the men will be punished even if you do report what happened. Paraguay is not a place where justice is the greatest virtue. This is a place where the highest value is power. Those who have power decide the morals."

"How can you say that?" I say reproachfully. "You are a priest!"

Padre's dark eyes show no emotion, not even offense. If anything, with his mess of tangled gray hair still uncombed, he looks a bit like an absent-minded professor.

"Peter, we do not have time to talk about this at length," he says, standing. "I will add, though, that you should trust that I know of what I speak. I have listened to confessions of many important men in this country."

"Wait, Padre," I say, standing in his path. "Does he really need to go all the way to another country?" I ask. "Couldn't he stay here with you—or go to some orphanage somewhere else in the country?"

"This country is too corrupt," he confesses, "and not even the church has escaped corruption. In Buenos Aires it is different. My seminary professor, a brilliant man, is now the archbishop. He has power, influence, and—most importantly—he is a man of integrity. He has a very good reputation caring for the *campesinos* who arrive in the capital. Edén need only find his way to Bishop Bergoglio and the bishop will see to it that the Jesuits take care of him. After some time, God willing, Amambay will be a distant memory. Peter, you must know that this is the best choice for him."

I look away because I don't want Father to see the tears welling up in my eyes. Father takes a few steps to join Edén in the kitchen, but I grab him by the arm.

"I'm going with him," I say, the words spilling out before I have a chance to think about them.

"No, Peter," Father says. "He will be fine. You will only attract more attention to him. This is not your world. You must call the embassy. He must get on a bus."

I feel desperate, as if this is my final chance to do anything of lasting value during my odyssey abroad.

"Padre, he is my Alypius," I blurt out. "We are supposed to find salvation together. I had a vision."

The words sound foreign in my mouth—I never use words like vision and salvation—but it seems like the only way to get the impatient old priest to stop and listen to me.

He turns to me and studies my face for a moment, his head cocked at an angle, eyes fixed on mine.

I hold his gaze, almost as if in challenge.

Finally, he sighs. "*Bueno.*"

He marches back to his armoire and, after a few seconds of rummaging, pulls out a handsome black cassock.

"You should wear this," he says, thrusting the outfit at me. "Yes, I was once a much slimmer man."

I give him a look that says I think the dress-like outfit looks ridiculous.

"And before you ask," he says. "No, this is not a joke."

Padre Roberto drives us to the bus station in a rough part of Pedro Juan Caballero, an area that is surprisingly lively at that hour of the early morning. The bus terminal is little more than a small, covered parking lot anchored by a modest kiosk where a dozing attendant sells tickets through a window with bars over it. As if to enclose the unwalled space, a variety of vendors have set up makeshift shops on the periphery of the parking lot to sell everything from grilled kabobs to housewares to knockoff sneakers. The wild-looking *vaqueros* waiting for buses pretend to ignore the gaggle of prostitutes eyeing them from the shadows just beyond the wan fluorescent lights.

"Two tickets to Ciudad del Este, please," Father Roberto says in Guaraní through the barred window. The attendant, a small unshaven man wearing a button-down short-sleeved shirt and stained tie, startles awake at the words.

He sees Padre at the window and glances at Edén and me standing close behind. If the attendant notices anything odd about our group, he doesn't let it show. It feels to me like it ought to be obvious to everyone—including the sleepy attendant—that I am a poorly disguised imposter. The cassock I am wearing is all black, including a sash that wraps around my waist like a belt, with a bright white clerical collar. Except for the way my feet are jammed into a pair of Padre's leather shoes, the outfit is a surprisingly good fit for me, physically. Still, I can't help suspecting that everyone knows that the clothes quite clearly do not match the wearer in some ineffable metaphysical way.

The attendant announces the price for the tickets and Padre Roberto passes some Guaranis through the window.

As we walk to an empty bench, no one—not the prostitutes, cowboys, nor the vendors—gives me a second look. In fact, I am surprised to find that most people quickly avert their eyes when they see me.

"You must make this lie your truth," Father says under his breath as we sit down on a rusty metal bench. "You must imagine yourself to be an actual priest."

"Is it so obvious that I am a fake?" I ask, my face feeling hot.

"No, not a person here thinks you are a fake," he mutters. "Except for you."

I frown and try to concentrate on getting into character. What would a travelling priest act like? I have the sense that priests tend to exude haughtiness bordering on sanctimony. Padre is not like this, but he is probably an exception. I sit up a bit straighter in my seat and look down my nose at the people gathered around us trying to imagine what sort of thoughts might be rattling around in a novice priest's mind.

"Take this," Father says, interrupting my daydream to thrust a rosary into my hand. "If you hold it like this, and mutter to yourself, people won't bother you." He demonstrates by thumbing another string of beads while mouthing a prayer, a faraway look in his eyes.

I mimic him and he nods approvingly.

On my other side, Edén elbows me in the ribs and I turn toward him. He glances at the rosary and winks, a big, mischievous grin on his face—the sort of look that says he is immensely enjoying our attempts at the sort of subterfuge in which he is an expert. I remember how we had planned our prevarications together back in Táva Rã, how he enjoyed the idea of being in cahoots with me to trick the world. The palpable delight in his countenance immediately annoys me.

"Go purchase yourself a pair of flip flops," Father suggests, passing Edén a colorful banknote. As Edén trots over to one of the nearby vendors, Padre deftly thrusts a wad of cash into the front pocket of my cassock.

"Don't take it out," he warns as I finger the money in my pocket.

I thank him and begin saying I plan to reimburse him, but he interrupts.

"*La zona tres frontera*," he continues, "*es muy peligroso.*"

"Yes," I agree. "Peace Corps told me to stay away from Ciudad del Este."

"But, thank God, even Jericho had a purpose," Father muses.

"*Jericó?*" I say

"Nevermind about that," he says. "*Ten cuidado, mijo.*"

"I'll be careful," I promise. "Like I said, he is my Alypius. We will do this together."

The bus is air conditioned with plush reclining seats, which—when combined with rhythmic swaying of the vehicle speeding along rural Paraguayan highways—serves to lull Edén into a deep sleep almost immediately. His head falls softly on my shoulder and his breathing is slow and calm.

Though sleep is tugging at fringes of my own consciousness, I will not succumb.

As the distance expands between me and the lynch mob, I feel a profound relief, as if an enormous weight has been lifted from my shoulders. But what I am feeling is more than relief. There is a sense of gratitude, peace even. Being a source of strength and comfort for my slumbering companion makes me think that all the turmoil and suffering might still have a purpose.

But none of these emotions, exactly, says what I am feeling. There is something more, something new, something that defies words.

As the morning light slowly gives form to the world outside the bus windows, I find the landscape of rural Paraguay an uncanny match for the strange feeling in my heart.

Sunrise over enormous, tidy farms on both sides for as far as the eye can see. Pastures dotted with fat cows. Oceans of crops—mostly soy—green sprouts, barely germinated, pushing up from the fertile earth. Modest huts, not unlike the one I recently inhabited, where occasionally there are children playing. It is as if the world has conspired to celebrate this unnamable feeling with me.

After so much fear and uncertainty and suffering, I refuse to let sleep rob me of this moment. My buzzing mind succumbs to a sort of hypnagogic lucid dream that feels both fully present in that particular time and place—this morning on a bus in rural Amambay, Concepción, San Pedro, my sleeping friend's head warm against my shoulder—but also outside of history, geography, and identity.

It is a moment that stretches to eternity, every fleeting moment a universe distilled through my eyes that also, at the same time, points to the limits of my own autonomy. I am in a Milan garden with my friend—somehow together, but also quite alone.

Before sleep takes me, at last, I have a premonition: our destination is not Ciudad del Este nor Foz nor Buenos Aires, nor America, nor even death. Our final destination is our first—and final—communion.

Chapter 9

COMMUNION

It is late afternoon when we are awakened by the stillness of the bus pulling into its destination. We have arrived at the Terminal de Omnibus de Ciudad del Este, a large and busy bus depot with multi-lingual signage that translates its name into many languages, including English: "International Bus Station of Ciudad del Este."

"Can you believe we made it?" I say, as we disembark the bus into the heavy tropical air, which smells vaguely of rotting trash. A long row of buses has pulled up to a sidewalk in front of the bus station where travelers lug cargo to and fro.

Edén does not say a word and looks somewhat overwhelmed by all the commotion. I realize that this may be the biggest city he has ever visited.

"Let's go inside," I say motioning toward the depot.

Inside is an even more frenzied hive of activity, travelers chatting and hurrying past, buying tickets, meals, and souvenirs. With a solid eight hours between me and my murderous pursuers, I have become much more comfortable in my cassock, no longer worried—or cognizant even—about being seen as an imposter. Edén and I shuffle through the building, past a long row of ticket booths, kitschy tourist shops, and fast-food restaurants.

It feels like I am back in a city—a real city—like New York, where the huge swarms of people offer the promise of anonymity. In this anonymity I feel like I can be anyone I want to be. Who is to say that I'm not actually a young priest?

As I watch the people walking past me, I become aware of the surreptitious bows and nods. It is more than respect. It is reverence.

"Edén," I say, turning to my companion, who still looks a bit like a fish out of water. "Do you see it? They really think I am a priest."

Edén nods without enthusiasm.

"What's wrong, friend?" I ask, slapping him on the back. "Cities aren't so scary when you get used to them."

"I'm not scared, Peter," Edén avers.

"Then what's wrong, *hombre*?" We have reached the far end of the bus station which looks out onto an enormous covered produce market that spills out into the street.

"Nothing," he says sullenly.

"Do not worry," I say, stepping out into the noisy street. "City life has its advantages. How about we go get dinner in a real restaurant?"

Edén looks unimpressed.

"Aren't you hungry?" I say, nodding toward a short, chubby woman with a mop of thick, shiny black hair who waves a tray of *chipas* under my nose. *Chipas* are sort of like a Paraguayan version of the bagel, traditionally baked in small brick ovens, made from cassava flour batter.

"*Chipa, chipa*?" she says, noting my interest. I look at Edén who appears determined to frown.

I shake my head no, but the smell makes me realize that I am hungry.

"How much?" I say in Guaraní.

"Eh ah," she says in astonishment. "Fala priest speaks Guaraní?" Fala is what some campesinos call Brazilians.

"I am not Brazilian," I say before I realize what I am saying. Then, in what is probably an unnecessary lie, I say, "I am Canadian."

"Amalia, Gregoria, come here and see this Canadian priest who speaks Guaraní," she yells to the other *chipa* girls working the crowd. Soon there is a small group of vendors surrounding me.

"Say it again Canadian boy," the *chipa* vendor says. "Say what you said again."

I am feeling a bit alarmed at having attracted so much attention in my first moments in the city.

"How much is the *chipa*?" I ask.

The crowd laughs.

"*Pa'i canadiense* speaks Guaraní," the *chipa* girl announces to the delighted crowd.

"Say something else," another girl yells from somewhere behind me.

"I just want to know how much?"

The crowd roars their approval. Edén maintains his frown.

"The *chipa* is yummy," the original *chipa* girl says waving the *chipa* at me like a prize. "Say the *chipa* is yummy."

"The *chipa* is very yummy," I say. She gives me a *chipa* like I am an animal that has performed a party trick for her.

"Canadian, Canadian!" a lady who is selling skewers of meat yells at me from the crowd. "Do you like to eat the Paraguayan *chipa*?"

I nod appreciatively, my mouth full.

"The Canadian likes to eat it!" she announces to the crowd. "But does the Canadian like to eat the Paraguayans?"

Everyone, even the shoeless little kids who are selling overripe fruit, laughs at this comment. She has employed the favorite Guaraní double entendre: "eat" can also mean "fuck" depending on the context. I am shaking my head no, but my denial just delights all the vendors. I look over at Edén, who smiles despite himself.

As much as I am enjoying the moment of levity, I realize that very few priests would entertain such lewd commentary from strangers. I flash a scandalized look at the motley crew around me and pull Edén toward the produce market across the street. The market is rows and rows of tables featuring all types of fruits and vegetables. It smells of sweat and spices, rotting compost and fermenting sugars. When we are far enough from the throng of admirers, I look over at my young companion, who is back to moping again.

"Come on," I say, pulling my friend with me. "A good meal will make you feel better."

I need not ask for directions as it seems quite clear from the activity in the streets which direction leads toward the city's commercial center where I am eager to treat Edén to his first real restaurant meal. The streets in Ciudad del Este are a mix of big retailers, dumpy shopping malls, and blocks upon blocks of street vendors who are almost all selling pirated retail goods—mostly of Chinese origin. The dirty sidewalks are cluttered with vendors who have set up shop under plastic tarps.

Due to my light skin and eyes, the street vendors continue to think that I am a Brazilian.

"Gaucho! Fala!" the vendors yell as I walk past them. Some rush up to me with bottles of cane rum and cigarettes explaining the benefits of their goods in broken Portuguese.

Occasionally, little barefoot indigenous children impede our progress, gathering around me with fists full of mottled mangoes.

"Mangas! Mangas!" they yell. "So um real!" I know that I must walk through the sea of eager faces as if they don't exist or else risk becoming the pied piper—which wouldn't be good if I want to pass unnoticed.

Every intersection, every storefront, every street booth selling bric-a-brac exudes the chaos of a city where order is generally neglected. Mostly, the city is block after block of run-down retail shops and apartments connected to each other by a tangle of overhead electrical wires. Occasionally there is a section of overgrown empty lot or a tall building that looks as if it was built decades ago.

I walk through the streets, block after block, which look, sound, and smell like desperation. The commerce is not for prosperity's sake, but rather to evade the direst consequences of stark urban poverty. Eventually, my feet take me to the city center, which is crowded around *El Puente Internacional de La Amistad*, Friendship Bridge, the connection between Ciudad del Este, Paraguay and Foz do Iguaçu, Brazil.

Downtown Ciudad del Este is dirty and chaotic, all squeezed into a few blocks located within steps of Friendship Bridge. It feels like a frontier city, not unlike Pedro Juan Caballero, that is trying hard—without much success—to be the sort of place that attracts tourists from major cities all over the world. There are a few nicer shopping centers, banks, and hotels here and there—all of which are distinguished from their surroundings by the cadres of SWAT-gear-clad private security officers carrying assault rifles.

A gleaming glass building ahead beckons to me. A sign above the doors reads "SHOPPING PARIS," with an Eiffel Tower in place of the "A." I guide Edén past the menacing security guards who seem unsure whether to try and dissuade us from entering. I hustle past them, as if I belong, and am inside before they can say anything to us.

SHOPPING PARIS turns out to be a shopping mall filled with people who are dressed like they belong in celebrity magazines. Although my cassock is strange, it is formal enough to make me look like I might belong there. Edén, on the other hand, gets pitying looks from the shoppers. In response, Edén scowls at anyone who looks at him sideways.

My plan is to find a decent restaurant and treat my young friend to a celebratory feast—but I realize that it will be hard for him to enjoy the meal if he feels embarrassed by the clothes he is wearing. I pull him into a clothing shop featuring mannequins wearing boys' clothes where upbeat Latin pop music plays a bit too loudly from overhead speakers. Everything in the store is much more expensive than I expect it to be, and I realize that I might not be able to afford the ticket to Buenos Aires if I buy him a new outfit and dinner.

For a moment I consider just leaving the store, but then a thought occurs to me: I could just call my parents and get them to wire me some money. After all that Edén and I had been through, I reasoned, didn't we deserve to really enjoy one last day together?

"Look at that," I say pointing at a mannequin sporting an outfit that wouldn't look out of place at a country club: khakis, polo shirt, and canvas shoes. "What do you think, Edén?"

Edén's eyes get wide. "Peter, but what about the ticket—"

"Let me worry about that," I interrupt. "What do you say?"

He doesn't have to answer because his beaming smile says everything.

The cashier is an attractive, if snooty, teenager in a scandalously short miniskirt who wears lots of makeup. She seems eager to quickly complete the transaction so that she may distance herself from the strange priest and campesino in her store. I do not hesitate to fork over the money when she tells me the cost.

In his new clothes, Edén still looks—to me anyway—like a poor campesino in disguise. But maybe that is because I know him. The outfit seems to fool everyone else, and none of the other shoppers look twice at us.

We saunter slowly past stores scrutinizing all the fancy things featured in the big picture windows: fashion, travel accessories, cosmetics, jewelry, electronics, sporting equipment. Edén is particularly thrilled to ride the escalators.

Then we see it: the CD shop.

"Come on, Peter," Edén says, pulling my arm. It is one of those stores—newly popular at the time—that lets customers listen to albums from headphones at special displays in the store. We spend a long time listening to the various American musicians featured in the rock section.

Edén is incredulous that they do not feature Eric Clapton on any of the stations and proceeds to share his opinion with a nearby staffer—a bored-looking young man who does a poor job of pretending to listen. Having thoroughly excoriated the man for his dearth of Clapton knowledge, Edén snorts that it is time for us to leave.

On the top floor of the mall, we find the food court and I pretend like the Burger King is a very fancy restaurant, which in truth it is for both of us, having eaten mostly beans and rice for the last few months. I treat myself to beers with dinner which I am surprised to see on the menu. Edén inhales a Whopper with French fries and a Coke and insists on eating another for good measure. Halfway through the second hamburger, he sits bolt upright and announces, alarm on his face, that he needs to find a bathroom.

I point at the restrooms nearby and manage to stifle the laughter until after he disappears from view. Once he can't see me, I laugh until my sides hurt.

By the time we leave SHOPPING PARIS later that evening, it is dark already, but the city seems even more busy and chaotic than it had been during daylight hours. Having enjoyed a few beers at the Burger King while Edén gorged himself on soft serve ice cream, I am feeling particularly jovial, and not at all in the mood for a long hike through two border crossings into unfamiliar foreign cities.

"What do you say we stay here tonight," I say, as we squeeze down a street full of shouting street vendors. "It is already late. We can go to Puerto Iguazú tomorrow."

Edén is quick to agree and we enjoy the evening wandering through the streets for many hours. The street vendors offer knockoff versions of every imaginable consumer good: liquor, pirated cigarettes, knock-off electronics, housewares, clothing, street food, knives, hardware, books, guns, furniture, toys and pharmaceuticals.

Later in the evening, just as the sex workers are beginning to appear on the streets, we decide it is time to find a room for the night. The problem, I soon find, is that hotel after hotel is insistent that I provide some form of personal identification in order to get a room for the night. It does not help my case that I appear to be a foreign priest with a young Paraguayan boy in tow. But even when I go into the hotels alone, the proprietors insist on seeing my passport.

"It's okay, Peter," Edén says when I return to the street after being rejected by another hotel clerk. "We don't have to get a room. We can sleep outside."

His consoling words make me realize that not having a place to stay is not completely foreign to my young friend. But it seems to me like being homeless is much more precarious in a city like Ciudad del Este than it is in rural Paraguay.

I pretend, for Edén's sake, that I am hopeful that we will find a place to stay. We need to continue looking, I say. The truth is, though, that I would rather walk the city all night than doze in some shadowy park or alleyway.

My enthusiasm for walking all night only lasts another hour or two before the buzz from the beers wears off and my feet blister in the leather shoes that are too small for me. Many street vendors are packing up their wares, leaving only groups of obviously drunk men and catcalling sex workers. An idea forms in my mind—a desperate one, maybe—but no more desperate than anything else I'd done in the last few days, I figure.

"Edén, I have an idea," I say, turning to my young friend, who still looks like an imposter in his new clothes. "I know what this might look like, but you're going to have to trust me."

We are on a particularly shadowy street, where I see that there are a lot of sex workers who stand under awnings calling out to passers-by: *tsk tsk tsk tsk*. I approach a pair of women standing in the shadows nearby.

"Good evening," I say politely. "How are you tonight?"

"*Alo sexi*," a whiskey-voiced woman purrs. "Want to party?"

"No, actually, I have a different service to ask of you," I propose.

"*Siii papi*," she says, stepping close enough to grab my hand. Up close I can see her in the dim glow of a nearby streetlight. She has tan skin and black hair, black eyes and broad shoulders. She wears a tight red dress that accentuates her bony body. Her face is gaunt.

"I do not want sex," I say. She immediately drops my hand and turns. "But I will still pay for a service."

"I do not play with children," she says, flipping her hair and walking back to her smaller friend, who remains silent, watching from the shadows.

"No, I'm not asking for that," I say, my face getting hot. "I am simply looking for a room for the night. One night to sleep. That is all."

"Do I look like a hotel?" she intones.

"No, but—"

"Do not waste my time, then," she says curtly.

"Let's go, Peter," Edén says, pulling at my arm. "It is okay, really. I will find us a place to stay. It is not so bad to sleep outside."

I stand there for a moment and, when I can't think of anything else to say, I turn to join my young companion, fully resigned to the idea that we are going to have to spend the night on the streets.

"Wait," another voice calls. The shorter woman approaches our spot under the streetlight from nearby shadows. She is wearing the sort of high heels that make it look like she is tiptoeing when she walks. She is dressed not unlike countless *campesinas* I had met during my Peace Corps service: stylized too-tight blue jeans with a halter top. She is younger than her companion, still obviously a teenager, with long, shiny brown hair, dark, sad eyes, and an angular face that may have been vaguely pretty was it not for the loud, bright makeup that makes her look like she is trying too hard to be noticed.

"How much do you have?" she asks.

"Enough," I say.

She laughs meanly saying, "You don't know what my time is worth."

"I am not asking for your time," I counter. "Just a place to sleep."

She considers this for a moment, then sticks out her hand.

"Room first," I say.

"Let me see it," she insists.

I pull a wad of bills out of my pocket and peel one from the top. "This is for your time," I say, placing it in her outstretched palm. "More once we have a bed."

Our new friend calls herself Yara and she is a serious and quiet woman whose modest studio apartment is a fairly long walk from the place where she plies her trade. She has one double bed, which is really just a sleeper sofa that sits in front of a television. The room is decorated with a few cheap Asian artifacts that look like they could have been stolen from a Chinese restaurant. The only other features of the room are a small table and two chairs, a window that looks out onto another building, a small, sparse kitchenette with a few cupboards, and an adjoining moldy bathroom.

"How much?" I ask after I have had a good look at the accommodations.

"How much do you have?" she says.

"That's not how this works," I say, smiling.

"That's exactly how this works," she says, undeterred.

I sigh and pull the wad of cash from my pocket. Tangled around the cash is Father Roberto's rosary.

"You can keep the rosary," she says. "I will take the rest."

I untangle the string of beads from the cash and hand her the small stack of bills.

While she counts the money, I thumb the rosary and pretend to pray. When she is satisfied with the payment, she turns to leave. But then she thinks better of it and turns back to me.

"You should learn to negotiate," she says, thrusting a 10,000 Guaraní note at me. "And I can tell by the way you do the rosary that you're not a real priest." She smiles at Edén, who is already making himself comfortable in the bed.

"And one more thing boys," she says, her angular face very serious again. "If you steal any of my stuff I will find you, and I will cut you."

I decide she won't find it funny if I tell her that I don't really see anything worth stealing.

Long after Yara has left us alone in her dumpy apartment for the evening, Edén and I are dozing in the narrow bed.

"Peter," Edén whispers, "Do you know New Jork en America?"

"Yes," I say.

"What is it like?"

"It is a lot like here," I say after a moment. "Lots of people and activity. It is like Buenos Aires, too, I am sure. Cities are all the same in some ways."

Edén is quiet for a time.

"Peter?" Edén whispers.

"Yes, Edén?"

"I like cities more than *el campo*."

A few months before this I might have felt the responsibility to talk about the benefits of living in rural Paraguay. But, at this point, I figure I owe it to Edén to tell him the truth.

"So does almost everyone in the world," I say.

Chapter 10

OPIATES

A dour, balding official from Western Union sits behind a thick glass window and tells me the requirements for receiving wired money with no identification.

Having received my instructions, I return to the asphalt where Edén is waiting for me. The street is full of the sort of businesses that require assault-rifle-toting security guards.

"We will need to call my parents," I report. "And we need a police report saying that my passport has been lost or stolen."

"You need a police report?" Edén asks, furrowing his brow.

"Yes," I say, already walking down the block in search of a *cabina telefonica* where I can make a collect call to my parents back in Florida.

"Peter, you will go to the police?" he says skeptically, half jogging to keep up with me.

"Edén, we don't need to ask them to do anything," I say. "They don't need to do an investigation. I'll just say my passport is lost."

"But, Peter, what about—"

"Don't worry about it," I insist. "I just need a report. Who is going to deny a report for a man of the church?"

I flash a roguish grin at my young friend, but Edén remains unconvinced. Still, he does not argue the point.

Down the street I find a Telecel shop where I make a collect call to my parents in Florida. They have been worried sick—my dad tries to be stern, my mother cannot speak for her weeping. They tell me that days ago Peace Corps officials had alerted them that I'd gone missing after a shooting in my village. I assure them that I am fine, that I need a few hundred dollars and would soon be home. I act as if it is all a big misunderstanding, but they know enough to not believe me. Still, they are good parents and promptly arrange to wire me the money.

Back outside the bright sun is baking the pavement. I tell Edén my plan: "Just keep your distance," I say. "Sit on the bench in front of the Western Union. I don't want the police to ask why we are together."

"Peter," Edén implores, "be careful, please. You cannot trust the police."

"Just wait near the Western Union," I say. "This will be done in no time."

Nearby, I spot a policeman in his khaki uniform and cap, patrolling the street on foot, charcoal black assault rifle strapped under his arm. I greet the cop in Spanish, speaking in a thicker accent than I actually have. I think having a very thick accent will help sell my story that I am just a hapless foreign priest who has lost his passport.

The policeman is young, perhaps my age, clean shaven and square jawed. He looks handsome in uniform with dark brown—almost black—eyes that seem perceptive. He politely listens as I spin a tale about losing my passport—maybe it was a pickpocket or maybe I just dropped it—somewhere in the commercial center.

"All I need is a police report," I explain. "I don't expect you to try and get it back for me or anything."

The policeman whistles for his partner down the street who is stationed at the corner of a busy intersection. His partner is middle-aged and pudgy with brown hair curling up from the edges of his khaki *Policía Nacional* cap.

The young one explains my predicament to the other in Guaraní. When he finishes his retelling, the older one smiles at me.

"You need a report then," he says, pulling a pad from a cargo pocket.

"*Sí señor*," I say, arranging my face into the most innocent look I can muster. The older cop scribbles some notes.

"Here you go," he says courteously, tearing a paper from the pad. "This should be all you need for the wire."

I thank the police for their service and saunter back to the Western Union. On my way past the armed security, I see Edén sitting on a bench down the street. I grin and wink at my friend, but he doesn't return the sentiment.

In the Western Union, the severe balding man behind the window counts my cash twice and then hands it through the drawer. My parents wire only $500, but this equals more than 3,000,000 Guaranis—a large, crisp stack of bills, which I take pains to stash in various pockets in my pants and cassock, even stuffing a few bills in my shoes.

But this effort makes little difference to the policemen who are waiting for me out on the street. They are stationed just outside the Western Union, in full view of the security guard, the courteous smiles on their faces turned into scowls.

The pain from their blows lasts only a few moments before sweet blackness takes me.

When I open my eyes, I am laying in a bed in a familiar studio apartment with Edén and Yara sitting vigil over me. As soon as I wake, I remember being beaten by the policemen, curled in the fetal position, combat boots raining blow after blow on my head and body. I wonder briefly if this is the end. And then, the soft embrace of unconsciousness.

But it is not the end. Instead, I wake to a world of pain that makes me wish for more blackness. And, for a time, God is merciful, letting me slip back into dreamless black. But eventually the dark will not come, and I am forced to speak to the two figures who remain at my bedside.

"How?" I croak in Guaraní. I am still wearing the cassock, though it now looks more like an old muumuu because it is torn in places and is missing the sash belting my waist.

"Peter, do not worry," Edén says. "We are safe."

One of my eyes is swollen shut, but through the other I can see Yara sitting next to Edén. She is still dressed in the jeans and halter top from the night before. I remember how she said she would cut us if we messed with anything.

I nod at Yara, as if to show my gratitude, and the movement sends waves of pain through my head and neck.

"They robbed you," Yara says in Guaraní.

I grunt in response, knowing any movement will bring waves of pain. My good eye roams about the room I slept in the night before, which looks even shabbier in the daylight. Shafts of sunlight fall through a window opposite me that looks out on a dirty cinder block wall with peeling orange paint.

"I told you not to go to the police," Edén says finally. Yara rises to attend to something beyond my field of vision. Soon I can hear the clinking of dishes and a refrigerator door opening and closing.

I don't feel like debating the details of my attempt to get money wired to me.

"How did I get here?" I ask.

"You are safe," Edén replies.

"Yes," I say through gritted teeth to express my frustration. "But how?" Edén begins to answer but is interrupted by the whirring sounds of a kitchen appliance—perhaps a blender—being used nearby.

"I brought you," Edén says finally.

"*Toma*," Yara says, rejoining Edén at the bedside, thrusting a drink in my face. "It is a *liquado*."

I take a sip of the smoothie, creamy banana and strawberry with a bitter tang that is either something rotten or a poorly masked drug.

"What is in it?" I ask Yara, who is holding it under my nose.

"*Es fortificado*," she says simply.

"Fortified with what?" I ask in Spanish.

I hear her say, "*Eedrocodona*." I ask her to repeat herself.

"Do not worry," she says when it becomes clear I won't understand. "It is a good medicine."

She is right: The pain fades quickly. It is still there—in the background—but the drug makes the pain feel like more of a nuisance than paralyzing agony.

Chapter 11

IDOLS

Edén announces he is going to work with the *sacoleros*, the smugglers who carry pirated goods between Brazil and Paraguay. He says that it is lucrative work and that he will save the money for passage to Buenos Aires in no time. This means that Edén and Yara keep opposite work schedules—Edén working during the daylight hours, Yara at night—leaving supper as the only time all three of us are together.

Yara likes to watch telenovelas on the TV in the evenings and thankfully Edén, who prefers bad Hollywood action flicks dubbed into Spanish, does not protest. Yara cooks dinner—oil fried *manioc*—in the late afternoon so that she can be ready to eat in time for her favorite soap opera, *Pedro El Escamoso*. Edén, Yara, and I sit together in the bed, backs against the wall, scooping bites of oily starch into our mouths while we learn about the titular Pedro, a goofy Columbian Lothario who sports a finely coiffed mullet and shirts that are much too small for him.

"They call him Petercito," Edén observes after a particularly hilarious scene where Pedro is once again unlucky in love. "Did you hear? They call him Petercito."

"Yes, Edén," I say, feigning indifference.

"I will call you Petercito now," he declares.

Yara snorts, her mouth full of *manioc*, half choking. Edén takes this as a sign of comedic brilliance and doubles down on this line of reasoning.

"*Petercito escamoso pirulino*," he sings. "You must dance your *pirulino*!"

Yara chokes again and spits her food back into her bowl, coughing in fits. This, apparently, is just the reaction Edén is looking for because he rises to his feet and begins dancing in such a contrived and ridiculous fashion that I can't help but join the laughter.

An excruciating pain radiates through my torso. The drugs do nothing to mask the pain, and I cry out in agony—making the mood somber again. When the shock of my scream and the wave of torture subsides, I apologize for ruining the moment of fun.

The first real conversation I have when I am alone with Yara is about a necklace she always wears: a delicate gold chain with a strange pendant that looks like a fired bullet.

"What's that?" I say, pointing at her necklace as she hands me a gourd of cool *tereré* tea.

It is the hottest part of midafternoon, and the apartment has no air conditioning, so it has become our custom to drink lots of ice cold *tereré,* which we share in the Paraguayan custom, passing a gourd back and forth at regular intervals.

On this particular day, I am sitting in my spot on the bed, and she is next to me in a chair pouring the tea. Yara has just woken up and her dark shoulder-length hair is a tangled mess. She is still wearing the oversized t-shirt and boxers she slept in. The t-shirt is threadbare and hangs loosely around her neck, framing the pendant on her olive skin. It is the first time I have noticed the necklace.

"Oh this?" she says in a singsong way, patting her chest where the pendant hangs. I have begun to notice that when Edén is not around, she prefers to speak Spanish. She talks like they do in the telenovelas, full of flirtation and intrigue.

"Yes," I say. "Is that a bullet?"

She giggles, pouring ice water from a pitcher into the gourd and then sipping slowly from the straw.

"Yes, it is," she says finally, then pouring another drink. I take my sip and pass it back.

"Why?" I ask.

Her demeanor changes at once and she is suddenly very serious. I assume this seriousness is contrived—an affect inspired by the mercurial characters we watch on her favorite soaps.

"This is for protection," she says somberly, pouring water. She has a faraway look in her eyes.

"I could use some protection," I say half-joking as I wave my hand across my battered face, trying to lighten the mood. "Does it work?"

She sits back in her chair, considering this question for a few moments, slowly sipping from the gourd.

"Well, I'm not dead yet," she says, but not in a joking way. *"Gracia a San la Muerte."*

"Thanks to which dead saint?" I ask.

She giggles again, pouring the tea into the gourd that we are sharing.

"What's so funny?" I protest.

"Not a dead saint," she explains, passing me the gourd. "Saint Death."

I take a long gulp of *tereré,* unsure what to say about Saint Death. She doesn't seem to be joking and I have no way to process this information. In my mind I have already put this in the same category as the superstitious things I hear from Edén about mythological forest goblins.

After a long silence: "You do not believe," she says furrowing her brow. She pours the cool water into the *guampa* without taking her scrutinizing gaze off me.

"How can I believe something I just learned about?" I answer.

"You are very clever," she says. "And very dumb at the same time. Are all Americans this way?"

This is the first time she has ever said anything critical of me, and it takes me by surprise.

"Come here," she says standing up and moving toward the kitchenette. I am still profoundly injured from my beating so it takes quite a while to wriggle from my spot on the bed to stand. It is my first time out of bed that day and I move like an arthritic old man.

I shuffle toward her kitchenette where she is standing, hands on her hips, looking into an open cabinet above the sink. Inside is a shrine decorated in the Catholic tradition with candles, incense, and various ornate containers. Standing taller than all the bric-a-brac, which includes a cross with suffering Jesus, is a small statue of a skeleton wrapped in black robes carrying a scythe.

"So, this is your Saint Death," I say, feigning interest in the weird devotional.

"Yes," she says, intensely searching my countenance. "But you do not believe."

Taking a closer look, I notice that the ornate bowls contain pills, blurry pictures, and handwritten notes. "No," I say finally.

"I like you," she says, her voice once again light, a furtive grin forming on her face. "You do not lie, even when lying would better serve you." The way she says this, it sounds sincere.

"Why is it better to lie?" I say reaching toward one of the photos in the shrine.

She swats my hand away and shuts the cabinet door firmly.

"Why is it better to lie?" I repeat, slowly turning around to shuffle back to my spot on the bed.

"You'll live longer," she says flatly.

Yara makes me her special medicinal smoothie every afternoon while she cooks dinner. One such day, I ask her how she knows so much about medicine.

"Transsexuals are like pharmacists," she says proudly, handing me the smoothie. She says this matter-of-factly, as if I already know she is a transsexual.

So many questions form in my mind, but I am not sure I should ask them.

She fills the silence by explaining that the transsexual sex workers in Ciudad del Este know everything about opiates because they're constantly buying hormone pills from the pharma vendors and getting lots of cheap cosmetic surgeries from uncredentialed surgeons. Self-medication is a way of life for them.

I decide it is probably more prudent to let my questions go unasked. Besides, I am beginning to find that Yara and I share a passion for telenovelas and hydrocodone—which we agree are best enjoyed at the same time. I tell myself that the pills are just to be taken until my broken ribs stop hurting so much. I don't think much—or don't want to think much—about the fact that Yara seems to always take the pills with me.

"Petercito!" Edén shouts as he bursts into the apartment. "Petercito! You are famous!"

I look over at Yara, who is in the kitchen fixing dinner. We share a knowing look. Edén tends to subscribe to all sorts of delusions of grandeur.

"No, it is the truth, Petercito," he says, gesticulating wildly. "Give me the remote and I will show you." Edén changes the channel to Telefuturo news.

I am feeling good, having just finished the *liquado* fortified with crushed hydrocodone that Yara makes for me every evening.

A pretty blonde anchor makes the introduction: "A breaking story tonight from the American embassy." A picture of me from my Peace Corps swearing-in ceremony in Asuncion flashes on the screen.

"Peter Jones was a Peace Corps volunteer serving in Táva Rã in the state of Amambay. He has been missing since a deadly shooting on the 7th of April. He has been in contact with Peace Corps officials in the days afterward but has been missing for over a week."

The screen flashes to a press conference at the US Embassy in Asunción. I can see my parents behind the official at the podium. They look as if they haven't slept in days. An American official speaks, and his words are translated into Spanish.

"Peter is thought to be in the Tri-border area. A reward is offered for any information that may lead local authorities to find him," the official says.

Suddenly they cut to a part of the press conference where my mother is speaking. She is a petite woman from whom I inherited my slight frame, light hair, and fair complexion. Her pretty green eyes are filled with tears.

"I just want to bring him home," she says hiccupping.

The news cuts back to the anchor: "A 60-million-Guaraní reward is offered for information that leads to locating Peter."

Edén whistles. Yara is more circumspect.

I am annoyed that the news has ruined my high.

All of us—me, Yara, and Edén—are invested emotionally in the vicissitudes of Pedro's semi-charmed life. By the time Edén and I start watching the telenovela *Pedro el Escamoso* with Yara, the titular Pedro Coral has escaped certain death in his rural hometown in the Colombian mountains and has found a job as a driver for the rich and powerful Pacheco family.

The evenings become my favorite time of day. Edén gets home from his *sacolero* work just before twilight and Yara has a hot meal of oil fried *manioc* waiting. And, better still, the hydrocodone begins its evening march through every nerve of my body.

We gather on the bed, three in a row, to watch what sort of trouble Pedro will get into that evening. His story is ours, and while we watch Pedro learn to navigate in the big city, we each secretly wonder if his story would somehow portend our own fates.

We, too, had escaped death in rural Latin America.

We, too, had made it to the big city, only to find that our provincial sensibilities helped us survive, but also got us into a lot of trouble.

We, too, longed for love, which went unrequited ostensibly because we were in the midst of some great odyssey, but—in reality—because we carried with us our hubris and foibles all along.

We are Pedro. Pedro is us.

And then there is Nidia and Cesar who are at once the most enthralling characters and the most foreign. They represent power and influence. A world apart. More forces of nature than people, it seems.

Nidia is always trying to seduce Pedro. Cesar seduces Pedro's love interest, Paula. What does this mean for us? Are we to be seduced by a lust for power? Or is the lust for power trying to seduce us?

I hatch a vague theory—as the days turn into weeks—that my Nidia is not the *Policía Nacional* nor the lynch mob in Táva Rã, but rather she is hydrocodone.

Edén is asleep on the bed next to me and I have been awake for hours. Yara is out working. It is maybe three or four in the morning, and I get out of bed very slowly because my ribs are still tender. I feel nauseous and know it is not a physical ailment—but worry. I have this stomach-churning sense of foreboding that is not logical. A void of blackness; yet more than nothing. Maybe I should just call the embassy or my parents? But what would the officials do with Edén? I can still pull this whole thing off. Just a little longer and this will all be over. It'll be worth all the suffering along the way if Edén makes it to Argentina, to the kind Bishop Bergoglio.

I need only watch my young friend sleeping soundly, so sweet and innocent, to convince myself that I need to ensure he gets his ticket. Plus, I can always take another hydrocodone if I need it.

Yara has gone out to work for the evening and Edén and I are alone in Yara's apartment watching a late-night variety show.

"What do you know about *San la Muerte*, Edén?" I ask.

He does not answer. I ask again, but Edén just shakes his head. I catch a glimpse of his eyes in the glow of the television. He is terrified.

I swing my feet over the side of the bed and stand. It is dark in the apartment, except for the glow of the television. I turn on a lamp and the brightness hurts my eyes. Moving very slowly to mitigate the pain from all the broken ribs, I shuffle over to the cabinet where Yara keeps her shrine. It looks just as it had days before, bejeweled, meticulously arranged, and, somehow, bric-a-brac at the same time.

I take a blurry picture from one of the chalices that is full of coins and various pills.

Edén leaps out of bed and bounds over to where I am standing.

"Put that back, Pedro," he says, his eyes wide in alarm. "Do not touch it. It is satanic."

"This?" I say grinning. I thrust the picture at Edén as if to touch him with it. With catlike reflexes, he leaps away from me.

"It is not funny, Pedro," he says, watching me as if I hold a dangerous weapon in my hand. "It is Satan."

"Satan is no more real than the *Pombero*," I say, reminding him of my longstanding doubts regarding his favorite mythological forest goblins.

"You are wrong, Pedro," Edén protests. "Satan is real. I know."

I scrutinize the photo. It is a family somewhere in rural Paraguay. A dozen or so people, three or four generations of Paraguayans, all of them looking at the camera, the older ones stolid, serious and the younger ones smiling jubilantly.

"Satan is just a way for people to blame their evil actions on a creature," I say finally. "Same with the *Pombero* or *Kurupi*. There is no forest goblin going around impregnating virgins. That's just men. Bad men. The same bad men that have been attacking me and you. The sooner you realize this, the better it will be for you."

Edén looks at me patronizingly, as if I am the one who won't accept reality. The look only emboldens me.

"Because I won't always be here to help you," I declare. "And you can't go around thinking that the whole world is full of evil spirits, Edén. It's just men. Bad men. Men like you and me who are scared and desperate and who want to force the world to conform to their evil desires. Most people are just evil, Edén—"

I stop because Edén is crying. Maybe I have gone too dark.

"I'm sorry," I say after a time. "It's not that bad. Most people are probably mostly good. It's just that we have had a lot of bad luck lately. It's not as bad—"

Edén is shaking his head, sobbing. I don't know what to say. When he has calmed enough to speak, he says this:

"When are you leaving me?"

I turn toward the shrine and spend a long time inspecting the various objects because I don't want Edén to see the tears in my eyes.

Early mornings are when I learn about Yara's life and work. Edén leaves around sunup for his work smuggling packages across the border, and usually sometime a little after dawn, Yara returns home. When she isn't high as a kite, we talk openly, our conversations meandering and aimless.

I still hold on to this silly idea that I shouldn't talk about adult matters in front of Edén—as if my conversations with Yara will cause him to lose his innocence. I guess I know, on some level, that I am the one who is losing innocence. And perhaps I am ashamed to let Edén see it. I tell myself it is all for Edén's sake.

It is in these early morning conversations that I hear about her nights turning tricks on the streets and truck stop motels. She talks with plain, almost clinical language about her work, wholly unashamed and unrestrained. She is a favorite among the men who like to be dominated because—in her words—she is really good at "choosing just the right amount of hormones to take." She takes just enough hormones to soften her features, she explains, but not so much that she can't sustain an erection.

I don't know the Guaraní words for things like "erection" and "blow job" so she often must stop in the middle of the lurid tales to explain what she is saying. She illustrates the words in pantomime and, as comprehension dawns, I can feel my face turning red.

I get the sense that she likes saying things that shock me. Sometimes it is just the weird things the johns tell her to say. Yara parrots the words like an incantation, she explains. Said in just the right way, with the right inflection, in the right order and she will ensure returning customers much more than anything she actually does with them.

But the early conversations aren't all sordid details from the night before. Sometimes she talks about her dreams, which mostly involve expensive surgeries that will give her a more permanent feminine appearance. She has this idea that she can get rich as a high-class call girl if she gets just the right combination of surgeries.

"I am lucky that I have small hands," she muses one morning while we sip our yerba mate together. "Look at them." She places her hand in mine. Her hands are much smaller, delicate even.

I nod. Usually when she talks about her appearance, I don't say much because I am worried I might say something wrong or insulting. And I don't want to betray my ignorance of her world, even though my inexperience is patently clear to both of us.

"Most *travestis* like me are not so lucky," she says. In America it might be an insult to call a transsexual a transvestite, but Yara simply uses the unnuanced local parlance everyone else does. "Often you can tell the difference between us and the genetic girls by the hands."

She calls naturally born women "*chicas geneticas*," especially when she wants to distinguish them from transsexuals. Her goal, though she never says so explicitly, is to look as much like the genetic girls as possible.

"The men like it because their penises look bigger when you have small hands," she says giggling. I force a smile, but I am mostly thinking about the fact that she said "penises" in the plural and am wondering how many penises she has touched in the last 24 hours. Then I begin wondering how many in her life. I can feel my face flushing.

I sometimes try to act like I'm not shocked by what she tells me in the morning conversations. But she almost always sees through this. She, like Edén, has spent the better part of her days surviving by reading the expression on the faces of men who can rapidly become violent. It is no use pretending with her.

The one thing she never talks about is her life before Ciudad del Este. One morning I ask her about the photo of the family she has in her shrine to Saint Death. She gets very serious.

"Do not ask me about this again," she says very slowly, carefully. "That person is dead. More than dead. That person is forgotten."

It is the weirdly third-person, emphatic way she says this that made me know better than to ask again.

Yara arrives at her apartment in the minutes just before dawn. She is high on some drug that makes her jumpy.

"Good morning sleeping boys," she says in singsong. Her words are slurred. She has a broom in hand and seems to be sweeping in circles.

Edén has just returned to Yara's apartment after working as a *sacolero* all day.

"Petercito," he says sitting down on the bed next to me. "I am getting closer to my goal. I have about half of my *pasaje* saved up. I will be able to go to Buenos Aires soon."

"Marvelous," I say, beaming. "How much longer do you think you might need?"

Edén does not look me in the eye when he says, "Not very long, I'm sure."

I am high on hydrocodone, having just snorted a line with Yara in the minutes before Edén arrives in the evening, euphoria crashing over me like waves in the ocean. "Snorting isn't so bad," I think, "But no needles. I won't ever do the needles. That will be a sign of a real problem."

On our favorite soap opera, Pedro makes love to the beautiful, vivacious Paula—but she is drunk. So drunk, in fact, that she does not remember the cloyingly poetic things Pedro has said to her about life, love, beauty and belonging. She is ashamed to have slept with Pedro, who is her subordinate, her driver.

"Petercito is crying!" Edén yells, pointing at me.

"No I'm not," I say.

"Look Yara! Look!" he shouts, hopping out of the bed where we are seated like a strange triumvirate.

Yara covers her mouth in mock horror.

"Shut up," I say wiping my eyes. "Both of you!"

"Have you evah love a woman," Edén croons. "So much yoooou tremble in paiiiin."

I look away so he can't see the smile forming on my face. Having not received the reaction he had hoped for, Edén stands, one hand on his heart, swaying, eyes closed tightly shut like an old bluesman.

"Have yooo evah love a woman, it is a shaaamme an' a seeen," he bellows.

Yara is the first to laugh and soon I can't contain myself.

I chuckle, but my broken ribs remind me that mirth has a price.

Chapter 12

BLOOD SACRIFICE

It is a simple sneeze that does it. We are watching *Pedro el Escamoso* together, as is our custom, and Edén sneezes into his hands. I glance at him and notice that the sneeze has ejected all sorts of dark flecks from his nose.

At first glance, I assume it is blood. Before he can wipe his hand on his pants, I grab his wrist and pull it close for a better look. Edén squirms, but it is no use. I realize that the hand is not covered with blood, but some sort of strange metallic flecks.

I look at him, but he is eager to extricate his hand from mine. He won't look me in the eye.

"Edén, what is that?" I ask.

He shrugs. I let go of his hand and he wipes it on his shorts. I notice that he has flecks of the same weird metallic stuff all over his shorts, as if he has been wiping it there all day long. He always comes home a bit dirty from his smuggling. It is hard work smuggling big packages down the riverbanks and back up them.

"Edén, what is this?" I ask, pointing at the place on his shorts where the silvery stuff is smeared. I look toward Yara, who is sitting on the other side of me, and there is something in her guilty expression that tells me she knows exactly what is happening.

"Yara?"

She fixes her eyes on the television.

"Well now I have to know," I announce. I stand up, slowly—my ribs still tender—and station myself in front of the television. I look at Edén and Yara, who sit on the bed looking a bit like naughty children who have been caught red handed. Neither looks me in the eye.

"Okay," I say, grinning. "I am not moving until someone answers me." I know I am on to something, based on the odd reactions I am getting. I can hear from the music and dialogue that something dramatic is happening on Pedro. It takes all my willpower not to turn and watch the television.

"Come on guys," I plead. "Just tell me. I don't want to miss any more of our show."

A few moments pass, but finally Yara relents: "He is sniffing paint," she says simply. This is not a response I am expecting, and it takes a few more moments for it to register.

As it dawns on me what Yara is saying—Edén had been huffing paint—I react in a way that feels more like instinct than reason. Suddenly I am on top of Edén, smacking him in the face savagely.

Yara is screaming for me to stop, pulling at my shirt. My ribs feel as if they are being rebroken; I do not care. I want Edén to be afraid. I want real fear, not some act. I do not stop until I see the fear in his eyes. The fear comes, finally, reluctantly even. It is the first time he looks at me that way. It is satisfying. Justified. Necessary. For his own good.

"No more," I say, breathing hard, still holding him by his shirt collar. His nose is bleeding, a trickle of red mixed with flecks of metallic paint dribbling over his lips and around his chin. "No more paint, understand?"

Edén says nothing, but I am confident that my point is made.

Yara has tears running down her cheeks.

I sit, as if to watch *Pedro*, as if we can resume the same as before. But everything has changed. I am no longer the uncompromising, naive Pedro Coral or the insurgent, innocent Paula. I have turned into Cesar: powerful and seductive, but wholly inscrutable.

I surprise myself with the savagery and violence with which I respond to the discovery of Edén's huffing paint. I keep telling myself over and over that Edén is only 12-years-old and that I am the closest thing he has to a parent. Beating him bloody is for his own good. It is the best way to ensure that he doesn't continue to huff with the band of misfit teenagers that work with him in the smuggling cartels. If I didn't soften my mind into such a deep opiate-induced stupor, I might realize that there is a reason I must tell myself this over and over, like a mantra. I might hear my conscience trying to tell me something different.

But the mantra is not the only tool I have. There is hydrocodone, which I have learned to enjoy as a snortable powder. I tell myself that this is just to help it work better. After all, I am still hurting from my broken ribs. And surely I am building up a tolerance to the drugs. Snorting just helps me get the same effect as before, I tell myself. And I'm not injecting it; injecting is a sign of a problem.

Deep down, I know I am taking too many pills, but I tell myself it is medicine for broken ribs. I know, on some deeply repressed level, that something has gone very, very wrong in my life and in the lives of people around me, but opiates short circuit normal ways of thinking and replace them with ways that lead back to the drugs. Every path leads to pills. It is the universal solution.

From the time that I beat Edén until the next evening—only 24 hours later—I snort at least four or five tabs, all the pills that I can find in the apartment.

When Edén does not come home the next evening, for dinner and to watch our favorite telenovela, I am so high that his absence barely registers. I don't know what happens on that evening's episode of *Pedro el Escamoso*, but I do have some sense that Yara leaves in the middle of it—looking a bit worried. She tells me that she is going to talk to her friends at the cartels to see why Edén hasn't come home.

Am I alone for one hour or six? I don't know. Time gets weird when you are committed to blocking out the world.

Later that evening, Yara comes home and sits next to me in the bed where I am blitzed out of my mind, watching flashes of color on the television. She crawls into bed somberly and, sitting beside me, takes my hand. Despite the haze of inebriation, I can feel in her touch that something is different. She is trembling.

"He is gone," she says in Spanish. It is simple, succinct. But I don't let myself think what is most obvious.

"He'll show up," I say. "Always does. Trust me. When we lived—"

"No, Peter," she interrupts, squeezing my hand tightly. "*Se fue para siempre.*"

I look at her, alarmed. Her sad eyes seem even more melancholy than usual, somehow.

"What do you mean, left for good?" I ask, my voice cracking.

As if anticipating this question, she thrusts something into my hand, saying, "He would have wanted you to have this." In my hand is the small Eric Clapton CD booklet that Edén always carried around. It is worn, faded, and torn in places, its pages as delicate as desiccated leaves. Yara and I both know what the booklet means to Edén. He doesn't carry around a wallet, never really has much money, but he always has his Clapton booklet, full of the precious old blues lyrics that he meticulously studies whenever he can.

"What do you mean, 'he would have wanted?'" I ask.

"Please, Peter," Yara croaks, pulling me into a surprisingly tight embrace. "You know what it means. He tried to steal from his boss. He got caught."

My mind is too numb from the drugs to feel much of anything at all. But I am conscious enough to know that I need to be quiet. I fix my eyes on the TV, because somehow I know that if I take my eyes off of it, I will have to process what Yara is telling me.

"He—he—he just wanted to buy his ticket to Buenos Aires," she says, grabbing my face, trying to make me look her in the eye. "That's what he told his boss before—before—you know."

I close my eyes. But it is of no use. There is a force that is not me—it is in me—and I vomit sobs. And then, as if by gravity, we are holding each other. I feel her shudder and, looking at her face, I see that she is silently sobbing. Small rivulets on her cheeks sparkle in the light from the television screen.

I kiss her forehead, her cheeks, and then her lips, which are soft and salty from the tears. She pulls away, bowing her head, as if ashamed. But I pull her close again and kiss her on the ear and cheeks and neck and, before long, she kisses me back.

Suddenly it is clear to me—when nothing has been clear for so long—that this is what I need more than anything else. I don't even care that there is an excruciating shock of pain in my broken ribs as we topple over awkwardly and I fall, twisted, on top of her. The pain isn't mine anymore. All that matters is Yara. I have never kissed so violently in all my life, her teeth clicking and clattering against mine.

We wriggle out of our shirts and her boyish chest presses against my broken one, but I want more. When I begin tugging at her shorts, she stops me.

"No," she says simply. "No, Peter."

"Siii," I hiss.

"No," she says more forcefully this time, extricating herself from under my weight and rolling toward the side of the bed. She stands by the bed, shirtless. In the glow of the television she looks small, skinny, vulnerable. "This is not your life. You have a different life that is not here."

"You tell me about all the things you do every night with men and when I want you, you say no," I say petulantly.

"You are not a customer," she says meekly.

I am infuriated: "You do this many times a night!" I cry. "What is one more?!"

"Go masturbate on a cactus," she spits, employing one of the favorite Guaraní curses.

We are quiet for a time and then I remember: Edén is gone. I am weeping so violently that I cannot catch my breath enough to say I am sorry for what I said— what I did—though I want to. I feel awful, but I presume she understands because she sits over me, rubbing my back for most of the night, saying things that she knows I want to hear.

She tells me sweet things about how much Edén loved me. How she could tell we had a special relationship when she first saw us on the streets of Ciudad del Este. She says that she knows that I loved him and that he is lucky to have been loved.

In the early morning hours, before sunrise, she confesses: "I will turn you in today. I get the reward money, okay?"

I nod because words won't come.

PART 2
MYMBA SIUDAPEGUA (City Animals)

Chapter 13

THERAPY

Though the Peace Corps promptly fires me, they are still obligated to pay for a hospital-administered detox program and six weeks of therapy from Dr. Mary Rook who deals almost exclusively with ex-Peace Corps Volunteers—all women—who have been raped abroad.

"The mind is like a muscle in a lot of ways," Dr. Rook says in our first session. "You must take care to exercise it properly or it will atrophy."

She has dark hair, streaked gray, that is cut short in the style of a shaggy teenaged boy. Both of her ears are bejeweled, pierced a bunch of times, all the way up her scapha. Her manner is very matter of fact with a loud, assertive voice. During our sessions, when I speak, she tends to nod and half smirk, as if to say she knows ahead of time what I am about to say.

I dislike her intensely from the get-go. And, to her credit, I'm pretty sure she knows it but never lets it get in the way of trying to give me the help she thinks I need.

The exercises she recommends seem ridiculous. A lot of "mindfulness" exercises that involve skip counting and focused breathing. She never tries to get me to talk about what has happened in Paraguay unless I mention it first. She is exasperating like that.

"I believe in God," I say in one session after I have decided I have heard enough about how to breathe from my diaphragm. If I were not so angry with the world, I might have confessed, more accurately, that *if* I believe in God, it is a belief rooted in a deep, abiding hate. But I am not really interested in therapy. All I want is to be difficult and I figure this will be a good way to piss her off.

"Good," she says placidly. "So do I." I am surprised by this response because I kind of expect her to worship at the altar of Freud or Jung.

"But my God is not so benevolent," I say petulantly.

"Ah, yes," she says after a pause, a knowing smirk on her face. "I was raised Catholic, so I think I can relate."

"But now you believe in a more loving God?" I ask condescendingly.

"Oh no, no, no," she protests. "It certainly would cause some cognitive dissonance if I had this job and believed in a God that didn't want us to suffer."

"Then why aren't you a Catholic anymore?" I ask, suddenly disarmed by her confession.

"I think that is a topic for conversation outside of this office," she says, as if we might grab coffee sometime to talk about it.

I never find out what she believes.

In our last session, she gives me a book, *Contemplative Prayer*, by a long dead Trappist monk named Thomas Merton. After I leave her office, I realize on the inside cover she has written a note: *"To Peter, who believes in God. May this book help you to 'learn to bear the beams of love.'"*

"The Little Black Boy"

My mother bore me in the southern wild,
And I am black, but O! my soul is white;
White as an angel is the English child:
But I am black as if bereav'd of light.

My mother taught me underneath a tree
And sitting down before the heat of day,
She took me on her lap and kissed me,
And pointing to the east began to say.

Look on the rising sun: there God does live
And gives his light, and gives his heat away.
And flowers and trees and beasts and men receive
Comfort in morning joy in the noonday.

And we are put on earth a little space,
That we may learn to bear the beams of love,
And these black bodies and this sun-burnt face
Is but a cloud, and like a shady grove.

For when our souls have learn'd the heat to bear
The cloud will vanish we shall hear his voice.
Saying: come out from the grove my love & care,
And round my golden tent like lambs rejoice.

Thus did my mother say and kissed me,
And thus I say to little English boy.
When I from black and he from white cloud free,

And round the tent of God like lambs we joy:

I'll shade him from the heat till he can bear,
To lean in joy upon our fathers knee.
And then I'll stand and stroke his silver hair,
And be like him and he will then love me.

—William Blake, 1789

I weep in my car when I read the inscription. It feels like a great mercy to finally have words to describe the turmoil in my heart. It feels like the night that I first read *Confessions*—maybe I am not alone in my suffering. Maybe it all has some purpose.

Why had I been so difficult with her? I try to return to Dr. Rook's office to thank her, but she is already visiting with another client.

That evening, I read the whole book in one sitting. Then, as if energized by some manic force, I drive through the night to the abbey in rural Kentucky where Merton lived.

The monks are used to desperate kooks like me arriving unannounced and accurately assess my fragile mental health almost immediately. But I persist and eventually they assign one of the Trappist brothers to tell me I am not ready for the monastic life.

After the Trappists reject me, I move to Tucson, Arizona because the Martian desert landscape looks nothing like the tropics of South America. There is comfort in my daily routine—a workaday job selling ad copy at a dying newspaper—and I become a daily attendee at a big, beautiful Catholic Church where, every few years, a new pastor is assigned to the congregation. The new priests inevitably try to persuade me to take communion.

I do not tell them that I am there for atonement, not repentance.

If a priest asks why I don't take communion, I tell him that I will have to do confession first. During confession, I tell him the story of my Peace Corps experience, of love and loss, of sin so deep that I cannot even begin to know what repentance means.

"So, as you see, Father," I say to the patient, balding priest sitting across from me, "I have been down this road before." We are sitting in his rectory office where we are surrounded by books with obtuse theological titles scrawled on the leather spines.

"I am not asking you to become a saint," he says gently. "I just think it is time for you to take communion."

"You can forgive me, Father," I say. "Perhaps God can too. But if I do not know what repentance looks like, then how can I honestly repent of my sins?"

He tells me of the power of prayer and God's great gift of mercy. I have heard it all before, and the truth—which I will never tell him—is that I would rather go to hell in penance for my sins than pretend like I believe I can inherit the Kingdom of Heaven after what I have done.

But I know the kind priest won't understand, so I simply offer that perhaps I am getting closer to communion.

"It has been years since a colony of killer bees saved my life," I say. "Anyone who has experienced trauma like that knows that the mind does funny things to those kinds of memories."

The priest nods.

"There will be long stretches of time, weeks, months even, when I don't think about it," I confess. "Then, for example, I'll hear 'I Shot the Sheriff' in a convenience store and find myself short of breath, feeling like I'm fighting for my life among the aisles of soft drinks and junk food."

"That is to be expected," he consoles. "You have been through a great loss. You are still grieving."

"Aside from the occasional anxiety attack," I continue, "which isn't all that dreadful, really, I am coping well. Also, since then, I've met a nice girl and she loves me even though she knows all my secrets."

"It is time for you to move on," he agrees. "Live for now. Think of your girlfriend. Of the future. Of eternity."

I tell the kind old man that I think I am making progress. I lie that he may be the one who finally convinces me to take communion. I tell him that I am not quite ready yet, but I am committed to trying.

He smiles, but something in his plaintive eyes makes me suspect that he knows the words are empty. Still he pretends, for the sake of propriety, that I am telling the truth.

I never do take communion, but I do end up marrying that lovely woman who knows all my secrets. I feel sure that the marriage is a sign that I have forged a pretty durable truce with the past. But those illusions are shattered sometime after our sixth anniversary when she announces that she wants a divorce. She moves back home with her parents and will only communicate with me via a court-appointed mediator. During mediation she describes me using clinical terminology like "major depression" and "manic episodes," which makes me feel irreparably broken. It doesn't help matters that, at about the same time, I begin to hear whispers from St. Augustine:

Men love truth when she bathes them in her light, but hate her when she proves them wrong.

I need more than a truce with the past. I know returning to Paraguay is not a matter of tying up loose ends or confronting old demons. Paraguay is not a place for answers. Instead, my return is a search for the right questions. It is a return to mystery, the source of which permeates the world and the very fabric of my being.

Chapter 14

CRUEL GARDEN

fly to Foz, the Brazilian city in the tri-border area, because I suspect that my application for a Paraguayan visa will be flagged by government officials if I fly directly to Paraguay. I had been involved in some official interviews at the American embassy before being unceremoniously fired by the Peace Corps and there is no telling what lists I might be on—and more importantly, who might be alerted about my arrival in the country.

My plan is simple: sneak into Paraguay by taking advantage of the porous open border between Paraguay and Brazil—the same plan, in reverse, that Padre Roberto had for us originally many years ago. I pack light—one small backpack with a couple of changes of clothes—to ensure that I can cross without attracting the attention of border officials. Once in Paraguay things get murkier in my mind. I have a premonition that once I get into the country, my journey will have to become extemporaneous.

I tell the Brazilian official scrutinizing my passport that I intend to visit the falls and she stamps it without so much as another word.

And then, almost as soon as I collect my passport, the panic begins. I lock myself in a bathroom stall and go through a series of breathing exercises that I learned from Dr. Rook years ago.

It is the freedom that does it to me. As soon as I leave the airport's orderly queues and clearly posted multi-lingual signage, the suffocation begins. Americans like to talk about their country being the "land of the free," but most have no idea how constrained they really are. Unless you have lived in a mostly lawless country, you won't know really how delicate and comforting and constraining law and order really is—and how confused most Americans are about the freedom that they worship.

The wave of panic passes. I change my dollars for Brazilian Reales and find a taxi to take me to the downtown market.

The taxi driver is a Brazilian who understands Spanish but does not speak it and seems to know that I am a foreigner. He plays Brazilian music low and hums along instead of trying to engage in conversation, which is fine by me.

Foz is like I remember it, a frontier city trying hard to be the sort of place that attracts tourists from major cities all over the world. There are a few nicer buildings but mostly block after block of run-down strip malls, apartments, and warehouses connected to each other by a tangle of overhead electrical wires.

I begin to think about Yara, wondering whether she is still here making her living among the *banditos, contrabandistas*, and *narcotraficantes* who are hidden only to those who don't know how to see them. Has her work killed her—either in body or spirit? How could it not? No one can maintain sanity in the profession for very long. Eventually, providing companionship to sweaty, unbathed long-haul truckers will catch up with you, right?

We pass through a familiar section of the city, resurrecting a viscerally excruciating series of memories. My mind floods with snippets of places in the city mixed with the old feelings associated with them.

"Please stop the car," I say in Spanish to the driver. "I will get out here." I hand him a wad of cash and hop out into the street, strapping on my small backpack. The unique smell of sultry jungle air mixed with rotting garbage makes still other memories come alive.

Pain itself can be pleasurable accidentally insofar as it is accompanied by wonder.

I needn't know exactly where my feet are carrying me because it seems clear that all paths lead to the city's center, to the city's *raison d'etre,* to its mother, to its own cruel Garden of Edén, named, unironically, *El Puente Internacional de La Amistad*, Friendship Bridge, which connects Ciudad del Este, Paraguay with Foz do Izguacu, Brazil

The bridge arches over the swirling brown waters of the Rio Paraná, the swift muddy river that divides Paraguay from Brazil. As I get closer to the bridge, the city comes to life. There are countless stalls and even more people, all on foot, walking to or from the bridge.

I buy a pair of cheap sunglasses and a cap, an unnecessary precaution given the general insouciance of the customs officials. They seem to be fulfilling more of a ceremonial role than a functional one.

The foot traffic on the bridge is as crowded as I remember it—thick with people walking in both directions, many with small sacks. Most of the people on the bridge are Brazilians or foreign tourists visiting Ciudad del Este for a thrill or a deal—or both.

Most who walk the bridge are the amateur smugglers. The real ones—the ones the Brazilians might call *laranjas* and the Paraguayans would call *sacoleros*—don't use the bridge. As soon as I get partway out onto Friendship Bridge I can see the professionals on the Paraguayan bank of the river, still working as they did decades before. Lines of *sacoleros* hike up and down the steep verdant banks of the Rio Paraná—in full view of the customs officials above—to the river where small boats ferry their goods across to the Brazilian side. From Friendship Bridge, these unbroken lines look like ants marching, the boxes of goods like crumbs.

On the Paraguayan side, as is the custom, the uniformed officials spend their time not inspecting the goods of pedestrians but rather catcalling to the women in the crowds.

And then, I am in Ciudad del Este, which has something for everyone: tariff-free liquor, pirated cigarettes, knock-off electronics, housewares, clothing, and pharmaceuticals. Only slightly less common are stores where you can buy a fully automatic AK-47 or restaurants that are fronts for Colombian cocaine dealers.

Amid this chaos a conversation without words is exchanged in the furtive glances I direct at the pharmaceutical vendors. All these years later, I can still tell which ones are selling black market opiates. They have a look: stony, hungry, vaguely wild and unkempt, usually with a taser or pistol prominently featured in their waistband. They have to be this way or the pill junkies will target them.

I suspect that they know from the way I look at them that I know what they're all about. All the other shoppers look at the goods on display. Only the junkies look at the dealers.

It is odd how full of hope I was last time I was here, but now, all these years later, the sad truth seems so crystal clear. At the time, I guess it was easier to pretend like things weren't so obviously doomed. As I walk the busy streets of Ciudad del Este, now a middle-aged man searching for more answers, I wonder, briefly, whether the reason for my current visit to the city won't seem so painfully obvious years from now when I look back.

Yara would say that these sorts of thoughts are dangerous because they assume that I'll live long enough to think back on my life years from now.

The memory of her dogged fatalism makes me smile.

But she is right. It is dangerous to get lost in your thoughts while walking in the streets of Ciudad del Este. Safety is best assured by living in the moment. All the private security officers cradling assault rifles who are stationed outside of every retail store should serve as a reminder that I need to stay focused on the here and now. The afternoon sun will soon be low in the sky and I know I need to find lodging or risk being out after dark. The streets look just as they did nearly two decades before and I remember the way to the main downtown bus terminal. It is not hard to find which bus route will take me to the outskirts of town; there is one main highway, *Ruta Nacional No 7*, to get there.

As I board the bus, I remember I haven't exchanged any Brazilian Reales for Guaranís. I pull out my cash and look at the portly bus driver with dismay.

"I am sorry," I say in Spanish. Then I switch to Guaraní, aiming to endear myself to the driver: "I forgot to change my money."

"*Eh ah*," the driver says with delight. "A Brazilian who speaks Guaraní!"

"Can I pay in Reales?" I ask, continuing to speak Guaraní, but the driver waves me on board without payment.

I sit among a group of little old ladies with sacks full of fresh produce. The lady sitting next to me must have heard me speaking Guaraní because, as soon as I sit next to her, she tells me that I am a dangerous *rubio* because I will make the girls in Paraguay crazy with my light eyes. The old lady is easily 60 or 70 years old with curly gray hair, and a modest ankle length skirt.

"Be careful who you look at *rubio*," she says. "Those eyes are too pretty."

The other old ladies sitting around us think this is hilarious, and they all begin half-frenzied speculation about my love life.

"He looks very tired," says one lady who is wearing a colorful scarf over her head.

"Yes, too much nighttime activity," another chimes in.

I explain that I am married, but this information only changes the conversation slightly, and the ladies begin speculating how many affairs I am having.

The one sitting next to me grabs my chin, turning my face toward hers. She has very dark brown, almost black eyes. Her eyes look deep and mysterious, and it makes me think she might have been strikingly beautiful at one time.

"*Rubio*, do not hide your pretty eyes from me," she chides. "*Rubio*, do you like the Paraguaya?"

I nod, knowing from experience there is no other acceptable answer. The bus is bouncing along the crowded roadway accelerating quickly between sudden stops to let people on and off. The whole bus has become quiet, and I get the feeling that everyone on board is watching our exchange.

"I bet he does enjoy the Paraguaya," another lady says. "He is very *letrado*, this rubio."

"It is hot, no?" another lady says. This is a favorite pun in Guaraní about being horny.

"Yes, I am very hot," I say. I haven't thought about this joke in years, but I remember it at once.

The whole bus erupts in laughter.

It continues like this for the remainder of the bus ride. Before long, a series of motels along the road signal that I have arrived at the outskirts of the city. I pull the cord to stop the bus.

When I rise to exit the lady next to me squeezes my hand and says that I will give her sweet dreams. The whole bus finds this hilarious, and I can feel my face flush while they hoot and whistle as I make my way toward the door. The bus driver gives an enthusiastic thumbs up as I climb down the steps to the street.

The bus lurches on down the road, and I am left alone in front of a motel called, Hotel Ña Fula. From the outside, it looks tidy and plain: A simple series of brick buildings surrounded by a brick wall just high enough so that passers-by can't see the cars parked in the courtyard. Next door is an empty field where a few 18-wheelers are already parked. In the middle of the wall is a metal gate that is painted in the red and blue of a favorite soccer club, *Cerro Porteno.*

My knowledge of these truck stops is somewhat limited. I have never actually been to any of them—but I feel pretty sure I know what they are like based on stories I had heard years ago from Yara. I have this idea that they basically operate like seedy motels in America—the sort of places in the States that might charge by the hour.

As soon as I darken the doorway of the hotel and my eyes adjust to the shadowy interior, I realize that all my ideas had been wrong, and that this hotel is much more obviously a *kilombo* than any seedy motels I had ever seen. Groups of young women in revealing skintight clothes and loud makeup are gathered at tables in the lobby under a glowing television mounted to one wall. They get eerily quiet when they see me enter.

The lobby of the brothel also serves as a sort of restaurant and bar. At the back end of the room, I can see the proprietor, a corpulent, swarthy man who sits vigil over gleaming refrigerated glass display cases featuring fat brown bottles of Pilsen beer and handmade empanadas. Even though the women say nothing to me as I pass, I can feel my face flushing. A few of them giggle and whisper to each other, which makes the short walk through the restaurant feel excruciatingly long.

"Do you have rooms?" I say in Spanish to the proprietor, a pot-bellied old man with curly salt and pepper hair who sits on a stool behind the display case.

"*Sí,*" he says, his eyes fixed on the telenovela.

"How much?" I say.

He glances at me, no doubt assessing whether to give me the tourist rate. I really don't feel like having a conversation with the man, but I also don't want to be gouged for a room. Before he can answer, I tell him in Guaraní that I don't need one that is air conditioned.

"You are not a Brazilian," the man says, his curious brown eyes fixed on me now. "Are you American?"

"Canadian," I lie.

The proprietor gives me the sort of look that says he does not believe me.

"Can I see your documents?" he asks casually.

"I am just here for the girls," I explain, as if this is a suitable reason not to produce the documents. "And I pay in advance."

He nods and gives me the local rate for a room. I give him a wad of Reales.

"What is your name?" he says, tossing me a key.

"Pedro," I say, adding, "like *Pedro el Escamoso.*" But his attention has already returned to the television.

My room is dirty and sparse. One naked incandescent bulb dangles from a black cord that is perilously close to the overhead electric fan making a low grinding sound as it spins. My room has Wi-Fi, and I want to call my soon-to-be ex-wife on Skype, but know it won't do any good. She probably won't even take the call. Besides, it is hard to pretend that I am doing anything other than initiating some sort of weird midlife crisis that has compelled me to travel halfway around the world to a place that is both dangerous and impossibly sad.

I feel generally pretty rotten about my latest life choices. I decide the best solution is to drink a lot of Pilsen in the lobby with the sex workers while we wait for nightfall.

In the lobby/restaurant, I sit alone and act like I don't notice the women making eyes at me. Instead I eat a pile of empanadas and focus on the telenovelas which are just as dramatic as I remember them.

Besides, the Pilsen is cold and delicious, and after a few fat bottles it slakes my thirst for oblivion.

Chapter 15

WEDDING RING

As the last of the evening telenovelas concludes the proprietor of the restaurant turns on loud cachaca music and, on the big TV I am watching, changes the channel to one that plays unabated softcore porn. The sudden change makes it hard for me to know what to do with my eyes. I don't want to make too much eye contact with the sex workers, but I also don't want to be the creepy middle-aged American who sits there by himself watching weird Brazilian porn. I settle on fixing my gaze upon the front door of the restaurant-bar where I can watch as the sex workers and truckers come and go.

I drink beer long into the evening watching the interactions of the restaurant patrons, trying to figure out how the whole process works. One ritual repeats itself: Brazilian or Paraguayan truckers come into the restaurant where they purchase an ice bucket of overpriced beer, which serves as a reason to invite one of the sex workers over to a little plastic table and negotiate for services. Most couples don't seem to need a room at the motel, preferring instead to return to the cabs of semi-trucks in the parking lot next door.

I am dangerously inebriated by the time I work up the courage to engage one of the women in conversation. Around midnight I invite a sex worker to share a beer with me. She looks slightly older than most of the women in the room—perhaps in her early 20s—short, skinny with long brown hair, loud makeup and obvious false eyelashes. Because of the blaring music, we must shout into each other's ears in order to communicate.

"Why you take so long to invite me?" she asks in Spanish sliding into the seat next to mine and squeezing my thigh as she leans in.

"What is your name?" I ask. She smells like cheap perfume and cigarettes.

"Estefani," she yells into my ear.

"Pedro," I yell smiling and patting my chest, "*como Pedro el Escamoso*."

The reference doesn't seem to register, and I realize she is probably still too young to be of any help to me. But it is too late, and I have already asked her to sit with me.

"Would you like some Pilsen?" I ask, passing her a jar full of the frosty beer.

"Yes," she says. "You are very cute, papi." I smile, assuming this is the sort of hollow compliment she always uses to put her johns at ease. I know I'm not ugly, but also that I don't really turn heads either. I am a smaller, skinny middle-aged man with graying hair who wears jeans, t-shirt, and tennis shoes—the sort of nondescript outfit that screams suburban gringo.

"You are not Brazilian?" Estefani observes.

"Canadian," I lie.

"*Canadiense*," she repeats. "Why do you come here?"

"I am here looking for a friend," I explain.

She leans in as if to say something and thrusts her tongue in my ear.

"I can be a friend," she purrs after probing my ear. Then, switching to a heavily accented English, she asks, "You like, baby?"

"You smoke?" I ask in Spanish, standing so suddenly that my head spins.

"*Sí papi*," she says.

"Let's go outside," I say nodding my head toward the door that leads to the courtyard. I purchase a pack of fake Marlboros from the proprietor who grins lasciviously at the woman on my arm.

Other truckers and women have spilled outside, mostly in pairs, either dancing or making out. A single floodlight fixed to the peak of the roof illuminates the whole courtyard, which is filled with compact cars and a few small trucks.

I rip the foil off the package and pull out two cigarettes.

"Have a light?" I ask.

"*Sí papi*," she says, producing a lighter. I light both cigarettes and pass one to her. I take a long draw, leading her to a secluded area at one side of the courtyard.

"You are shaking," she says grabbing my hand. "Do not worry, papi, I will not bite."

I take another long pull from the cigarette.

"So quiet, Papi," she observes. "My mother always said to be careful of the quiet ones."

The thought of the woman having a family makes me feel wretched.

"Look mami," I say, "I do not want to waste your time, and I know it is valuable."

"*Sí papi*. Tell me what you want, baby," she says, flicking the cigarette away, then grabbing the hand with my wedding ring, she adds, "I will do what your wife will not."

"I am looking for someone else, mami," I say pulling my hand from hers taking another long pull from the cigarette. My head is spinning from the cigarette smoke. "Maybe you can help me find her?"

"Papi, I can do anything she can do and more," she says, grabbing my crotch. "You won't be disappointed, I promise."

"No, mami," I say. "I am looking for a transsexual girl. Her name is Yara. Maybe you—"

She pushes herself away from me.

"You are a *puto?*" she says incredulously, looking at me like a leper. I try to grab her to pull her close because she is making a scene and people are beginning to look.

"No, I am—"

"Disgusting!" she says shrilly, pushing herself away. "I should have known you were a *puto.*"

"I'm not—"

"Don't touch me, faggot," she spits. And with that she runs back to the restaurant.

I take one long last pull from the cigarette trying hard to pretend like I don't notice everyone in the courtyard looking at me.

Before I finish my cigarette, the proprietor approaches me.

"Go get your stuff, *maricón*," he says.

"What?"

"I said go get your stuff," he repeats through gritted teeth. "From your room. This place is not for faggots."

"I'm not—"

"Damn faggot," he hisses. "Get your things."

He escorts me to my room where he watches me as I grab my backpack. We walk back through the courtyard together toward the restaurant.

As we step into the restaurant, he grabs me by the arm and neck roughly, cursing as if we had been struggling. A few truckers laugh and take drunken swipes at me as we pass between the tables. The sex worker with whom I had chosen to speak is stationed by the front door.

"Damn faggot," she yells and spits in my face. The proprietor pushes me roughly out the front door, still cursing. Some working women and truckers are gathered out front and they laugh as I stumble out of the restaurant.

A pair of big Brazilian truckers wearing cowboy boots approaches me. They look like they could be brothers, heavily freckled with eyes that are obscured by the dark shadows of their wide-brimmed cowboy hats. Though I don't know what they are saying, I can tell from their body language and the way everyone is encouraging them that they intend to hurt me. They are on me before I can turn to run, and we begin to wrestle awkwardly. I manage to push one into the other and extricate myself from their clawing hands. Everyone gathered outside the motel finds this hilarious except for the two Brazilians who have murder in their eyes. I turn to run away, parallel to the highway—into the darkness.

I don't stop running until I can no longer hear the laughing crowd. When I catch my breath for long enough to gather my wits, there is a whisper:

If the present should always be present, and not pass into the past, it cannot be anything but eternity.

I walk along the shoulder of the roadway catching my breath, feeling generally like a fool for the scene I had caused at the brothel.

Even on the outskirts of Ciudad del Este there are lots of little shops—all closed at night—and seedier motels like the one from which I had been ejected. The roadside is not built for pedestrian traffic, but a footpath has nonetheless been worn onto the shoulder of the highway. I buy a lighter from a toothless street vendor and smoke four or five more cigarettes before I stop shaking.

I stumble upon a 24-hour gyro place run by a bunch of Lebanese men who are doing brisk business even at that hour of the early morning. They serve lamb gyros sliced off of a vertical rotisserie from a narrow stall. I am not hungry but I like the feeling of the crowd gathered there. It's not just truckers and sex workers, though there are some, but also teenagers and all sorts of drunk men and women who appear to need a greasy meal before returning home. They are clustered at picnic tables set out along a concrete slab, talking to each other too loudly

I order a gyro and wonder whether getting kicked out of the motel is a sign that I should just give up and go home.

I find an empty seat at one of the tables where there is a group of drunk teenagers reliving the evening's fun. The group of teenagers sharing my bench are obviously drunk and very loud. They ignore me as they chat about the evening. I can tell that they are city kids by their shaggy haircuts and the way their clothes look well-worn. Campesinos tend to keep their hair short and their clothes for going out on the town are usually hardly worn, starched, and appropriate for church.

The group is a mix of young men and women, all of whom possess the general nonchalance of a group accustomed to urban comforts. Unlike the last time I lived in Paraguay they carry smartphones. They attend to the glowing devices in the midst of conversation, texting and scrolling through social media while talking to their friends.

That's when a new strategy comes to mind: maybe I can use the Internet to narrow my search. If the transsexual sex workers in Ciudad del Este are still a tightknit group—supporting each other throughout the process of physical and social traumas of transition—then perhaps I can find one on the Internet who will help me. Searching the Internet would be easier than getting beat up for asking impertinent questions in Ciudad del Este's truck stop motel-brothels.

I hadn't thought of it before because the Internet revolution hadn't reached Paraguay when I was there twenty years ago.

I rise without finishing my gyro and head to the nearest motel, one called Hotel Amorcito. It's just like the last one, full of truckers and sex workers but I ignore them and get a key for a room. I only care about one thing: they have Wi-Fi.

In my dumpy room I scroll through the ads for transsexual sex workers. They are all between 18 and 20 years old. Pages and pages of listings. One ad for "Yenifer Travesti" says that she is 27. I call her on WhatsApp.

"*Alo*," a voice answers.

"Hello, is this Yenifer?" I ask in Spanish, my voice trembling.

"*Sí, papi*," she answers. "Are you American?"

"Canadian," I say automatically.

"Where are you, papi?" she asks.

"Motel Amorcito," I say. "*Kilometro 7*. You can come here?"

"Are you active, passive, or versatile, papi?"

I don't know how to answer this.

"Papi?"

"Versatile," I say finally.

"Okay, Papi, it will be *cien mil Guaranís*," she says. "And I need you to pay my Uber to travel there. Okay, papi?"

"*Dale*," I say.

She tells me how to pay for her Uber ride and I hang up.

My room seems suddenly eerily quiet and I feel that old familiar panic—a deafening, black chasm—in the pit of my stomach creeping upward toward my chest, threatening to swallow me whole, to consume my mind, my soul. I find myself wishing St. Augustine would whisper something obtuse or sanctimonious. But he says nothing.

Chapter 16

PRIAPUS

The minutes pass excruciatingly slowly while I wait for Yenifer to arrive at my motel room. Doubt and Panic are circling like wolves—licking their chops—knowing, somehow, that I am wounded, easy prey.

I am trying to control my breathing, and it is not working at all. I can see Dr. Rook, my old Peace Corps therapist, in my mind's eye. She is sitting across the desk from me, nodding as if to say she knew all along that I would eventually pay the price for failing to do the work I ought to have done.

Many thoughts are running through my head at once and none of them are cathartic. I try to pray but it is no use. It has been years since I've prayed earnestly. Most of my prayers, like church liturgies, had become nothing more than a comforting ritual.

Panic is settling in my stomach like a lead weight. In my mind, all I can picture is Dr. Rook, smirking.

My mind spins for what feels like a long time.

And then, finally, mercifully, a knock at the door.

As I move to answer the door, I feel as if I am watching myself in the third person, as if I am not in my own body.

In the hallway outside my room, I find the woman I had contacted online. She has tan skin and black hair, black eyes and broad shoulders. She wears a tight red dress that accentuates her bony, angular body, her ribs clearly visible. The online pictures had cleverly disguised acne scars and bruises on her arms and legs, which are impossible to hide in the vapid florescent lights of the hotel hallway.

"Yenifer?" I croak.

She nods, grinning coyly.

"Please come in," I say in Spanish turning back into the room. "Have a seat," I say as calmly as I can given my shortness of breath. My words come out half-choked, a full octave higher than normal.

I shut myself in the bathroom, which is more like one big shower stall that feels crowded with the toilet and sink. As is the custom in Paraguay, the toilet and sink are located in the tiled shower area.   I turn on cool water and splash it on my face, looking at myself in the mirror. With my light complexion and practical clothes I exude an unmistakable unsophisticated *gringo* vibe. The face in the mirror looks how I feel: bags under my eyes, a sort of "deer in the headlights" expression on my face. But I know I am delaying the inevitable, which is its own form of torture. If I stay in the bathroom much longer it will seem strange.

I open the door and take one step out into the small hotel room which is crowded with one simple bed with two bedside tables, a modern looking lamp on each. Yenifer has turned on one of the bedside lamps and laying on the bed, still propped up on her elbows, smiling sweetly, her dress pulled up around her waist, her panties pulled aside and a semi-turgid, uncircumcised penis bobbing in the space between us.

"Come here, papi," she says.

I am rendered temporarily without a voice, and I stand there looking at her, my mind blank.

"You like this, papi?" she asks, moving her hips back and forth.

"*Sí, mami*," I say, finding my voice, which is unnaturally high.

"Then come here," she beckons.

My mind is racing.

"Want to get high?" I ask, the words spill out of me before I can think about them.

"You party?" she says eagerly, hopping out of bed, closing the space between us in a few steps. She wraps her spindly arms around my neck, pressing her hips into mine. "You do not look like you party, papi." This is an obvious understatement. I haven't done drugs in years. And it shows.

Her breath is hot and smells like cigarettes. She grinds her crotch on mine.

"I don't have a connection here, and I don't want to get sick," I say. I am fairly sure she is an IV drug user, something I learned to identify when I was in detox after getting kicked out of the Peace Corps.

"Ooh, daddy," she beams. "You are a cute partier. You want to play first?"

"Party first. Then play, mami," I say. I pull out a wad of Brazilian Reales, as if to accentuate the point.

"I knew I liked your voice," she says, releasing me from her embrace, stepping back as if to get a better look at me. "You are going to be so, so delicious, papi."

I try to force a grin on my face.

"Let me call my friend," she says. "I know a good place where we can party if you are buying."

"*Sí mami*," I say, waving the wad of cash at her emphatically.

She turns to grab her cell phone, which is sitting on the bed where she was laying. While she is making arrangements on the phone, I sit at the foot of the bed enjoying a wave of relief when I see her smooth it more discreetly over her hips.

While Yenifer chats on the phone, I wonder if this is how Yara was with her clients. Was she a fixer like Yenifer, doing whatever she could to please the johns? I presume some are tolerable, kind even. But some, no doubt, were disgusting or violent; she never told me about those ones.

How did she do it? Going out at night, turning tricks, while still modeling domestic tranquility in the daytime with Edén and me. Every evening she made dinner, and we would all sit watching our favorite telenovela, fully investing ourselves in the life of goofy Pedro Coral—our tragic hero, our oracle. I knew, pretty much all along, that Yara led this double life, but I also didn't want to think about it. The human mind is very adept at making horrible things seem tolerable and then even normal, especially when softened by drugs.

"The Uber is here," Yenifer says grabbing me by my elbow. "Let's go."

I stand and she hooks her arm in mine. She is a bit taller than me in heels. Arm in arm, we pass through the lobby. The Motel Amorcito attendant doesn't even look up from the television when we pass by the front desk. It is still dark and warm outside. Waiting out front is a small Toyota. Yenifer and I scoot into the backseat. A Pitbull song is playing on the radio.

"You go to Remansito?" the driver asks in Spanish.

"*Sí*," Yenifer confirms.

Yenifer pulls my arm around her shoulders and snuggles into the crook of it while we bounce around in the back of the Toyota. The car speeds through the potholed streets, some paved, others just dirt roads, weaving in and out of traffic. According to the dashboard clock, it is past three in the morning.

"*Ya llegamos*," the driver says, pulling to a stop. Yenifer and I climb out of the car onto a posh residential street, the kind of neighborhood where all the houses are enclosed behind 8-foot walls.

"Here we are," Yenifer says to me as she walks up to the front gate of one of the houses. "Stay with me Yankee," the way she says Yankee, it sounds like *junkie*. "This is a *sauna*. It is not a place where you should wander, okay?"

I nod.

"We are going to have fun, baby!" she exclaims, kissing me on the cheek.

She presses a button next to the gate and we wait, hand in hand, like some degenerate version of Dorothy and the Tin Man petitioning at the gates of Emerald City.

"Yennnnifer, bay-bee!" a man says through the intercom. Yenifer strikes a pose for the intercom camera as if she were in a photo shoot at a fashion magazine. We are buzzed through the gate and onto the driveway of a large, modern house. Inside the gate is a guardhouse from which two armed private security officers, in all black, emerge to search us thoroughly, one pats us down, the other waves a wand over us. Yenifer makes lewd comments about the search, but the officers are very serious about their jobs and do not smile.

When they are satisfied, Yenifer tells me to pay one of the men 100 Reales. I hand over the cash and she takes my hand, leading me through a lushly manicured yard to the front door of the house. She enters without knocking.

Inside is a landing between two flights of stairs in a split level ultra-modern home. It is the sort of home that wouldn't look out of place as the setting of a telenovela. The lighting both downstairs and upstairs is soft and, though we cannot see anyone, we can hear many voices coming from rooms out of sight on both levels.

"You stay with me Yankee," Yenifer warns.

I nod.

She takes me by the hand and leads me upstairs and through a short hallway that opens into a large, ultra-modern, well-appointed living area where there is a dozen or so men, mostly in pairs or trios, at least half of whom are in some state of undress, or nude. No one seems to take much notice of Yenifer and me—which is good because I imagine the shock on my face is quite obvious.

Priapus, stretched out in vile nakedness, is preferred to those who shine from their supernal abode.

While I usually disparage Augustine's obtuse comments, this is one of those times when I'm grateful for his strange form of companionship. The interruption gets me out of my head just long enough to remember to try to arrange an expression on my face that does not exude complete naiveté.

"Come," Yenifer says, pulling at my hand.

We weave our way through the room toward another hallway on the other side. I catch the eye of a chubby, middle-aged Asian man in a three-piece suit who is whispering in the ear of someone much younger. Three handsome, tan men wearing towels are talking loudly in an unfamiliar language. An older, potbellied man with a bushy mustache and curly salt-and-pepper hair stands near the hallway alone, in a t-shirt and briefs, drink in hand, leering at Yenifer as we pass.

"You like?" she says when we have passed through the room.

I nod, sensing that my words might come out choked were I to try and say anything.

"Good, baby," she says, kissing my cheek sweetly. Then she knocks at a closed door.

The door is opened by a fat man dressed in black like the other security officers, a matching black pistol holstered on his hip like an accessory.

"*Flaca! Ven!*" a man shouts from somewhere out of sight. Once inside, I can see that the room is a large bedroom. The furniture is all ultra-modern, perhaps Scandinavian. Toward one end of the room is an enormous bed and, beyond it, a marble-tiled bathroom with sparkling fixtures. We climb a short flight of stairs and turn to see the other end of the room, which is arranged as a study. A youngish man rises from the desk where he is sitting to greet us.

"*Hola mamita,*" he says, coming out from behind the desk to give Yenifer two kisses. The man is lanky and wears a tight polo shirt with slacks and boat shoes. He is handsome, dark-haired, with quick, darting eyes and a 5 o'clock shadow of stubble. "And who is with you?" he asks in Spanish, winking at me.

"Roberto, this is my friend," Yenifer says. I realize she probably doesn't know my name.

"*Hola, amigo!*" Roberto exclaims, gripping Yenifer's hands. "He is a cute one."

"My name is Peter," I say extending my hand. Roberto grins at Yenifer for just long enough to make me think he might not shake my hand.

"Peter!" he says loudly. "I am Roberto." He grabs my hand and pulls me close with the handshake.

"Nice to meet you," I say.

"You don't look like you party," he says, searching my eyes as if diagnosing me. "Where'd you find this guy, Yenifer?" He is still holding my hand tightly, though we'd stopped shaking.

"He found me, papi," Yenifer says, flipping her hair as if insulted by this question. Roberto turns his attention back to me. My breath is rapid, and I try to disguise it by looking around the room, which has been decorated with care—but with nothing that might hold one's attention. The walls are somewhat sparse with an occasional, wholly uninteresting, abstract painting. His eyes dart so much that I find it hard to hold his gaze. I want to pull my hand away and take a step back, but he holds me firmly and I don't want to make a scene. I settle my gaze on the desk where he was sitting. There is nothing on it except an electronic tablet, its screen dark.

"Are you American?" he asks in English with very little trace of an accent.

"I'm Canadian," I say. My words come out choked.

"Canadian!" he exclaims, gripping my hand tighter. Then, staying in English: "I hope you're not one of those Americans who claims to be Canadian because you're ashamed of Trump."

"No, but I sometimes pretend to be American because I'm ashamed of Trudeau," I say, regretting it almost immediately. I don't know anything about Canadian politics. He lets my hand go and I take a step back.

"Good," he says, staying in English, winking. "I like Trump. He does not try to be someone he is not. That is what I hate. I can't stand people who pretend."

I can't look him in the eyes for fear he will see some truth in them. I turn toward Yenifer who crosses her arms, clearly annoyed by the conversation in a language she cannot understand.

"My apologies, Yenifer," Roberto says in Spanish, returning to his seat behind the desk. Yenifer grabs my arm, and we stand on the other side of the desk like petitioners at a royal court. "So what do you want?"

"*Chiva y cabello, papi*," Yenifer reports.

Roberto raises his eyebrows. He and Yenifer begin negotiations. I understand only about half of what they say.

"Pills for me," I interrupt. "No points."

They hear me, but neither acknowledge it, and they continue their negotiations. When it seems like the conversation is over, I reach into my pocket to fish out cash, but Yenifer stops me, shaking her head emphatically.

"*Vamos*," she says turning me around.

"Goodbye Roberto," I say, in English, over my shoulder.

"No, this is just the beginning," he says, a twinkle in his eye. He is holding his tablet now. "Hello and welcome!"

As we walk down the stairs toward the fat security guard, I am told to give him 500 Reales, which he takes without saying a word. I figure if I can get her high maybe it will be easier to ask about Yara.

She leads me back out into the large gathering room, which looks a lot like it had before. There are some new faces, others have gone. We find a seat next to the Asian man who is still flirting with the much younger man. I turn toward Yenifer because the odd pair next to me gives me the creeps.

"You want to go downstairs and play?" she asks, grinning.

"Party first," I reply squeezing her knee. I am noticing furtive glances in my direction from more than a few folks gathered in the room.

"What's downstairs?" I ask, not because I am interested, but because I want to look engaged in conversation.

"Rooms for everything," she says. "We find our *ambiente*."

"Like what?" I ask, forcing a grin.

Before she can answer, we are approached by the three Middle Eastern men in towels I had noticed earlier.

"Hello Yenifer," the short one says in heavily accented Spanish. "Who is your friend?" It feels like they are looming over us while we sit on the couch. I rise, pulling Yenifer up with me, so that we are all standing. The men are all in their 20s or early 30s, tan, with hairy chests and shoulders, though their faces, in contrast, are clean-shaven. The two taller men could be brothers and have a full head of longish black hair. The short one, the instigator, is balding with short-cropped hair and has a well-chewed, unlit cigar in his mouth.

"Name is Peter," I say in Spanish after a silence that feels too long.

"Join us," the short one says, cigar still in his mouth, taking a step toward me. I instinctively retreat as he approaches me, having no interest in joining a group of men I don't know.

Sensing my discomfort, Yenifer mercifully intercedes, "Let's go out back. We can just be alone by the pool."

I nod sheepishly.

"Come on," she insists, running her fingers through my hair, rubbing her leg on mine. "Just the two of us. We will get high, and no one will bother us."

I let her lead me to a sliding glass door toward the back of the room that leads into a lushly landscaped space similar to the front. It's enclosed by a high wall, and has a small pool, sparkling with lights that shine from under the water. There is a row of small cabanas facing the pool, inside of which there are pairs of people making out. We find an unoccupied cabana and sit down together in a lounge chair. She snuggles into the crook of my arm, massaging my chest, shoulder, and arm. I have a hard time pretending I don't hear the men in the cabanas next to us.

I begin thinking about my soon-to-be ex-wife back home and the thought makes me feel very alone.

I am saved from my thoughts when we are interrupted by a teenage boy who brings us a small pill case with a variety of drugs and paraphernalia. Yenifer passes me a pill, which I promptly cheek. The taste is almost unbearable, but I do my best not to let it show. She pulls a band from the case and tourniquets her arm to inject heroin. She sits back against me, and I can feel her body relaxing. Though I never injected the drug I remember the feeling, like your blood has become light, almost like air, taking your breath away. After a few moments she sits up again to prepare the cocaine on a small table next to our lounge chair.

"*Cabello* makes everything better. Trust," Yennifer says.

"No thanks," I say, careful to speak in respectful tone so as not to offend her while trying not to talk in a way that will reveal I have cheeked the pill.

"I mean, you can snort it if you want," she offers. "You don't need to inject it."

"No, baby." I say casually.

Her words are becoming a bit slurred while meticulously cutting a small dose of cocaine with vinegar. I see this as my opportunity.

"I used to do both," I say. "But then I met this one girl named Yara. It got too crazy."

Yenifer has her back turned to me, so I cannot gauge her reaction to this information, but I can see her silhouette nodding.

"Do you know Yara?" I say, half-forgetting that I have a pill in my cheek. The words come out a little garbled. Yenifer doesn't seem to notice. She is still nodding slightly.

"You do?"

"Yes, baby," she says, leaning back on me in the lounge chair with me. She sounds very drunk.

"How do you know Yara?" I ask as casually as I can. But she doesn't respond. I don't want to seem overzealous, so I wait a few moments before I ask again. When she does not respond, I extricate my arm from under her head and shake her. Gently, at first, then more firmly.

"Yenifer…Yenifer?"

I shake her face, trying to wake her. Suddenly I am 23 years old again, desperate, losing control.

Yenifer has nodded off. I smack her a few times, firmly, but without violence. I put my head on her chest to listen to her heartbeat. Her breathing is slow but regular.

Before I can figure out what to do next, Roberto is standing over us.

"Come on," he says in English. "Don't worry about her. She'll be all right."

He pulls at my shoulder as if to separate me from the unconscious person next to me. But I feel a certain degree of responsibility for her, given my role in helping her score.

She is fine," Roberto pledges as he pulls me to my feet. "Do not worry. I gave her the good stuff. She will have the best sleep she's had in weeks."

"But—"

"—you can just spit that pill out if you don't want it," he admonishes.

I have forgotten about the cheeked pill. I spit it into the bushes.

"Come, there are plenty of fish in the sea," he says walking me past the other cabanas. "I did you a favor. She has the bug, you know."

I stop in my tracks as it dawns on me that Roberto is right: Perhaps he has done me a favor. If anyone could get in touch with Yara, it would be a man with connections, a man like him. Besides, I figure, what do I have to lose at this point anyway?

"Roberto," I say, looking into the mesmerizing pool, which twinkles with underwater lighting. "You have been here for quite a while, no?"

"Yes, friend, you don't get all this without hard work." He sweeps his hand through the air to accentuate his point.

"Do you know a *travesti* named Yara?" I ask.

"Of course," he says, a hint of lasciviousness in his voice. "You have very expensive taste."

"Do you know how to get in touch with her?" I ask eagerly.

"I do." He holds up his cell phone as if to demonstrate it. "But it would be much less expensive for you to just visit any of my other friends here tonight."

"Yes, it would," I agree archly. "Still, would you call her for me?"

"Certainly," he says, crestfallen. He pokes at the phone then thrusts it at me. I put the phone to my ear; it is ringing.

Chapter 17

DESPERATE WISHES

Yara lives in a high-rise condominium building downtown called El Rafa. In the lobby, a uniformed doorman asks me for my documents. It is mid-morning and the lobby is empty except for me, the doorman, and an out-of-order fountain full of angels. The ornate fountain is in the middle of the lobby and features a spiraling group of little, fat frolicking cherubs. It appears to have fallen into disrepair, layers of dust collecting on the statues, a few coins still laying in the basin—a reminder of a time when the fountain still had water or evidence of a few desperate wishes.

"The reason for your visit?" the doorman asks in Spanish, scrutinizing my passport.

"Only to visit *no más*," I say.

He writes down my information in a register then returns my passport, winking at me. I walk past the desk to the elevator bank. Yara is on the fourth floor. Like the rest of the building, the elevator seems tidy and perfectly functional, if a bit rundown, which is probably as nice as one could expect in a place like Ciudad del Este.

The elevator walls are mirrored, and I can't help but notice how exhausted I look. I note the bags under my eyes and now two days of stubble shadowing my face. My light brown hair is turning gray at the temples and I wonder if Yara will think I look old and sad. I certainly think my countenance and the bland clothes I wear—an old pair of jeans with a t-shirt and tennis shoes—exude a "middle-aged suburban dad" vibe. Despite appearances, I don't feel tired at all. The thrill of finding my long-lost friend has me feeling punchy and a bit nervous.

As I navigate down a hallway toward her apartment, I wonder whether other men have made the same journey. Other johns looking for companionship. Was that why the doorman winked at me in the lobby? Is it possible that she is still turning tricks after all these years? What would that do to a person? I wish I wasn't thinking these thoughts right before seeing her again for the first time in years, but I can't seem to keep my mind from spinning.

I find Yara's door and pause for a moment, wondering if I am really ready for whatever lies ahead. For so many years I built up narratives, ways to think about what exactly had happened when I was in Paraguay, what probably happened after I left, what I might do and say if I ever returned.

In the intervening years I'd gotten sober, learned to manage the panic attacks and my unruly mind. I'd gotten married, found a decent job. Life seemed pretty tidy. Even my impending divorce didn't seem quite as bad as my Paraguayan detour into darkness, which has become fairly well-compartmentalized. Sure, it is something that informed my outlook on the world but does not loom over it like a dark shadow.

Did I really need to dredge all this up?

I knock.

Yara answers it almost immediately and I worry that perhaps she had seen me hesitate in the hallway.

"Petercito!" she cries, pulling me in for a tight hug. I hardly have time to look at her before she is squeezing me. It takes only a glance to know that she looks very different from what I remember. A combination of hormones and at least a few major cosmetic surgeries have turned her boyish body into a woman's—which is accentuated by the form fitting skirt and blouse she is wearing.

When she lets me go, I take a step back and look at her again. She is wearing an outfit that wouldn't look out of place in an executive office: high heels, a black pencil skirt, and a colorful floral blouse that tastefully accentuates her ample cleavage. Her brown hair has blonde highlights and looks like it has been styled at an expensive salon. Her face looks just like I remember it—angular, pretty—and either age or surgeries have left her with even sharper features than when I last saw her. The thought enters my mind that she looks like she belongs on a telenovela.

"I am sorry about the way I look," I say in Spanish, suddenly aware that she has probably gone to some trouble to look nice and I am a stark contrast.

"Do not worry," she says smiling. "I am happy to see you. Please come in and let's catch up."

Her apartment is like the rest of the building, very comfortable, if dated, beginning to show signs of disrepair. Yara camouflages the defects by crowding the walls with a mishmash of European and East Asian cultural artifacts. Big metallic and stone statues of Buddhas sit prominently on pedestals or built-in shelves. On the walls, there is an array of large framed posters featuring either pictures of Japanese temples or bucolic scenes from mountain villages somewhere in the Swiss Alps. Tying together this eclectic mix of East and West are a variety of bells—cow bells, meditation bells, strings of bells, shiny metal bells.

"Nice place," I say as she leads me into her living room. "What is with all the— how you say?" I point at a bell nearby. I can only remember the word for doorbell, but vaguely remember, somehow, that it is not the same word for the sorts of bells she is collecting.

"*Las campanas*?" she says. "Yes, I love them. They help me relax." She motions for me to sit on an impossibly clean, bright white L-shaped couch that wraps around a glass coffee table on which there sits a tray with all the equipment needed to begin sharing the traditional Paraguayan tea, *terere*. Before I sit, I walk to a large picture window, which looks out over the northern portion of Ciudad del Este—and, in the distance, parts of Brazil. It is not so close to the river that I can see smugglers traipsing up and down the riverbanks.

"Beautiful view," I say, finding a seat opposite Yara on the couch. She hands me the *terere* gourd.

"Remind you of old times?" I say, taking the gourd to take a gulp and then passing it back. She always served me the hot version, *mate*, when she got home in the mornings, when we lived together.

"Sí, Petercito," she says. When she calls me Petercito, it reminds me of our third roommate, Edén, and I can't help but feel an acute twinge of grief. She sees this in my countenance and furrows her brow into a look of concern.

"Are you okay?" she asks. I feel like it is much too soon in our visit to say all the things I have been wanting to say, ask all the questions I have been wanting to ask.

"Yes, yes," I say, trying to put a smile on my face. "Of course. I'm so happy to have found you. I kind of thought I might not be able to find you after all these years. You're not so easy to find, you know."

"That is for a reason," she says enigmatically, passing me a refilled gourd. "So how is the wife?"

"How do you know about her?" I ask, fingering my wedding band.

"I have my methods," she says winking. "It is not so hard with the Internet and the Facebook."

I wonder what my life might look like if pieced together only through Facebook posts. I have a sudden desire to explain myself, to fill in the gaps. I want to tell her that I had not taken my life for granted in the intervening years—no matter how mundane it may seem on Facebook. But it would be too much.

"I looked for you on the Internet many times," I say. "There's no trace of you."

"I have nothing to put there," she says mournfully. "Unlike you! Please, tell me about the *señora*."

In the years since I have been away from Paraguay, I have imagined this conversation many times. In all the times I dreamed of it, I did not think that the first thing we would talk about would be my wife, her personality, passions, hidden talents. Yara is eager to hear all sorts of details about my life: how my wife and I met, whether we wanted to have kids. I had sort of forgotten how quickly most Paraguayans tended to ask innocent, disarmingly personal questions about one's private life.

She asks me to show her the photos I have on my phone and scrolls through the pictures employing her favorite adjectives for cuteness: *"Ayyy chulinnna!"* and *"Preciosa!"* and *"Iporãiterei nde rembyreko!"*

She thrusts the phone back at me when she has scrolled through all the pictures.

"You are a good husband, no?" she says.

"Well, I try to be—" I say, sliding the phone back into my pocket.

"No, Pedro," she interrupts, handing me the tea gourd. Something in her voice has changed the tenor of the conversation from lighthearted to serious. "Are you loyal?"

"Yes," I say. "I am loyal." I feel like I can't tell her—at this point—that my wife wants to end it all.

She puts her hand on my knee and leans in, as if to study my face for signs of equivocation. Her melancholy dark brown eyes are clear and inscrutable.

I hold her gaze as long as I can; it gets uncomfortable for a moment and then she starts laughing uncontrollably. It is a genuine laugh and relieves the tension. I had forgotten how her laugh reminded me of a squeaky hinge.

"Of course you are!" she chuckles. "You are a terrible liar! You have no choice!"

I smile obligingly, though I am not sure if what she says is really meant to be a compliment.

"You are not *letrado* at all," she says employing a Paraguayan slang word that has no translation in English. *Letrado* is the near-ubiquitous adjective that describes a clever womanizer, one who schemes and manipulates others to satisfy his appetite for sexual conquest.

"What is a word we can use for you," she says putting a finger on her chin as if thinking. "Yes, you are *in-letrado*, no? Yes, I have created a new word, *inletrado*. It is good, no?"

I nod, finding the whole conversation about my relative guilelessness much less amusing than she does.

"I am sorry, Petercito," she says. "It is a good thing. I know too many men who spend their lives lying to the ones they love most. It will ruin your soul."

There is a pause, and I take a big gulp of tea, passing the gourd back to Yara. I want to ask her about her life but am not sure how to do so without seeming prurient or, at least, impolite.

"It appears that you are doing well," I say waving my hand in the air toward a wall of built-in shelves that feature an array of shiny bells. "A big improvement on the old place."

"It is much better," she confesses, passing me the gourd. "I was living in hell before."

I take a sip without saying anything. Given what Yara has seen in her life, it would seem silly to pretend to know anything about hell.

"But it all changed when I got these," she says with a chuckle, grabbing her boobs. "I bought these with the reward money I got for you. Well, not these, exactly, but my first pair. They changed my life."

She is still holding her boobs and I am not sure where to look, so I look at the ground and can feel my face turning hot. She laughs like a squeaky hinge again.

"You are just the same, Petercito," she says squeezing my knee. "It makes me happy. Are you hungry? Would you like lunch?" she asks standing.

"Yes," I say. "I am hungry. Would you like to go somewhere?"

"No," she says exiting the room. "I will prepare some empanadas for us." I can hear the clatter of dishes being moved around in the kitchen. I rise and join her in a modern, if narrow, galley kitchen where she is arranging and stuffing empanadas on a greased pan. I lean on the door frame.

"Beats *mandi'o chyryry*," I say, reminding her of the oil-fried yucca we ate three meals a day when I was living with her.

"Ahh, to be fourteen again," she says wistfully. "I couldn't eat that stuff nowadays without getting fat."

I never knew how old she was, but presumed she was seventeen or eighteen at least.

"You are surprised," she says looking up from her work to gauge my reaction. "I have lived many lives. I am like an old lady now."

I am not sure what to say to this. I am still trying to come to terms with the fact that she was only fourteen when I met her. The thought of her working the truck stops so young makes me feel like the human race is beyond redemption.

"There is a saying in Russian, *vinagax pr'avdi nyet*," she says. "It means there is not truth in the legs. Please, sit down." She nods toward a pair of chairs and a small table at the far end of the kitchen.

"How did you learn Russian?" I ask.

"That is why you need to sit down," she says. "There is so much we need to talk about."

I squeeze past Yara and sit at the table.

"Yara, do you remember that you used to have that shrine?"

She giggles, nodding. "Yes, Petercito. What a horror, no?"

"You were not a horror!" I argue. "You always took such good care of me!"

She laughs dismissively, rolling her eyes.

"Yara, do you remember when I asked you about the picture?" I ask. She stops stuffing the empanadas and looks at me, a small line of consternation between her thin eyebrows. "Sometimes I still wonder about it. You know all about me, but I never knew anything about you. I still don't."

"And you remember what I said then?" she asks, her voice faltering.

I nod.

"And if I answer the same way now?" she asks.

"I will tell you something I have learned since then," I say. "I will say that there is a lot I wish I could forget. A lot of things that I wish I didn't have in my head. And I have spent the last twenty years—"

But I don't finish because as I say it, tears start to roll down her face and then mine, and then we are both trembling and crying. I rise to hug her and we hug awkwardly in the middle of her kitchen. Her hands are covered in empanada filling so she only sort of squeezes me with her forearms her head in my chest.

When we have both finished crying she looks up at me, streaks of mascara running down her cheeks.

"Now see what you did!" she says, awkwardly trying to wipe her face with her forearm because her hands are covered with meat filling. "This is why I don't talk about it. You see?"

I grab a dish rag and wet it for her to wipe her face then return to my seat at the table.

She wipes off her face and then slides the pan of empandas into a small oven.

"Why didn't you ever send me a message?" I say while she washes her hands and face at the kitchen sink. "All this time."

I was compelled to learn about the wanderings of a certain Aeneas, oblivious of my own wanderings, and to weep for Dido dead, who slew herself for love.

She shrugs at the sink and then sits down heavily in the kitchen chair next to me, her eyes puffy. The obvious answer to this question is that she has nothing good to tell me. But that clearly isn't true. She has done well for herself in the intervening years.

We are quiet for a time, the kitchen filling with the delicious aroma of baking empanadas.

"I am sitting now," I say finally. "You never did tell me how you learned Russian."

Her countenance brightens in an instant. "Oh, that is a long story," she says, rising to rifle through a kitchen drawer. "A very long story. And a good one. Ah, here it is." She hands me a photo of a luxury yacht moored at a wooden dock.

I look at her with raised eyebrows.

"I lived there," she boasts.

"You lived on a boat?"

"A yacht," she corrects.

"How?" I ask, astonished.

"That is why I say you must sit," she says, obviously relishing my intense curiosity. "It is a long story." She saunters to the oven and sets a timer. "Come," she says, inviting me back to the living room. "We have thirty minutes, and maybe I can tell you some of it before the empanadas are ready."

Chapter 18

ECONOMY

My side of the sofa faces a wall with built-in shelves that is full of baubles and bells—things she seems to have collected from her travels abroad—but my attention is fixed on her. She sits, her legs crossed in the way that her pencil skirt requires, with the sort of impeccable posture of someone who attracts a lot of attention and is keenly aware of how she is seen by others.

"I will tell you about the Yacht," she begins, "but first how I got there."

She pauses, looking out her large picture window, a faraway look in her doleful eyes. Her handsome, angular face makes her look almost severe when she is serious.

"After I got my surgery," she grabs her boobs again for emphasis, "I got a lot of attention. At first it was just trips over to Foz. But the men I visited were from all over the world. Not just Paraguayans and Brazilians, but Europeans and Americans and Lebanese and Chinese too. It was the first time I earned these different types of money.

"I used to think there were tricks to being rich," she explains. "Like there were secrets at all the banks and if I could learn them I would also have access to money. You smile like I am making a joke, but truly I thought this way. I thought that if I dressed a certain way—like they do in the *telenovelas*—that I would be given access." Yara shakes her head, grinning at the memory of her naiveté.

She explains how, in her mind, it never made sense that the currency with greater purchasing power was the easiest to earn. How men from rich countries were easiest to rip off. It was a contradiction to her that the people whose money made them richest, at the same time, seemed to merit the wealth the least.

"I realized that there was something else I did not see or understand happening in exchanges. How is it the rich men from America and Europe and China get ripped off all the time, but still had their wealth? It didn't matter if it was drugs or girls, they almost always paid too much for too little. You know?"

Over time, Yara learned that wealth was full of contradictions.

"For example, lots of wealth is just cost," she says. "I did not know this at first."

She cites another contradiction: poor people tended to value money much more than the rich people did.

"It was like a light came on," she explains. "Being poor is the best way to understand the value of money. It is something you cannot know without experience. It is a hell, yes? It is worse than hell because hell is for human beings. Poverty and starvation make you an animal. And once you know it, you cannot forget."

I nod, but the truth is I have never really experienced deprivation in the way she describes it.

"What I found out was that there is a secret to money," Yara says accentuating the point by making a quick motion with her hands. "It is this: Wealth follows *deseo*." I understand the word *deseo* means both wish and desire. "And I am making all this money because I am an expert in *deseo*.

"This difference made the foreigners easy targets. It became like this game I played," she says, a shadow of guilt passing over her face. "If they came from a rich country, I would see how much I could get out of them. I started making more than 10,000 *reales* in a night. That is like 2,000 or 3,000 dollars."

I try to arrange my face into a look that says I am proud of her for this success, even though I don't feel that way because I know how the money is earned.

"You look surprised," she says, smiling. "But yes, I actually made that much. I do not say this to brag, but I did. I was very good. Perhaps the best in the city."

Her voice did not express pride as much as a sort of wistfulness.

"But you know what happens in a place like this," she laments. "Ciudad del Este is not a place where one can excel for very long. One of the cartels began to notice the money I was taking, and they wanted a cut for protection. I knew it was over."

"Because the cartel knew what I knew," she explains. "And the tricks that I played with the foreigners was what they were beginning to use on me. I knew it would be only a matter of time before I would once again be making very little and turning all of my money over to the cartel bosses.

"So I decided to go to a big city," Yara says, a twinkle in her eye. "Somewhere I could make this sort of money and go unnoticed. By then I had made many Brazilian friends in my work and some of them had been to Rio de Janiero where I was told there are thousands of *travestis* and they make a very good living and go unbothered by cartels and pimps.

"At first, I really did not believe what they told me. It seemed too good to be true. Was there really a city where millions of rich tourists from all over the world come every year, where they celebrate sex in the streets and where prostitutes are hard to distinguish from half-naked carnival revelers? This could not be."

...there is continually the noise of the mad and abominable revelry of effeminates and mutilated men, and men who cut themselves, and indulge in frantic gesticulation...

"It seemed even to me," Yara explains, "that such a city would just fall apart or explode, no? Everything I knew seemed to be upside down. How could there not be hungry people looking to take advantage of such a place?

"It really is like how it was described to me. I arrive in Rio and I move into the *sobrado*."

"What's that?" I ask.

"Oh I forgot, you do not speak Portuguese," she says. She explains that a *sobrado* is the Rio version of a New York City brownstone.

"The *sobrado* is run by an old *travesti*," she continues, "the *madraste*, who I know through a friend. The *madraste* teaches me all about the carnival season. She knows where the rich tourists stay, what streets to work, what parades to attend, what bars to frequent. I make a lot of money right away, but like everything in a city like Rio, there are bigger costs. There are costs for what my *madraste* teaches me, costs to stay in the *sobrado*, costs to go to the right bars, costs for the right parties, costs for all the surgeries, costs to bribe the police, costs to bribe the gangs.

"I still make a lot of money. Much more than I did in Foz. Even after paying all the costs. But everything in Rio costs more and more. And what I don't realize is that I am getting accustomed to the expensive things that all these rich people have. It happens slowly—so slowly that I do not even notice—but one day I wake up and I am eating only at nice restaurants and staying in the nice hotels more than I am in the *sobrado*. It is like at once I am richer than I could ever imagine and hungrier than ever. Does that make sense?"

I nod, thinking of *Bonfire of the Vanities*, but knowing she wouldn't get the reference.

"I did not understand what I do now about money," she explains. "I still thought that the stuff rich people had was wealth. I did not know it was all just cost. Because of this, I began to work the yachts in Rio. It is even better money, but it is dangerous. Anything goes out in the sea. They do these drugs that I do not even know. And I know a lot of drugs! My *madraste* says I should not go on the yachts. But you know I never have done what is safe. Safety has always been like a prison to me. I know girls that go out on these trips and never return. But still I go."

She pauses for effect. Images of sex workers being thrown overboard on fancy million-dollar yachts flash in my mind.

"I used to think I was just clever," she continues. "But now I don't think I am so clever. I think it is karma. I am good to people, so they are good in return. The yachts were never dangerous for me. Maybe I was just lucky. But I do not believe in luck anymore. If I did, I would have to believe I was very unlucky, you know? Why should I be born into this life and you into yours?"

I nod, even though I am not sure I really understand what she is trying to say.

"And it was during one of the yacht parties that I met Mikhail Guramishvili," she says, pronouncing the name without Spanish accent. "He invited me to stay on the yacht and go to Europe with him. At first I said no. It was not that I thought it was dangerous, but it still seemed scary to me. I guess I kind of thought I might become a slave. Many *travestis* lived on his yacht from all over the world. There were a few *chinas* and *tailandeses* and I did not want to be one of his collection. And I could not speak to them—because they did not speak Spanish, of course—but I got the feeling from the way they acted that they belonged to him. I did not want to belong to anyone, even if he was rich. You understand?"

I nod, fidgeting with my hands in the hopes that it might distract from the look of discomfort on my face. Knowing how the story will end—that she will end up on the yacht—breaks my heart.

"But he told me about Europe and it seemed even better than Rio. And he gave me expensive jewelry and took me shopping and soon my no became a yes. I was so hungry, Petercito." She looks ashamed of this, as if pleading for forgiveness.

"It is strange," she continues. "I am a *puta*. I work in the streets. But I never felt cheap until this time. I am making more than ever in my life and I feel cheap. I don't know why, but I do. I think it is because I sell my freedom, which is the only thing I have, which I never sold before. It is really a silly thing."

"It is not silly," I interject. "I think I understand."

"You are so sweet, Pedro," she says patting my hand patronizingly.

"So you went with him," I say after a moment of awkward silence. "Why did you not stay with him?"

"I just decided to leave one day," she says simply. "I got homesick. I spent almost a year living on that yacht and it was supposed to be wonderful. Everything I imagined. But the whole time I just thought about home. I guess I realized that there was nothing else for me. This was it. I finally accomplished what I wanted and found out that it was very lonely. I was so hungry to be rich and suddenly I was as rich as I'd ever be. I ate in all the nicest restaurants, partied with *multimillionarios* all over Europe. Went to the best clubs. Enjoyed beautiful lovers. And through it all, I only thought about Paraguay. I guess I must always long for something," she says wistfully. "It is how I am broken."

"I don't think you are broken," I say.

"Oh ho, Petercito," she says smiling sweetly. "You always were a terrible liar."

"No, really," I insist. "I don't."

"Pedro, I am just an old *puta*," she says, laughing like a squeaky hinge. "I am more broken than you will ever know."

"You are—"

The timer in the kitchen buzzes.

"Ah, the empanadas," she says, rising. "They will be too hot. Let me pull them out of the oven and let them cool. Come. Let's sit in the kitchen."

Yara disappears into the kitchen and I follow. She pulls the baking sheet out of the oven with an oven mitt. The empanadas—in neat rows—are now golden brown. The smell of the meat pastry is pungent, and I am suddenly ravenous.

"I am hungry," I say.

"Yes, me too. We must let them cool though first. Come. Sit down," she says pointing at the kitchen chair.

I take a seat and she shuffles around the kitchen pulling plates, cups, and silverware from cabinets and drawers, arranging them on the small kitchen table. It reminds me of how she used to cook for Edén and me in the evenings—after Edén got home from working as a *sacolero* and before she left for the truck stops.

"Remember how we used to eat dinner together?" I ask, trying to pretend a geyser of emotions are not bubbling up in my chest. "We would all watch *Pedro el Escamoso*."

"Of course, Petercito," Yara says smiling as she lays out napkins.

"I never saw how it ended," I lament.

"Ah, no?" she says. "You never saw it in the States?"

"No," I say glumly. I consider telling her that I went straight into detox when I got back to the States but don't actually know the Spanish word for detox and don't feel like trying to describe that particular hell.

"Pedro got his girl, of course" she says happily. "Could it have been any other way?"

"So it was happy?" I ask.

"Yes," she says squinting. "I believe so."

Yara brings the baking pan over to the table and places a few empanadas on each of our plates.

"So it was just a happy ending," I say. "No twists? No unexpected events?"

Yara puts the pan back on the stove top and put her hands on her hips, squinting, as if trying to remember.

"There were twists," she says. "There are always twists. It is a telenovela. It was so long ago, and I do not remember everything."

"What do you remember?" I ask.

She sits across from me at the kitchen table and I can tell from the long pause and her furrowed brow that she is weighing her answer carefully.

"Peter," she says, grabbing my hand with hers, "I remember everything. And I tried very hard to not remember. And even despite the drugs—a lot of drugs—many, many drugs—I cannot forget. But, Peter, I do not like to remember that time. It was not so good for me. I don't know how I can explain." Yara looks up at the ceiling, as if searching for the right words. She is still holding my hand in hers and I can feel her trembling.

"I am sorry, I—"

Yara puts her finger on my lips and shushes me.

"No apologies," she says finally, letting my hand go. "Let's remember later when we are not hungry and when I can have a glass of wine in my hand. After we have eaten. Okay?"

I nod.

"Now, would you like to bless the food?"

I look at Yara in surprise, who seems to have arranged herself in a pious pose, head bowed.

"Are you making fun of me?" I ask.

"Of course not," Yara says. "I see on the Internets that you go to church with your señora. Not just pretending to be a priest."

"I go, yes," I concede. I briefly consider explaining that even though I go to church, I do it as penance, not because I am a believer. But this seems very complicated to translate into Spanish. Instead I say simply, "But I do not take communion."

"So you cannot bless the food?" she asks simply, cocking her head at an angle.

"I can bless the food, of course," I concede. "But I want to explain something first."

"*Dale.*"

"I do go to church, but I need you to know something," I say. "I will never judge you."

"No?" she says, her still head tilted at an angle, as if studying me.

"Of course not," I cry. "I could never judge you!"

"You elect not to judge me," Yara asks, a furtive grin appearing on her face, "or you are not able to judge me?"

"I don't think I understand," I say.

"I think you understand me," she contends. "The question is very simple: Do you elect not to judge me or you cannot judge me?"

I squint at her for a moment before answering: "I believe that... I elect not to judge."

"So you can judge me then, no?" she says, still grinning slightly.

I feel like she is tricking me and don't see any way to answer this question. Finally, I shrug.

Yara gets very serious for a moment and I wonder, briefly, if I said something irredeemably offensive. I fidget, wishing I had just said the prayer instead of making this whole weird profession of tolerance.

Then her squeaky-hinge laughter fills the room: "You are so funny, Petercito!" she says between fits of laughter. "You are just the same. Just the same as always."

I try to smile but can see in Yara's eyes that she knows it is not genuine.

"I am sorry Pedro," she says, patting my hand. "I should not make what you say into a joke. But this is Paraguay where we elect a bishop to be president and then remove him. We remove him not because he is proven to have many, many children from many different women, but because he does not rule the *campesinos sin tierra* with a firm hand."

"Paraguay had a president who was a bishop?" I ask. "When was this?" I hadn't really kept up with Paraguayan politics since leaving the country.

"*Presidente Lugo*," Yara says. "Bishop of the Poor, we called him. He was elected just after you left. He was just like your pope. He said the poor will inherit heaven, but he also wanted that no one would suffer in poverty! How is that possible? I never understood that." Yara's voice became quietly reflective for a moment. "Enough! We must eat. Will you pray, Father Petercito?"

I force a weak smile and bow my head, trying to think about how to translate the traditional mealtime prayer. Then I hear Yara:

> *Dios mio,*
> *me arrepiento de todo corazon*
> *de todo lo malo que he hecho*
> *y de todo lo bueno que he dejando de hacer,*
> *porque pecando te he ofendido a ti*
> *que eres el sumo bien*
> *y digno de ser amado sobre todas las cosas.*
> *Propongo firmemente, con tu gracia*
> *cumplir la penitencia,*
> *no volver a pecar y evitar las ocasiones de pecado.*
> *Perdoname, Senor,*
> *por los meritos de la pasion*
> *de nuestro Salvador Jesucristo*
> *Amen.*

I look at Yara with arched eyebrows.

"Don't be so surprised," she chides. "This is Paraguay. Everyone is Catholic here. Even if we don't want to be."

The prayer wasn't a mealtime prayer, but a prayer of penitence. I wonder, briefly, if I can ask her why she chose it. But I can't figure out how to ask the question in a way that doesn't sound critical or too personal.

"Please," she says motioning toward the food on my plate. "Eat."

I take a bite of the empanada, which is crispy on the outside and a steaming mush of sweet and savory on the inside.

"They are perfect," I say, my mouth already full of another bite.

Though she nibbles at her own empanada, I notice that she mostly just wants to watch me. It feels weird being watched, but somehow I know it gives her satisfaction, so I eat six or eight of them. I eat until I cannot eat any more.

Chapter 19

KOKUE

After lunch, Yara says she wants to go on a short trip to the *campo*. I demur, saying that lunch left me in a food coma and much too tired for an excursion to the countryside. But she is insistent:

"You can sleep in the car," she says, handing me two bottles of Argentinian Cabernet.

She leads me out of the apartment to somewhere in the bowels of her building, where we find her meticulously maintained Land Rover. It is the sort of vehicle only corrupt politicians tended to have.

We climb into the SUV and I look at her with raised eyebrows.

"Remember: none of this is wealth," she says waving her hand dismissively. "It is only a cost."

I roll my eyes.

The winding ramps of the parking garage spit us out into the chaotic streets of Ciudad del Este. Yara drives aggressively—like most of the other drivers on the road—cutting off pedestrians when she can, nosing into intersections to gain the right of way. Paraguayan traffic customs reflect priorities of the culture: the bigger and more aggressive cars are rewarded for their boldness. I might have said something about this if I didn't fall asleep almost immediately.

I am jostled awake as we bounce down a dirt road, surrounded on all sides by verdant hills of soy as far as the eye can see.

"Good morning sleepy head," Yara says in Spanish, her words singsong.

I grunt, feeling even more tired than before. The clock on the console tells me it is mid-afternoon, which means I must have been sleeping for at least an hour or two.

"We are almost there," she says.

"Where are we?"

"*El campo*," she says brightly.

"Yes, I can see that," I say. "But where in the countryside?"

"In Alto Paraná," she says.

"Where in Alto Paraná?" I ask.

"Southern part of the *departamento*," she says.

We are quiet for a long stretch and the only sound is that of dirt crunching beneath the tires.

"This is not a place for a picnic," I observe.

"Just wait," she says. "You will see."

Presently, a small cottage appears on the horizon. As we get closer, I can see that it is a simple, sturdy brick house with a yard of swept dirt around it. The yard is empty except for a well in front of the home and, next to it, a tall, solitary Lapacho tree—a regal hardwood with a broad canopy of small leaves that has beautiful flowers for a few weeks during the year. The red earth yard looks especially crimson in contrast to the shin-high rows of soy all around it.

As soon as I hop out of the SUV, the suffocating heat and humidity make me regret the whole excursion. Since returning to the States, I have become accustomed to ubiquitous climate control. Plus, I am wearing jeans, which just makes the swelter worse.

Yara doesn't look much better. Her pencil skirt and high heels look ridiculously out of place in the Paraguayan *campo*.

"Look at us," I say chortling. "We look like we have never been to the *campo*."

She smiles and leads me toward the front porch, which is a shaded area of concrete slab that extends across the front of the home. In the middle of the porch is the front door, which she unlocks with a key. Inside, it is dark; and the air is stuffy, as if it hasn't been disturbed for some time. She motions for me to wait near the door while she walks through the home, opening the wooden shutters all around. As light pours in the windows, the sparsely decorated interior begins to emerge from the darkness.

Even with all the windows open, it takes a few moments for my eyes to adjust to the shadowy room. There is a small bed tucked into one corner over which hangs a big crumpled ball of gossamer mosquito netting. Opposite the bed, is a wooden table with a few chairs and a gracefully curved old-time icebox with big chrome handles. Next to the icebox are a few cabinets and a stack of a particular kind of outdoor lounge chair—popular among Paraguayan campesinos—which is made of a metal frame and thin straps of rubber.

Twirling in the middle of the room, arms outstretched, Yara says, "This is home."

"This is *your* house?" I ask in disbelief.

She nods. "Grab some chairs, will you?" she says pointing at the stack in the corner of the room. She is already working to uncork the Cabernet.

I grab two of the chairs and head outside onto the front porch. Except for a few solitary trees here and there in the distance, there is nothing to see except for miles and miles of soy in all directions. It is peaceful, if austere. I wonder if the idea of a country house isn't more of a comfort in theory than reality.

"Do you come here often?" I ask as she joins me on the porch, two glasses of wine in hand.

"Not as often as I'd like," she says. "Bring the chairs over here." She leads me toward a shady spot under the tall Lapacho tree, walking precariously on the balls of her feet to avoid pushing her expensive heels into the dirt.

She hands me a glass and sits in one of the chairs. Wine in hand, I walk around to see the back side of the house. The landscape is the same as the front, except in back there is an outhouse and another wooden stall enclosed on three sides where one might take bucket baths. I smile, wondering if Yara has ever used them. It is hard to imagine she has.

I return to the shady spot in the yard where Yara is sitting. "*Tranquilo-pá ko-ape!*" I say, employing Guaraní to emphasize the idyllic surroundings.

"Yes," she says. "My heart is here."

"But tell the truth," I tease, "you don't stay here for very long."

She gives me a wounded look. "Not now," she confesses. "But I will."

I take a sip of wine trying to imagine her living in a home without any electricity or running water. The image seems ridiculous.

"Why do you smile?" she asks.

"Because you don't fit here," I say. "Look at you. There is a reason *campesinos* do not wear shoes like that."

She takes the high heels off her feet and stands up, barefoot. It is striking how different her body looks without the heels. Though shorter, she looks somehow more powerful.

"This is how I grew up," she says, waving her hand in the air, a faraway look in her eyes. "I didn't have any shoes until I left my village." She paces to and fro, barefoot, sipping the wine in her hand.

"But surely you do not want to live like that again," I say. "I mean, once you have experienced modern comforts it is difficult to go back, right?"

"Yes and no," she says enigmatically, sitting back down in her chair. "Maybe I do not *want* to live like this. But I *need* it." Yara looks at the sky, which is a vibrant blue and full of incredible curved towers of clouds exploding upward. I get the sense that she has more to say, so I remain quiet. There is an eerie silence in our pauses—not even the sound of a bird.

"The *campo* is who I am," she continues after a time. "Everything good that has ever happened to me comes from the *campo*. And every terrible thing too. It is two sides of the same coin. I do not *like* it here, but it is where I belong. I must sound crazy to you."

I nod, thinking that she does sound crazy—but afflicted with the same sort of madness that has plagued me all these years.

"This is my retirement," she says, taking a gulp of wine, as if to accentuate the finality of her decision. "I know I won't look like this forever. Doctors can do only so much before time has its way."

I understand her to be saying that she is still making a living as a sex worker. A litany of questions forms in my mind, but they all seem impertinent.

"In Rio, my *madraste* gave me a glimpse into the future. She was too old to work in the streets anymore, so she made her living running the *sobrado*. Unless I want to run a house full of working ladies, there is not much else for me to do. And I know I do not want to do what she did."

"I can imagine," I lie. In reality I have no idea what life must be like in the situation she describes. I can't even really imagine how she reconciles her life of such genteel comforts while still earning a living as a sex worker.

There is a long silence between us while I contemplate these thoughts and Yara, enigmatic as ever, considers others. When there is an occasional breeze, the rolling fields of soy look like a wavy green sea. Yara turns the glass in her hand slowly. The wine looks vaguely like an enormous gem in the bright afternoon sun.

"You lease this land?" I ask, knowing the answer cannot be anything but affirmative. There is no way she is doing the farming.

"Yes."

"To Brazilians?" I ask, again knowing the answer.

"Yes."

"How much land do you have?" I ask.

"220 *hectares*."

The biggest landowner in the tiny subsistence farming village where I lived during my time in the Peace Corps might have owned 50 hectares. 220 hectares put her in a different class.

"This is not a *kokue*," I say, smiling, employing the Guaraní word for farm. "This is an *estancia*."

Yara does not find this distinction as amusing as I do. She refills both of our glasses, emptying the bottle completely.

"Sí, Petercito," she says gravely. "This is the only thing I own that is not actually a cost. It's the only thing I own that makes money. Other than my body, of course." She laughs like a squeaky hinge. Even though what she says makes me uneasy, I laugh along with her. Her laugh always was contagious.

"But, of course, my body has a big cost," she says chuckling. "Good surgeons are not cheap!"

I force a guffaw.

"I am sorry, Petercito," she says, still smiling sweetly. "I forgot how uncomfortable I make you."

"You do not make me uncomfortable," I protest. "If I remember correctly, you were the one who rejected me."

Her smile fades. "Pedro, you were not in your right mind."

I did not mean for my comment to be taken so seriously and wish that I could take it back.

"Yara, I'm not sure I'll ever be *en sano juicio* after my time in Paraguay," I muse.

"You are doing just fine," she says brightening. "Your woman, she seems to be quite happy, no?"

"No, Yara," I confess. "She is not."

Yara does not look particularly surprised by this news. A silence grows between us as we sip our wine and survey the fields of soy. We both have a sheen of sweat collecting on our faces in the afternoon heat. I consider whether I could ever ask her if she wants a family. But I am afraid I might dredge up some sadness from her past or sound silly for asking at all. After all, how can a transgender sex worker have a family in a country like Paraguay? Then a thought comes to me, a way to talk about it:

"Yara, when Edén and I lived with you before," I begin. "We were kind of like a family, no?"

"A really, really bad family, yes," she says, a despondent look in her eyes.

"But there were good parts, no?" I say, thinking about our evenings watching *Pedro el Escamoso* together.

Yara shrugs.

"You don't think so?" I try.

Yara takes a gulp of wine, nearly draining the glass. She does not answer or give me any indication that she has even heard my question. The silence stretches on for quite a while and, before long, I assume she simply has decided not to engage at all with this question. I know better than to press it further. And then:

"Pedro, a few years after you left, I found you on Facebook and I always checked the pictures. I saw every new picture you put on there. I saw when you bought your house. I saw when you got married in the church. I saw the pictures from all the holidays. It made me sad, but happy at the same time, you know?"

"I think I understand," I say.

"Sometimes, when I am looking at the photos, I think it is like the legend of the Iguazu Falls. Do you know the legend?"

I shake my head.

"It is like all the Guaraní legends: the gods always jealous of human love. In the legend of Iguazu, the god *Mbói Tu'ĩ* was so jealous of this couple that he broke the earth to separate the lovers. In this way he created the Falls. To punish the couple,

Mbói turned the man into a palm tree above the Falls and the woman into a rock at the bottom. They could always see each other, but never be together."

There is a moment of quiet where I wait to see if there is more to the story. When I am satisfied there is not, I speak:

"Well, that was pretty depressing," I say, laughing and taking a big gulp of wine. Yara does not laugh, or even smile.

"Sometimes when I looked at your Facebook, I felt like we are like the couple in the legend," she says finally. "I could look at you, but we could never be together."

"But now we are together," I say smiling, patting her hand. "So it is not so sad, now, right?"

"I still feel like it is the same," she says, a twinge of annoyance in her voice. "I don't know why I do. It is a feeling."

I can tell by the tone and the look in her eyes that she is serious and, somehow, I will ruin the beautiful thing she has just told me by asking her to explain too much. Instead I nod slowly like the significance of what she is saying is now dawning on me.

I am beginning to feel the effects of the wine, which is compounded by the afternoon heat. I decide it is time to talk about all those things that I had been longing to ask ever since I first spoke to her on the phone that morning:

"Yara," I begin, "Do you ever think about Edén?"

She stands, and walks toward the soy, as if to survey the fields. I stand too, wanting to see her face as she considers my question. Her countenance is as enigmatic as ever.

"Tell me, Yara," I plead. "Do you?"

"Yes," she says sighing.

Chapter 20

DREAMS

"I suspected this is what you want to talk about," Yara says, still surveying the field of soy. "It is the only thing you would not say. You are very easy to read, Petercito. If we are going to have this conversation, we will need the second bottle."

She hands me her empty glass and saunters barefoot into the house, leaving me outside sitting in the shade of the Lapacho tree. I finish the wine in my hand and watch the clouds as they dance in slow motion above me.

It is eerily quiet in the middle of the orderly rows of soy. No songbirds, no sounds of civilization, no animals. Even the occasional breeze is silent, a hot blast of wind evoking the hypnagogic. The feeling gives me a sense of déjà vu—as if I'd lived through some sort of sweltering waking dream before—but couldn't quite remember the exact details.

"Is it really that bad?" I ask when Yara returns and fills my glass almost to the rim.

She nods and generously fills her own glass, taking a long drink. She sits heavily, fixing her inscrutable eyes on me.

"Petercito?" Yara says, studying me.

I nod, squinting.

"Do you remember the necklace I wore?" she asks. "The one with the bullet?"

"Of course," I say.

"It was pulled out of a dead man," she says. "I believed it gave me favor with San la Muerte."

I nod, unsure of how this relates to Edén. But the tone of her voice tells me that she considers this all gravely serious.

"I was young," she continues, "but I had already seen so much death. Many lifetimes. But that is not the whole reason I believed. I did not choose San la Muerte. He chose me. After you left, I threw away the necklace, the shrine, all of it. I could not believe in anything except for myself. And, believe me, you get to the end of yourself very quickly and soon the world seems very bleak."

I nod slowly.

"Do you remember that picture that you asked me about?" she asks. "The one in the shrine?"

"Yes. Of course," I say. "The one you said to never ask you about."

"That was me and my family," she explains. "And, yes, it was me as a boy. I note that you do not look surprised to hear this. So you knew?" She searches my face for a reaction.

I nod, though I am only half honest. Although I did guess the picture was her family, I never thought to wonder if anyone in it might have been her. I try to remember the photo, but the only thing that comes to mind is a vague memory of the old folks looking dour and the young people smiling jubilantly. I hadn't thought to inspect the faces to see if any of the boys looked like Yara.

"You are trying to remember which one was me, no?"

I fervently deny this and she flashes a patronizing smile.

"I was loved and happy," she says without seeming to relish the memory. "I was different, yes, but my family did not care. For as long as I can remember, everyone whispered about me, teased me. The *maricón*, they called me. They told my father he need to be harder on me. If he beat me, they said, I would be like a normal boy. But he never laid a hand on me. He was a gentle, kind man. He died when I was eleven." Yara pauses, as if creating space for emotion, though she is as impassive as ever.

"A snake bit him," she continues. "He got sick from the snakebite, but he had been bitten before and told us he would be fine. He did not wake up the next morning."

I search her face for some trace of emotion. I put my hand on hers, hoping to express sympathy without having to resort to words—which seemed wholly inadequate.

"My life became a nightmare after that," she says, extracting her hand from my grasp as if to say that she doesn't want sympathy. "Look, Petercito," she leans toward me, "It was so bad that when I came to the city, I thought I was the luckiest person in the world. My farm was very far north—very far from the city, from any city. Things were so bad, so terrible that I thought I was *lucky* to be homeless on the streets of Ciudad del Este. I will never say the terrible things that happened to me after my father died. Never."

Extreme, sickening scenes parade through my imagination.

"I thought I was lucky to have escaped death. I thought San la Muerte favored me. His favor may be a curse, really. It is no blessing to see death up close and escape it so many times. But at least I believed in something besides what is in my own head. But now I no longer believe in anything except myself. I don't know if any of this makes any sense to you."

"I understand," I say quickly, not because I really comprehend all of what she is trying to say, but because I am worried if I don't assent, she might not tell me anything else.

"You do not understand," she says blithely. "You are a good man, gentle, honest, like my father. I do not want you to know the things that I know. It is good that you are sad and you search for a way to go back to being happy. It is how a person who is not broken is supposed to feel." Her tone sounds more like a warning than a compliment.

"You know, I am not so fragile," I offer. "You do not need to protect me from all the bad things."

There is a long silence where Yara seems to contemplate these words. I keep my eyes fixed on her as she stares blankly into the middle distance.

"Petercito, why do you come back after so long? There is nothing but sadness and misery here. Go. Be happy with your wife. Or find a new señora if she does not love you right. Do not come back here."

"Yara," I groan. "Don't you see that I am not okay. I am not happy. Every day I feel sad about what happened with you and Edén."

Yara nods in the knowing way that Dr. Rook used to do.

"Is it possible, Petercito," she says, her voice cracking, "that you are happy with this sadness? Is it possible that sadness is how you should feel? You should not be empty like me."

She looks away from me, as if ashamed of herself.

"Yara," I say, grabbing her hand firmly so she cannot shake free. "You are not empty. You know you feel something because there was a time when you cried for Edén."

Yara closes her eyes, a small tear forming at the corner of each.

"Look at me, please!" I insist. I realize I am speaking English and I say it again in Spanish.

"Look at me," I beg. "Yara, please."

"Petercito, I did not cry for Edén," she says, her eyes somehow sadder than usual. "I cried for you. I did not want you to become broken like me." She holds my gaze and I cannot bear it for more than a moment. I release her and then I am on my knees, sobbing as she awkwardly cradles my head in her stomach.

It feels like a lifetime has passed when I stand again, squinting. The whole world seems too bright, too colorful.

"Have another glass of wine," Yara says, pouring the ruby liquid into my glass, which sits precariously in the dirt next to my chair.

I nod, suppressing a sob.

"What is important is that you remember that you loved him," she coos, pouring another glass of wine. "And that you know he loved you."

"What is love?" I ask, thumbing the ring on my finger. "I think maybe I never did love at all really. And if I did, I sure did it wrong."

"No," Yara says flatly. "No, there was love."

"How can you say that?" I protest. "My love has all turned bad. Edén is dead and my wife won't talk to me."

"That is true," she concedes, "but that is life. You would encounter sadness and loss whether you loved or not."

Her wisdom is of little consolation. We fall silent and I drink the wine too quickly thinking about questions that make me progressively angrier: Why couldn't I have a normal life like everyone else? Why did I have to be so unlucky in love? I punctuate my anger by throwing my empty wine glass on the ground, scattering shards in every direction. Yara rolls her eyes and then glances at her feet, reminding me that she is barefoot.

"Oh, I'm sorry," I say, suddenly deflated. "I forgot that you were barefoot. Here let me get your—" I try to get past Yara to retrieve her heels, which lay on the other side of her chair, but she grabs me by the hand.

"No, Pedro," she says. "If you get my shoes I will run. And running never helps."

In her eyes I see a new emotion, something I'd never seen on her. Perhaps it is resignation. Or mourning. Whatever it is, the look makes me want to be still. She sighs heavily and looks toward the heavens.

At last, she says, "You want to know if you are alone in that sadness. You are not. There. I said it. I am sad too. But what is the use of thinking of it?"

"I don't know," I say, shrugging. "I believed that seeing you would help in some way."

"Do you see, Petercito?" Yara says emphatically.

"See what?"

"*Tenes fe*," she says. "You are sad, yes, but you still believe that there is hope for something more or something better. I am different. I only believe in myself. And when you only believe in yourself, the only hope left is that death does not take you from the world very soon. And that is no hope at all."

"Are you not overwhelmed by regret? Don't you wish you could have—"

"—I could not regret what I have done or who I am—"

"—If I had known, I could have—"

"—Nothing! You could have done nothing, Pedro. This is not your world. You cannot just change—"

"—I could have—"

"—Stop, Pedro, please," she says, standing to stroke my cheek. I fix my eyes on the dirt, as if the earth might diminish the shame that I feel burning in the space between us. "Pedro, you cannot change the world."

"But I can change the world for one person," I sob.

Yara places both of her hands on my cheeks. "You did," she says. "You did change his world."

"I just made it all worse," I blubber. "He would have been better back in Táva Rã."

"Pedro, it is bad, maybe worse in *el campo*," Yara says placidly, pulling my head up so that I must look her in the eyes. "You believe. Even after all of the bad stuff, you still believe, or you would not be here. And your faith gave Eden hope. Maybe you do not think this is important, but it is. Even as he left, he believed he could have a better life in Buenos Aires. Maybe he was sad or mad at you. But he has been sad and angry many times for many reasons. Perhaps he was. So what? He still believed in the possibility of a good life and happy future. You cannot change the past, but if you are not as broken as me, you will hope for a future."

I extract my face from her grasp and turn around, fixing my gaze on the horizon where a bright blue sky meets the soy.

Yara continues speaking, but I barely hear her. For the moment, I feel numb, hollow, physically weak. I return to my chair and sit down heavily. Yara is still talking, now sitting next to me, but I am not listening; I am still lost in my own thoughts.

"Yara," I interrupt, turning to face her.

"Yes?"

"How did you get the Clapton booklet?" I ask. "You saw him?"

"Pedro, please," she pleads, grabbing my hand. "You know enough. You know it all."

"I believe you," I say, fixing my eyes on the crimson earth at my feet. "I trust you. I do not *want* to know, but I must know how it ended."

The human mind so blind and sick, so base and illmannered, desires to lie hidden, but does not wish that anything should be hidden from it.

"Pedro, it is all the same," she intones. "Dead is dead is dead."

"But did he—" I ask, my voice shaking. "Did he suffer?"

After a moment, Yara reluctantly nods.

Yara talks about how suffering is part of life for street kids, how dangerous it is, even for the clever ones like Edén. Murder happens all the time, she says, and it could have happened to anyone, at any time, doing the work that he did. She speaks as if teaching a lesson, using the sort of empty platitudes you might tell a child who has tried very hard to do a difficult, complicated task for the first time, but has failed.

Besides, the remaining details don't matter and I only half listen anyway. I remember, vaguely, the first thing that Augustine whispered to me while I was listening to my wife's court-appointed mediator. I don't remember it exactly—it was something obtuse—but I do remember the jist of what the old saint said: truth is like a woman who may evoke both love and hate.

Augustine didn't explain how much suffering is involved in the latter emotion. It turns out that hatred cannot be directed at the truth, but only at oneself.

Or maybe he had been warning me all along?

Chapter 21

SUFFERING

The airport in Foz is small and dumpy with spotty Wi-Fi, a fitting portent for what awaits me on my string of flights back to Arizona. I can think of nothing quite so excruciating as being alone with myself for the next 16 hours. That my thought torrent is sometimes interrupted by a long dead Algerian saint is little consolation.

While I wait to board, I log into Facebook, hoping to distract myself.

I see Facebook through Yara's eyes, scrolling through pictures, trying to imagine how she might have seen them. This is my life, I think, curated for anyone who might see it. Smiling photos of me with my wife in which she doesn't yet harbor thoughts of divorcing me, and I don't suffer from "major depressive disorder." Vacations, holidays, weddings, and parties with lots of pretty people. In them, there's not one shred of evidence that I have been carrying an enormous burden of guilt. In them, you would never know the metastasizing regret I carried for decades. Surely no evidence that I sometimes think about Paraguay.

It's not so different from the ads for *travestis* in Ciudad del Este. In the right light, at the right angle, we present an idealized version of ourselves. Our internet profiles hide the acne scars and track marks.

I find my seat on the plane and strap into the seat, which feels too constraining for my unruly mind. There is a hell in my heart—always festering, roiling—which no amount of therapy, time, or church can exorcize. The only person in the world that knows this particular hell is Yara. Somehow she lives in it as if it is the only life she has ever known.

Who can teach me, save He that enlightens my heart, and discovers its dark corners?

My seatmate on the plane is a middle-aged Brazilian businessman who mercifully pretends not to notice the tears I can't staunch.

As the plane takes off, I conjure Éden, as if the memory of him, his dogged optimism that flourished despite the world in which he lived, might in some way provide a bulwark against this darkness.

For the first time I see his pantheon of mythological figures—forest goblins, cannibalistic sirens, kung fu cowboys—not as manifestation of evil men, like I once told him, but rather as the turmoil in my own heart.

And perhaps that is why Yara, too, believed in San La Muerte: the darkness inside is just too much for one heart to hold.

that crimes might be not longer crimes, and whoso commits them might seem to imitate not abandoned men, but the celestial gods

One mistake that continues to haunt me is that of a precious, decaying booklet of Clapton liner notes. In my quest to purge all memories of the ordeal, I trashed it not long after I was fired from the Peace Corps. The desiccated tract had become a holy relic, sanctified by the force of Éden's will. I was under the delusion that the physical contained the metaphysical and it wasn't the other way around.

For whither should my heart flee from my heart?

The problem with the geographic cure is that no matter where you go, there you are.

I had heard something similar in my mandatory NA meetings, and so I knew going into it that my return to Paraguay wouldn't provide any answers. Answers would suggest that I have reached the end of the mystery of how Éden lives in my heart, how he has made me into who I am today, how our time together continues to shape me.

It makes me smile despite the tears when I think of how sure Éden was that we were just like Cordell Walker and his trusty sidekick, Jimmy "Go Long" Trivette. It was us against the world and no amount of evil would prevail so long as we could stick together.

The problem, of course, is that television episodes are tidy and prosaic, not an odyssey complicated by Sisyphean struggles with mental health. Also, the good guys always win, which might as well belong to the realm of fantasy.

A truer tale would be the one that all of us—Yara, Éden, and I—watched with such anticipation in the shabby Ciudad del Este apartment that we called home. The conclusion of *Pedro el Escamoso* reveals a hero that does not prevail over the evil in the world, or even the darkness in his own heart.

The titular Pedro is a man, who like most of us, aspires to greatness, wants to be good, but who, in reality, is much more gullible, silly, provincial, and foolish than he thinks himself to be.

If I am a hero, I am Pedro, whose swollen pride and excessive sentimentality has gotten me, and everyone around me, into a great deal of trouble over the years, but who, by the grace of God, has escaped mostly unscathed, even if others were not so lucky.

I am a man who consumes love and cannot fathom a love that consumes me.

purified and molten by the fire of Thy love

I am now hurtling 30,000 feet above the earth headed to a place I call home. Even after all I've been through, part of me still longs to be the old Pedro, the one with the mullet and the ridiculous dances and the starry-eyed trust.

I want to go through life with unshakable faith, to be the beloved protagonist of a hero's tale, willfully ignorant that I am the subject of some heartbreaking tragedy.

But there is reality: There are divorce papers to sign back in Tucson, putting my name and consent to something that might have appeared like an inevitable consequence, or, at the very least, an avoidable outcome had I objectively considered, for even a short time, what I had experienced so long ago in a land far away.

No, I am Pedro at the end of the beloved telenovela who, in shocking fit of passion, cuts off his iconic mullet. Maybe I do this because I recognize that the price for true love is ego, pride, the self. And it is a miracle—magic really—that somehow, in giving up my very self, I am not diminished at all.

This is the truth of my story, or more properly, Éden's. It does not point to any larger truth—other than, perhaps, to show that the stories we all tell ourselves are the stuff of magic. An ancient witchcraft, even—like beekeeping—which requires the sort of wonder that only children possess and adults see in glimpses through their eyes.

A few months later, the divorce is finalized. I quit my job selling ads for the dying newspaper and move to Nogales, a straight shot south on I-19 from Tucson, to work for an agency that serves undocumented migrants. If I can't outrun my ghosts, I figure, I might as well learn to make use of them.

Nogales, on both sides of the border, is poor, dusty, hot, dangerous, and ugly—at least to the untrained eye.

To me, it's different. It's a place where the world around me matches the turmoil in my heart. And, somehow, there is beauty in that equilibrium. There's no pretense that this is anything other than a miserable last stop on the way to the land of milk and honey.

Borderlands are all the same in some ways. They are full of people like Yara and Éden. Full of people just trying to eke out a life for themselves that is a little less dismal than the one from whence they came.

I'm not doing that much good here, at least not in my official capacity as "migrant advocate." My title sounds noble. The reality is that it makes me just another bureaucrat in a long line of bureaucrats that will for years, burden the lives of these resolutely hopeful people. A Kafkaesque series of immigration hurdles await them.

This job provides a way to pay the bills so that on the weekends, and sometimes in the early evenings after work, I can go to Mexico.
In the makeshift migrant camps street kids, sex workers, hardscrabble *campesinos*, coyotes, political dissidents, fugitives, *narcotraficantes* become acquaintances, temporary friends. They're from all over the world, Latin America mostly, but also from as far away as Africa and South Asia.

I talk to them about safe houses and checkpoints, warn them about agencies that promise help but don't. Sometimes I'll just buy them a Coke and talk about their journeys. There are Haitians that fly to South America and make their way to the border on foot. There are Congolese who fly into Mexico City and somehow hitchhike their way north. Once I met a Bangladeshi man who made it to the border alone.

Besides the coyotes, there are only a handful of other Americans like me. Only a few who also frequent the Mexican side of the border to visit the camps. They're mostly wild-eyed pastors whose evangelistic style tends toward eschatological horrors.

I'm sympathetic. After all, I once had a long dead Algerian saint whispering in my ear.

Sadly, St. Augustine doesn't talk to me anymore. Sometimes I wish he would. On my bad days I'm sure he gave up on me. Either that or he was some manifestation of an acute mental illness. On my better days, which increasingly outnumber the bad, I am just grateful he spoke to me at all.

One of those fire and brimstone pastors, a pale, skinny, dreadlocked Puerto Rican man who goes by Jesús, isn't completely insufferable. Over time, I begin to trust that his companionship doesn't appear to be rooted in a surreptitious evangelistic impulse. Jesús and I never discuss God or church or even theological stuff. Mostly, we talk about the people in the makeshift camps, and their material concerns: food, water, shelter.

It takes me a few months before I work up the courage to call him Reverend Maslow, which is the nickname I'd been calling him, in my mind, for quite some time.

"Maslow, as in Maslow's Hierarchy?" Jesús asks, amused. It is the hour just past sunset, when the sky is on fire and everyone, migrants and locals alike, is out on the littered, potholed streets, enjoying the cool twilight. We are making our way back to the border because only a fool stays on the Mexican side after dark.

"Yeah," I say.

"I've been called worse," he observes. The two of us shuffle past a liquor store blaring *cumbia norteña*, Mexican pop music that is popular throughout rural Latin America, including Paraguay. It is the kind of music that was played when the carnival came to my small village in Amambay. The memory buzzes into my mind like a bee, a wonder with a tiny dagger.

Jesús, seeing my change in countenance, assures me he isn't offended by the moniker.

"No, I just hate this music," I grumble, quickening my pace to the big iron gate ahead, and the never-ending pedestrian queue that waits patiently for Customs and Border Protection to vet their documents.

"It is much better than the *raggaetón* that is popular back home," he offers.

"Yeah, maybe," I concede. "There is this band called *Lalo y Los Descalzos* that is super popular in Paraguay. A Mexican band from LA."

"Lalo and the Barefoots," he translates, chuckling, "seems about right for, where did you say, Paraguay?"

I nod, acknowledging both the country and the tacit invitation to tell Jesús more about this land far away where I once lived, for a time. Maybe one day I will tell him more. But not tonight. For tonight, it is enough to let the word of that place—Paraguay—live on the lips of someone else.

ACKNOWLEDGMENTS & THANKS

A book like *White Cloud Free* does not get written without the support and encouragement of lots of people.

First and foremost, I need to thank my mom and dad, two writers who showed me that words are sacred. I also want to thank a couple of editors without whose encouragement I might have never thought myself capable of writing a novel: Julie Riddle (a great writer in her own right) and Morgan Lee. Other writers who have encouraged me along the way include Darin Strauss, Irini Spanidou, Marc Cirino, and Tom Franklin; I'll never forget that time when you (Tom) bought me a beer and a stack of books in downtown Oxford, MS the day we met.

Of course, this story was inspired by my real-life experiences in Paraguay. I am deeply grateful for all the Paraguayans who loved me despite my obvious limitations, including Felix, Éden, Kiki, *la familia Anzoategui, y la gente de Tuna, Caazapá.*

I want to thank all my Peace Corps friends—especially beekeepers, Evans, Rebecca, Eva—and the Peace Corps staff, Don Antonio, Josue, Don Diosnel, and Ña Sonias.

I am forever indebted to Brad Word (who has the best name ever) for sharing AW Tozer with me. I'm also thankful for Father Robert Sirico and Rabbi Yosef Weingarten, who deepened my faith.

My lovely sisters, Kate and Alex, and my buddy David, thank you for your unfailing support and unflinching feedback when I asked you to read early versions of the novel.

To Torie Amarie Dale, Katherine Anderson, and the small, but mighty, staff at V Press LC: Thank you for your meticulousness and hard work.

Finally, a simple thanks seems insufficient for my wife and three children, who give my life meaning and inspire me every day with their kindness, creativity, and unconditional love.

ABOUT THE AUTHOR

Peter Johnson grew up in Colorado, Wisconsin, and Alabama and is a graduate of New York University. From 2002-2004, he served as a beekeeper in the US Peace Corps, Paraguay. After the Peace Corps, Peter lived in Dakar, Senegal, where he competed on the local beach wrestling circuit.

His writing has appeared in *Rock & Sling*, *Hiedra Magazine*, *Provo Canyon Review*, *Dappled Things*, *Seven Hills Review*, and *Christianity Today*.

He currently lives in Naples, Florida, where he and his wife produce a weekly podcast called *Romance with a Cocktail*. He is at work on his second book.

9 789898 546704